Children of the Undead

Books by David Dvorkin

Fiction

The Arm and Flanagan

Budspy

Business Secrets from the Stars

The Cavaradossi Killings

Central Heat

The Children of Shiny Mountain

Children of the Undead

Damon the Caiman

Dawn Crescent (with Daniel Dvorkin)

Earthmen and Other Aliens

The Green God

Pit Planet

The Prisoner of the Blood series

- *Insatiable*
- *Unquenchable*

The Seekers

Slit

Star Trek novels

- *The Trellisane Confrontation*
- *Time Trap*
- *The Captains' Honor (with Daniel Dvorkin)*

Time and the Soldier

Time for Sherlock Holmes

Ursus

Non-Fiction

At Home with Solar Energy

The Dead Hand of Mrs. Stifle

Dust Net

Once a Jew, Always a Jew?

Self-Publishing Tools, Tips, and Techniques

The Surprising Benefits of Being Unemployed

When We Landed on the Moon: A Memoir

Children of the Undead

David Dvorkin

ISBN: 978-1-7345636-4-1

CHAPTER ONE

Lily Morgenstern Flicker groaned. "Christ, look at this place."

"The sooner we start," Jerry Morgenstern said, "the sooner we can put it on the market. You take the bedroom closet. I'll take the hall closet."

"You're taking the easy one."

Jerry sighed. "Let's not argue, now that it's finally over. Okay, we'll switch. I'll take the bedroom."

"Wait a minute. That's where all the valuable stuff is. Maybe I should take the bedroom, after all."

"Jesus Christ."

Jerry was about to say more when he realized that his sister was looking with horror at something behind him. Her face was pale, her mouth was open, and her eyes were wide.

He spun around and found himself facing his father. Jerry's expression began to resemble his sister's.

The old man was dressed in the suit he had been wearing when the coffin lid was closed on him. The undertaker's caked-on makeup still covered his face, but it was cracking and falling off in pieces. Or maybe it was his skin that was falling off. Jerry couldn't tell for sure.

"Still bickering," his father said. "You kids will never stop. What are you doing in my condo?"

"Who are you?" Lily asked.

"I've been dead for a week, and already you've forgotten me? I'm not surprised. I told your mother it would be that way."

"But you're dead," Jerry said. "You can't be Dad."

"I *was* dead. Didn't like it. Told them I was going home."

"You can do that?" Jerry asked. "When you're dead?"

"You think I was going to let them tell me what to do? What are you doing in my condo?" he repeated.

Ignoring him, Jerry said to Lily, "It's some sort of scam. This guy's pretending to be Dad so he can get hold of the condo and sell it."

"Sell it?" the older man said. "Of course not. We're going to live in it, just like always."

Lily looked around the place, her nose wrinkling. "You call this living?"

"We?" Jerry said.

"I had to walk all the way from the cemetery," his father said. "In my condition. Why didn't you leave my car there?"

"We didn't think you'd ever need it again," Lily said. "We, um, we got rid of it."

"You sold it? I bet you didn't get enough for it. You always let people take advantage of you. Where's the money?"

"We gave it away," Jerry said. "To a charity. It was for a good cause."

"You mean someone told you it was for a good cause, and you believed them," his father said. He shook his head from side to side. His neck creaked and cracked, and small bits of leathery tissue floated down.

Jerry was afraid the head would fall off. He was torn between an urge to leap forward and hold the head in place and an urge to run like hell.

"You were always so naïve," his father said. "Such a good brain, but so naïve. Brain," he repeated. "I'm hungry." He turned away and opened the door of the refrigerator. The refrigerator was empty. "Where are the pickled peppers?"

"Pickles?" Lily said.

"Piper's Pickled Peppers. We always keep a jar or two in here. I love them." He turned back toward Jerry and glared at him accusingly. "Did you eat them? Just because you work there doesn't give you the right to eat up all the Piper's Pickled Peppers."

"I didn't touch the damned things."

"Watch your language when you're in my house!" Jerry's father stepped forward threateningly.

Jerry stepped back. "After you, er, after you left, there was a lot of old food in there. We had to get rid of it."

"You threw away the Piper's Pickled Peppers?" his father roared. "What's wrong with you?"

"I'll get you some more, okay? Never mind that right now. You said *we're* going to live here. Who's we?"

The front door opened and a woman walked in.

She looked like their mother but less so than the old man looked like their father. He looked like a dead man fresh from the coffin. She looked like a dead woman who was very unfresh. Bone showed through here and there on her face, and the dress she had been buried in hung limply on her in a way that made Jerry suspect that she was mostly bone underneath it. If this was a scam, the makeup was remarkable.

"I'm exhausted," she said. "That was a long walk." She noticed the brother and sister, and her face contorted stiffly into what could have been an expression of pleasure.

"Lily!" she said. "Jerry! It's so wonderful to see you children again!"

Before Jerry could react, she had stepped forward and embraced him.

He responded automatically by putting his arms around her. On one side of her back, he could feel her ribs and the spaces between them. The other side felt normal. Up close, the smell of decay was staggering.

He managed to escape and to step away from her. "It's not a scam," he said to Lily. "They're real."

"Oh, Jesus. It's not possible!"

"I read that there's more solar flux in Florida because of global warming."

"What's solar flux?"

"Something to do with the sun. Maybe it energized them."

His father stared at Jerry's forehead. "You always were the one with the brains." He tore his eyes away. "I don't know how long you kids were planning to stay. Lily, you can have the guest bedroom. Jerry, you'll sleep on the couch. You'll have to find your own food. Except for those pickled peppers, your mother and I don't eat in the old way anymore." His gaze drifted back to Jerry's forehead.

"Dinner," Jerry said to his sister. "Out. Now." He grabbed her arm and steered her out the front door.

On the balcony outside the front door, looking out over the lights twinkling peacefully on the waters of the bay, Lily said, "You've always been such a damned bully. You've always pushed me around."

"I've always protected you," Jerry said. "That's what I'm doing now."

"You're protecting yourself. It's *your* brains they want. They always preferred your brains."

"That's because I've always had more. Just like the old bastard said."

"You shouldn't call him that."

"He's a fucking zombie!"

"He's still our father."

"It's the end of the world. It's the Zombie Apocalypse."

"No, it's just Florida."

"Yeah. It's 99 degrees, 100% humidity, our parents are zombies, and this is the armpit of hell."

"Oh, come on. That's not fair. It's not the armpit of hell."

"You're right, it's not. Texas is the armpit of hell. Florida is the butt crack of hell."

"What's so great about where you live?" Lily said. "Arapahoe? You have terrible winters. You even had exploding cows a couple of years ago."

"There were no exploding cows. That was something the media made up."

"I saw pictures on the evening news."

"It was exaggerated. One cow," Jerry said. "Maybe two."

"They showed a whole field covered with cow parts."

"One cow makes a lot of parts. It was probably just something they ate."

"Maybe it's that awful weather you have."

"Awful weather?" Jerry said. "You think the weather in Piketon is worse than it is in this hellhole?"

"It's at least ten degrees hotter in the summer in Piketon than here."

"It's a dry heat."

"And at least it doesn't get cold here in the winter. Normally, anyway. It's always cold in the winter where you live. Very cold."

"It's a dry cold."

"Tell that to the exploding cows."

"The cows only exploded that one summer. It hasn't happened since then."

"I bet it has," his sister said. "I bet they're just covering it up. Exploding cows! It's because of the way you people up there treat our planet. Mother Earth is complaining, Jerry."

"Oh, God."

"Exploding cows," she repeated. She waved her hands, imitating something blowing up, and said, "Psht!"

"You can't make explosion sounds. You never could. It's because you're a girl. Girls can't make explosion sounds. Only boys can do that."

She stuck her tongue out at him. "You were always mean to me."

"You always ratted on me to Mom and Dad."

There was no riposte. Instead, Lily smiled in satisfaction. Whether it was satisfaction at the memory of betraying him to their parents or at having gotten under his skin so thoroughly, Jerry couldn't tell.

Her mention of exploding cows reminded him of another strange story from his home state of Arapahoe.

Not long after the exploding cows had been in the news, he had read a small item in the local newspaper about exploding bodies in a Piketon funeral home. There had been no follow–up stories in the newspaper or on television or online, so he assumed the story was false. It might have been repeated in out–of–state newspapers, though, and possibly his sister had seen it. If so, he didn't want the exploding cows to remind her of the exploding bodies. That was a conversation he didn't want to have, especially now.

"Hey," Lily said. "I just remembered another weird story from Arapahoe. Something about exploding dead bodies. Right after the exploding cows."

Jerry groaned.

"You can't say that's because of something they ate," she said triumphantly. "Dead bodies don't eat."

"You mean like Mom and Dad? They're eating stuff, and they're dead bodies."

"You don't know that they're dead."

It was definitely time to change the subject.

"What I do know," Jerry said, "is that Florida is hell. The only thing that saves this place is the seafood. How about that place we went to last time? The Gourmet Pirate."

"The place with the hot waiter? Sure!" Lily said.

"Hot waiter?" Jerry had noticed the hot waitress and the hot bikini babes on the beach beyond the window that formed the restaurant's west wall. Youth and beauty and sex on display. If his sister saw her version of the same thing there, maybe that would make her cooperative for once.

When they got to the restaurant, Jerry discovered that the hot waitress had been promoted to hostess since his last trip to Florida. She glanced at the two of them without any hint of recognition. "Two for lunch? Would you like a table by the window, for the view?"

"Oh, I love the view," Jerry said, staring hard at her because he naïvely thought that that would pique her interest.

The woman smiled perfunctorily, picked up two menus, and led the way. Fortunately, despite her new job, she still wore one of the Gourmet Pirate's waitress uniforms, which included brief, tight-fitting shorts with a giant red lobster painted on the back. The lobster's tail and the rest of its body undulated separately as she walked in front of them.

Lily looked annoyed. She leaned toward Jerry and whispered, "She's way out of your league."

"Thanks, sis."

Lily looked around and gave a disappointed *hmph*.

No hot waiter, Jerry guessed. "Maybe he found someone in his own league," he said. "Probably a guy."

As they were sitting down, with the wall of glass to Jerry's left and Lily's right, the hostess said, "Would you like anything to drink?"

"Pitcher of beer," Jerry said. It would wash away memory of the smell of his mother. He hoped.

"I'm not having any beer," Lily said.

"Just one pitcher, then," Jerry told the hostess.

After the woman had left, Lily shook her head. "Dad always did say that you drink too much."

"He said that to you? He never mentioned it to me."

Lily smirked.

Ignoring each other and the bodies baking in the sun just beyond the window, they both focused on the menu.

"What's the least kosher thing on here?" Jerry said. "That's what I'm having."

"Good God," Lily said.

"I don't think anything on here *is* kosher. Great!" He put down the menu, turned at last to gaze out the window at the sun-blasted beach, and froze.

Lily noticed his movement. "They're all out of your league," she said. She looked where he was looking and said, "What the hell?"

It was a public beach, accessible via a pathway that ran beside the restaurant. Thanks to the oily sluggishness of the Gulf's waves, there were no surfers, but it was popular with sunbathers, swimmers, parasailers, and young and beautiful exhibitionists.

At about the same time that Jerry and Lily were reading their menus, a group of the latter was walking along the path beside The Gourmet Pirate, on their way to working on their tans. The young people were flirting idly with each other, eyeing each other's bodies, and planning ahead. It was too hot for very active flirting. Anything more vigorous would have to wait for air conditioned bedrooms.

The young man at the front of the group came round the curve of the path past the corner of the restaurant, to where he could see the beach. He stopped. "Guys..."

The others piled up behind him, like slow-moving, sleek, beautiful, and very expensive sports cars sliding on ice into a brick wall. He was rooted to the spot. The rest of them saw what he saw and stopped trying to push him forward.

There were no parasailers, no swimmers, no families, no gamboling young people. The beach—their beach!—was covered with bodies.

These were bodies very unlike theirs. These bodies were brown, but it wasn't the brown of carefully tanned Caucasians. It was the brown of old, stained wood, of old, dried leather, of ancient people who shouldn't be above ground. They lay side by side, row after row, covering the beach, the feet of those in one row almost touching the heads of those in the next row. Their feet pointed toward the water and their heads toward The Gourmet Pirate. Their arms were by their sides. They stared up at the sun unblinkingly. They were immobile. They were like an army that had fallen on its backs. Here and there, the brown was broken by the white of exposed bone.

One of the new arrivals, a young woman, said loudly, "Gross!"

At the sound, the army of baking ancients simultaneously turned its heads toward the young people. The army of mouths opened. A sound somewhat like a human voice but leathery, dry, raspy, and multiple, groaned: "Catching some rays."

The beautiful young race cars shrieked in unison, backed up, turned around, spun their wheels for a moment, and then sped away.

The army turned its face back toward the sun in satisfaction. The hoarse, multipart voice spoke again: "Soaking it up."

The thick windows blocked all sound. Jerry and Lily hadn't heard the army's words. Even so, watching the interplay had been unsettling. Looking at the ancient bodies motionlessly bathing in sunlight was even worse.

"They're all like Mom and Dad," Jerry said. "Their bones are showing. They're dead. They're drawing energy from the sun."

"It makes sense," Lily said. The earth is the Great Mother, and the sun is the Great Father. Together, they're the source of all life. All the food we eat really comes about in the same way," she gestured toward the window, "as whatever it is that's going on out there."

"I've lost my appetite," Jerry said.

"A lot of folks say that." It was their waitress. They hadn't noticed her arrival. She was even hotter than the one who had become the hostess, but for once Jerry was oblivious. She was looking out of the window, too. "All those weirdoes out there are bad for business."

"Weirdoes?" Lily said.

"They started showing up a couple of days ago. Just a few of them at first. Then more and more. All of them laying there like that, all day long."

"Lying there," Jerry said.

"Yeah, like I said. They show up around sunrise, and they stay there, just covering the beach, till the sun goes down. All the normal people stopped coming to the beach. Then the normal people stopped coming in here, too."

Jerry looked around. He had been too focused on the hostess during their walk to their table to notice how empty the usually bustling restaurant was. Only two other tables were occupied in the huge space.

"Where do they go after sunset?" Jerry asked. Back to the grave, he thought. Or to their condos, to freak out their adult kids who made a special trip down to hell to clean out all the old junk.

The waitress shrugged. "All I know is, I'm scared to go out of the restaurant after dark now. Last night, after my shift, I made a run for my car. I know I heard one of them behind me."

"Heavy breathing?" Lily asked.

The waitress frowned. "No, I didn't hear any breathing. More like a shuffling sound. There's a cot in the back. I think I'm gonna just stay here tonight." She pasted on a smile. "You folks ready to order?"

Brother and sister looked at each other.

"We've changed our minds," Lily said.

"Yeah," Jerry said. "Sorry."

They pushed back their chairs and stood up. The waitress tried to mask her disappointment behind another smile. "Well, y'all come back."

Outside, Lily walked ahead and kept turning around and urging Jerry to hurry.

"Don't worry," he said. "The sun's still up. They're all lying on the beach."

"Yeah, but maybe they move real fast in the sunlight. They'll catch us and suck out our brains."

"It's too late for me," Jerry said. "Mom and Dad sucked out my brains years ago." But he stepped up the pace.

They got into Jerry's car and locked their doors.

Lily seemed to relax a bit at that point. "This is your own car, isn't it?" she asked. "I mean, it's not a rental. You drove all the way down here?"

"Yeah."

"You're crazy. I flew. I fly everywhere."

"I drive everywhere. I hate flying. It feels like you're in a herd of cattle being jammed into trucks to be driven to the slaughter. Or maybe a corpse crammed into a coffin."

"You're crazy," she repeated. "You're worse every time I see you. Even Mom and Dad are saner than you. Even the way they are now."

"The way they are now is fucking zombies. You're not staying there, are you? In the condo?"

"I always stay there when I visit. So do you."

"Yeah, but...I'd be out there on that damned sofa bed. Out in the open. I'm going to a motel. You should do the same."

"They're our parents, Jerry. You go where you want. I'm staying at Mom and Dad's place."

They'd squabbled since they were children. Often, the squabbles had turned into vicious physical fights—vicious only on one side, because Jerry would be punished severely if he hit his sister. In spite of that, he retained a kind of vague sibling affection for her, and he felt obligated to persuade her to protect herself now.

"You're scared of those zombies on the beach," he said. "Mom and Dad are just like them."

"It's all natural," Lily said. "You have to learn to accept the natural world. We're all the natural children of the Great Mother."

He started the car and pulled out of the parking lot, not quite sure where to go. The street ran the length of the barrier island and was lined with restaurants and motels. In the summer, the street was crowded with cars and the sidewalks were crowded with pedestrians, but now both looked empty.

By the time they got back to the condo complex, the sun was low. The air wasn't any cooler—it never was, here—but at least the light was no longer so blinding.

Jerry pulled into one of the visitor spaces in the parking lot and turned off the engine. The air conditioning stopped, and the outside heat and humidity began to force their way inside the car.

"I'm not going back in there," he said. "You shouldn't, either."

"Stop being stupid." Lily held up one hand. "Okay, I know. You can't help it. You're stupid."

"No, I'm the one with the brains."

"You're still stupid."

He had always hated the way his parents and his sister were

able to turn him back into a little boy again. "Your brain is so small, it'll just be an appetizer," he said. "They'll want mine for the main course."

Lily stuck her tongue out at him.

"You want to walk to the pier? Before it gets dark?"

Lily looked up at the sky. "I guess there's time."

They headed across the parking lot toward the sidewalk. It was a walk they often took in the evening when they happened to be visiting their parents at the same time, not because of feelings of sibling friendship, which didn't exist between them, but to get a few minutes of escape from their mother's prying and their father's lectures.

The sidewalk ran along a quiet street. To their left, across the street, was a row of houses that were rented to tourists during the summer and shuttered during the winter. Sometimes families rented them, sometimes groups of young people on vacation did so. In both cases, there was normally a lot of shouting and activity in those houses. They seemed to be quiet now, and no lights showed in them.

"That's weird," Jerry said, pointing across the street. "Where is everyone?"

"Maybe it's the economy," Lily said. "No one can afford to come down here. Or maybe it's that solar fucks thing you were talking about." She snorted derisively.

"Flux."

To their right was the beach, beginning at the edge of the sidewalk, and beyond the strip of sand was the water of the bay. A steady succession of tiny waves—ripples, really—lapped at the sand, making the most pleasant and relaxing sound Jerry had heard in days. Beyond the water, where the land curved around at the other end of the bay, lights shone from the hotels and restaurants of the business district, reflecting in the still water.

"It looks so pleasant from here," Jerry said. "You'd never guess that it's hell."

"Give it a rest."

On the way, they passed the senior center. Ancient dance music crackled faintly from ancient speakers. Through one of the lighted windows they could see ancient people dancing slowly. It looked the way it had when they'd walked past it on previous visits. There were usually some old folks standing outside the building, no doubt complaining about today's young people and their awful music and the direction of the country. Tonight seemed to be no exception.

"At least this place looks normal," Jerry said.

Then the moving figures inside all drifted to the window and pressed against it, seeming to stare out at the brother and sister. The murmuring groups outside the building stopped talking and faced toward them as well. The only sound was the music.

Jerry grasped his sister's arm and hurried her along, past the building and along the sidewalk toward the pier.

Lily kept looking over her shoulder. After a while, she said, "You're hurting me. Stop it. They're not following us."

He released her arm and slowed to a more normal walking pace. His heart was hammering. "So you're going to spend a night alone in a condo with two of *them*?"

"Mom and Dad, not 'two of *them*.' I think we're both overreacting. It was the light, or something. Those people back there are just normal old people. It looks the same here as it always does."

She stopped talking while an old couple shuffled past, hand in hand, cheekbones shining through their skin in the light from the senior center.

"See?" Lily said.

"You've always had a problem with reality. We saw Mom and Dad buried."

"Not exactly. We saw them in their coffins, and then later we saw those coffins put in the graves. We don't know who was really inside. Maybe there was a mix-up at the funeral parlor. Maybe both of them had some kind of disease that put them in a coma, and everyone thought they were dead, even the doctors. Then they woke up in the funeral parlor and panicked and put someone else's body in the coffin and ran away."

"I think I've seen that movie. So the same thing happened to both of them? A year apart? And then they hid away and let us think they were dead? Mom hid for almost a year? And now they both decided to show up again?"

"Maybe."

"That's ridiculous." Jerry looked at the old people, shadows in the dark, standing silently or moving slowly, randomly, on the sidewalk and the beach. "You're right that it looks the same as it always has. Except for the fact that they're all—" he shouted "—GODDAMNED ZOMBIES!"

Even in the dark, he could tell that all the shambling figures had turned to look at him and his sister, and they were all beginning to move toward them.

Brother and sister turned around and walked quickly, almost running, back toward the condo parking lot. They brushed past the group standing in front of the senior center and the hands reaching out from the dark.

Back at the car, in the brightly lit parking lot, they stopped, panting, covered with sweat.

"See?" Jerry gasped. "You were scared, too. You agree with me."

"I just wanted to make sure you didn't trip in the dark and hurt yourself."

He knew she would refuse to admit that she agreed with him. It had always seemed to be a point of pride with her to do that.

Nonetheless, he tried.

"They only look like our parents," he said. "Mom and Dad are dead."

"Obviously they're not dead."

"Obviously they are dead. They stink, and their skin is falling off. This place is filled with zombies, and that includes our parents."

"They're still our parents. Blood is thicker than water."

"Whatever the hell that's supposed to mean. I think they're thinking about our brains more than our blood."

"You watch too many stupid movies."

"We're in the middle of a stupid movie. This is the one where you go back to that condo and two old zombies eat your brains."

"You're an idiot. It was kind of fun when we were kids. Now you're just an idiot. I'm all sweaty from running because you panicked. I'm going to go back to the condo and have a shower. Then I'll spend some family time with Mom and Dad. And then I'll go to bed."

"Lock the bedroom door tonight," Jerry said as he unlocked the car.

"You're crazy. You're also an idiot."

"I'm just trying to protect you. Didn't I always protect you when you were little?"

"No. Never."

"Okay, but I'm trying to protect you now."

"Oh, please." She turned away.

Jerry watched her walk across the parking lot toward the building's entrance. He tried to conjure up nostalgia for the moments of warmth between them in childhood, but all he could remember were the fights. He shrugged, got in the car, and drove away.

Jerry drove until he found a motel with lots of bright lights around it.

The middleaged man at the front desk seemed to be normal and alive.

Jerry got a room for the night. He would sleep, and then he would reevaluate the situation in the morning.

Once he was in the room, he locked the door and attached the door's safety chain. The room had a small desk with a chair. He tried to wedge the chair under the doorknob, the way people always did in movies, but the chair was on wheels and the doorknob was a lever instead of a knob, so he gave up on that idea. He told himself he'd be perfectly safe. Nonetheless, he slept fitfully, waking repeatedly at the slightest noise outside the door.

In the morning, he stared at his haggard face in the mirror, at the dark shadows under his eyes, and thought that he was beginning to look like a zombie himself.

His mother would probably say something to him about not taking care of himself. Great, he thought. Health lectures from a corpse.

The motel provided a free, hot breakfast. He joined a few other sleepy people in the small breakfast room, where he piled bacon, ham, sausage, and scrambled eggs on his plate. He chewed and swallowed the food without much joy. The idea of lots of pork had appealed to him more than the actual food did. Pork always had a special appeal for him when he was visiting his parents, but this time the forbidden food lacked its usual magic. He wondered if the Gourmet Pirate served breakfast and if the scene outside the restaurant's big window was different in the morning.

A television set high on one wall was showing some kind of morning talk show. The sound was turned off, but the closed captions were turned on. Jerry chewed mechanically and watched idly. A group of slender, attractive women with earnest expressions were discussing the myriad faults of men in general and their boyfriends and husbands in particular.

Jerry's attention drifted away from the TV set. He looked at the other people in the room, none of them either slender or attractive.

He looked, and he grew suddenly alarmed.

The people he was watching walked as if their brains were dead and they had no souls. They were zombies!

But then he noticed that they perked up when they had some coffee. He realized that they were just typical exhausted travelers.

They're all normal, he thought, and they're all visitors from elsewhere. They're non–Floridians. Lucky them. Maybe this contagion is limited to Florida.

He hoped so. He'd pay a quick visit to the condo, and then he'd be a traveler, too. Back on the road, he thought. Back to civilization. Even without zombies, he had spent as much time here as he could stand. He had always hated Florida with a hatred so great, so intense, that the addition of zombies couldn't make the place more hateful.

He checked out, put his bags in the trunk of his car, and drove toward his parents' condo complex.

He wondered if he had dreamed everything. Maybe there were no zombies. Maybe Florida was just its usual hellish self without anything supernatural added.

Traffic was light. He scanned the sidewalks as he drove. There was normally a mix of ages on the sidewalks -- old people who lived here, young people on vacation from school, and families, also on vacation. The families strolled, taking in the sights, the young people zoomed along while eyeing each other, and the old people shuffled. Today he saw only old people, and they weren't shuffling. They were standing still, eyes closed, faces tilted toward the sun.

He drove slowly, staring at them. Their skin was dry and dark and cracked, their flesh sunken. Bones showed.

Nope, he thought. It wasn't a dream. It's a waking nightmare.

He shivered and focused on the traffic. Which now seemed even lighter than before. Any visitor who could still drive was leaving, he guessed.

What about the natives? he asked himself.

They're being eaten, he replied.

His route took him close to a long beach, a place where he had once spent a pleasant if sweaty afternoon standing in what little shade there was and girl watching. He wasn't surprised to see that the sand was now covered with close–packed, silent, leathery bodies. Here and there, the white of exposed bone gleamed amidst the darkened skins.

Sun–worshipers, he thought. That term had a whole new meaning now.

On the way, he stopped at a Publix supermarket and bought a big jar of Piper's Pickled Peppers, shuddering as he did so.

That was the last jar of the peppers on the shelf.

The older Morgensterns had never liked the beach. Years earlier, when Jerry had asked them why they had chosen Florida for their retirement, his father had said, "Because it's warm and it doesn't snow."

"But it's hell," Jerry had said.

"When you get to be our age," his mother had said, "you'll understand."

I'll never be your age, Jerry had thought, like every young person before him.

To his relief, there were cars but no people in the condo parking lot. The old people he was used to seeing shuffling across the parking lot had always bothered him—repelled him, to tell the truth—but they hadn't scared him. Zombies did.

He looked around carefully before he got out. He hesitated about locking the car. What if he needed to make a quite getaway? But there were still live, human predators here in hell, and he had to protect his property against them, so he locked the door.

He walked quickly across the lot, his head down and shoulders hunched, as though that would protect him against zombies and human thugs and the malevolent sun and the heavy, wet air.

His mother opened the door when he rang the bell. She looked slightly better than the day before—still a walking corpse, but a bit livelier.

She tried to hug him, but he held out the jar of pickles quickly and made her take it. Her eyes lit up and she seemed to forget about the hug. He held his breath until he could push past her and get a few feet away from her. That didn't help, though. The smell of death now pervaded the condo.

The hallway led directly into the dining room. His father was there, sitting at the table and eating messily. The older man had never been a gracious diner, and death had not improved him. The plate in front of him was covered with a red, jelly–like substance, which he was spooning into his mouth. Jerry thought that death had not improved his mother's cooking, either.

"Where's Lily?" Jerry asked.

His father stopped moving with his mouth open and the spoon in midair. The red jelly oozed over the side of the spoon and drooled down to the plate.

"She's gone," his mother said.

"She went out? When?" She won't have gone far on foot in this weather, he thought.

"No, she's gone. Away. You don't have to wait for her."

His father turned to look at Jerry. He stared at Jerry's forehead.

"Unless you want to wait. Have a seat. You must be tired. Take a nap."

"I'm not tired, and I don't need a nap. I need to be on the road. I just came by to say goodbye and to make sure that Lily's okay."

His father looked back at the plate. "She's excellent." He started spooning the jelly into his mouth again.

At the touch of a hand on his shoulder, Jerry started. It was his mother, standing suddenly beside him. She was between him and the door. He heard the sound of a chair being pushed back and turned to see his father standing up.

A feeling of panic overcame him. He stepped back quickly and around his mother. "Tell Lily I stopped by. I have to go."

His mother gave him the guilt–trip look that Jewish parents have honed to perfection over the millennia. "You're always in such a rush. We never get to see you."

"Stay," his father said. "Come to the beach with us. Get some sunlight."

"You hate the beach," Jerry said. "And the sun."

"Nonsense," his father said, looking at him as though he were a fool. He had often looked at Jerry that way, and it had always annoyed Jerry, but this was the zombie version of that look, which made it more unsettling than annoying. "We love the beach and the sun. It's good for us. All our friends will be there."

"Gotta run," Jerry said, and he did, down the hallway, down the rickety stairway outside, and across the parking lot to his car. Fumbling with his keys, he got the car door open, threw himself inside, and locked the door.

The parking lot was still empty of people of any kind. Jerry gave himself a few minutes while he waited for his heart to slow down. Then he started the car and turned the air conditioning on full blast, with all the blowers pointed toward him. He was sweating even more than he usually did in this hellhole. The air turned cold after a while, and he sat leaning forward into the artificial breeze, drying off and calming down. At last he sat back, buckled his seat belt, and drove out of the parking lot and toward the Interstate.

CHAPTER TWO

On the Interstate, everything looked normal, although he thought there was less traffic than normal.

The usual glare of sunlight was dimmed by a cloud cover that thickened as he drove. That made Jerry think of solar flux.

He wondered if his earlier speculation about solar flux made any sense. He also wondered what solar flux was. He had read the term and liked the sound of it, but he hadn't bothered to look for a definition. He wasn't really the brainy one in the family, as his father had called him, but from childhood on he had had the knack of making people think that he was brainy. He had been fooling people all of his life. Having hungry zombie parents who believed that he had more brains inside his skull than other people did was some kind of cosmic payback.

Maybe it's not the sun, he thought. Maybe it's a virus, or pollution in the Gulf of Mexico, or weird vapors being released by the oil platforms. But if it's one of those, then it's probably not limited to Florida.

That was a terrifying thought.

Fortunately, his gas tank was almost full. He didn't stop to refuel until he was well into Georgia.

He pulled into a service station overlooking the Interstate. He stopped beside a gas tank, but he didn't unlock his door until he had stared for long minutes at the other travelers filling their own tanks.

When he was convinced that they were all normal, he got out, moving quickly, prepaid at the pump with his credit card, filled his car, looking around nervously all the while, and then got back on the road.

He was feeling hungry, but he didn't dare stop at a restaurant yet. He wanted to eat; he didn't want to be the meal. He thought about watching his father eating that morning. Jerry had a strong suspicion about what that disgusting substance on the plate was, but he didn't want to think any further about that.

For the first time, he turned on the car radio. He found a news broadcast. It was just the usual stuff about sports, the economy, murder, war, and mayhem. There was nothing about a zombie invasion.

In Washington, the Republicans were posturing and pandering to their base. Social programs were un-American and should be eliminated in order to force the parasitical poor to get jobs and lift themselves up by their bootstraps right after they bought boots. Democrats were responding with instantaneous capitulation. In the Senate, Fred Foxtrot, Republican from the great State of Arapahoe, was babbling his usual nonsense about strength, destiny, cowboys, oilmen, assorted other rugged individualists, and the sainted Ronald Reagan. Jerry voted against Foxtrot whenever he had the opportunity, but the vile man's political career kept prospering.

It was business as usual, and while it made Jerry mutter and curse and yell at the radio, it provided a comforting sense of normality. This was the America he knew and alternately loved and hated. This, not a zombie apocalypse. He wanted to believe that he had imagined all the weirdness in Florida, but the image of the plate of red glop his father had been eating that morning intruded and undermined his attempt.

That image made it all real again. His mind wandered into

speculation about zombies.

Were zombies slow or fast? In the movies, they shambled stiffly and slowly. His parents weren't fast, but they never had been. The other old zombies he'd seen in Florida were also slow. But they were old people, and he assumed they'd moved slowly before dying. Would someone who died young and then came back to life be a fast zombie?

That was an alarming thought.

I could outrun a slow zombie, he thought. Maybe defend myself, if I had to. Well, I could if I knew anything about self–defense. I should take some martial arts lessons. Tai Chi, maybe. That would be good for defending yourself against slow zombies.

As for the fast ones...

His mind skittered away from the thought and kept skittering in random directions as he drove north.

A zombie apocalypse might not be all bad, he thought. Maybe the great composers of old would come back to life and start composing again. Wouldn't it be wonderful to have new symphonies from Beethoven? Even though all the movements would be slow ones.

He spent the night in a motel south of Atlanta. He slept late, barely getting out before checkout time. Before getting under way again, he had breakfast at a restaurant next door to the motel. Grits with gravy, fried eggs, and ham. The South wasn't all bad, he thought. As long as there was air conditioning.

The zombies seemed to need the sun. He wondered if they also needed heat. Would air conditioning kill them, or at least make them even slower?

Can't you just stop thinking about the damned things? he asked himself.

Apparently not, he answered.

Jerry made a long, slow trip of it, driving shorter distances than usual before finding a motel, and making frequent stops during each leg of the trip. He had extra time before being due back at work, thanks to leaving Florida sooner than he had originally planned. He needed the solitude of the long drive back home to help him reenter the real world.

When Jerry finally entered his apartment in Piketon and checked his voicemail for the first time since leaving the city more than a week earlier, there was a message from George Gordon imploring him to come into the office as soon as possible. "I didn't want to call your cell phone," George said in the voicemail, "because of the nature of your trip. But we really need you here, Jerry."

It was late and he had to pick up a few groceries, so Jerry didn't call back.

At the grocery store, he examined his fellow customers carefully, but they all seemed normal. Relieved, he picked up what he needed and went home. That evening, he watched the local news, and there, too, all seemed normal. There was no mention of zombies in Piketon. There was no mention of zombies in Florida, either. That made Jerry nervous again. Was the government suppressing all terrifying news from the butt crack of hell?

Because the station he was watching was the local Fixed News outlet, it always gave extra and favorable coverage to Arapahoe's Republican senator, Fred Foxtrot. Earlier that day, Foxtrot had given a speech in the Senate about voting rights. Long excerpts were shown on the news.

Jerry watched the excerpts, but he could make little sense of them. Foxtrot never made sense, and yet he had a devoted following in the state and had won every election comfortably, starting with his first, a city council race in a small town up north near the Wyoming border. Now Foxtrot was being mentioned as a possible presidential or vice–presidential candidate.

That would be even worse than a zombie apocalypse, Jerry thought. Then he remembered the zombies in Florida and his reaction to them, and he changed his mind.

Voting rights, though. That was odd. Why was Foxtrot giving a speech about that? The only respect in which Foxtrot and his kind cared about voting rights was taking them away from likely Democratic voters.

Jerry tried again to pay attention to the obnoxious whiny, nasal voice of Arapahoe's senior senator.

"Deprived of their God–given, American right to vote because of their age!" Foxtrot was saying.

He wants to lower the voting age? Jerry thought. That didn't sound like Foxtrot. He would never get the votes of younger voters. He'd be more likely to want to raise the age back to 21. Or even higher.

"This is a new era," Foxtrot shouted. He pounded on the lectern in front of him. "We won't go back to taxation without representation! Citizens must have the right to vote, and it must not be taken away from them because of an insignificant and merely temporary change of domicile. Justice must be done and voting rights must be restored to our Interrupted Existence Compatriots, the IECs."

The camera panned briefly around the almost empty chamber. A few of Foxtrot's fellow senators were standing in the open space at the front of the room, talking to each other, clearly ignoring the Arapahoan's passionate speech.

What an embarrassment to this state the man is, Jerry thought. They're right to ignore him.

Foxtrot disappeared from the screen. A commercial took his place. It showed a slender, attractive woman with an alert, intelligent expression making lunch for her rowdy children and dull-witted, slack-jawed husband. A smug female voiceover said, "You know they'll just make a mess of it, no matter how carefully you prepare it." The husband reached hungrily for the sandwich the wife was preparing. She slapped his hand away. "So outwit them with the plastic wrap that's smarter than they are." Picture of a box of plastic wrap with a big, red letter M on it distorted into the shape of a heart. "Mom Wrap! It keeps everything in its place." Smart mother wraps all the lunches in Mom Wrap while husband and children look on in stupid defeat.

Jerry turned off the TV set and went to bed. Tomorrow he'd be back in the office. It would be a relief, a full return to normality.

Jerry took an early bus into downtown Piketon. His fellow passengers were sleepy humans, but they *were* humans. The sun was shining. The pedestrians he saw through the bus window were human. The cars in the adjacent lanes contained humans.

It's good to be alive, Jerry thought. And it's good to be surrounded by other people who are also genuinely alive.

He got off the bus and walked the remaining half mile to the office. The sidewalks were filled with other people on their way to work. Most of them were young or middle aged, and they weren't shuffling. Even the few old people didn't shuffle. No one stood unmoving, staring up at the sun.

Good, old, placid Piketon, Jerry thought. Nothing weird ever happens here.

Ahead of him, he could see the high-rise where he worked. The building was fifteen stories high. The top three stories were occupied by the headquarters of Piper's Pickled Peppers, Inc. A huge sign consisting of the letters PPP in bright green stood atop the building, practically glowing in the sunlight. The same triple-p logo was plastered on walls throughout the company.

Jerry remembered how silly he had felt coming to work here on his first day, almost ten years earlier, and how sure he had been that he would be embarrassed to tell people that he worked at Piper's Pickled Peppers. But he had come to love the company and its people, with the sole exception of the founder and president, Frank Pistole, a tall, saturnine man, who was irascible on his few good days and evil on every other day.

For years, up until Pistole died, the only other thing that Jerry had hated was the big bowl of fresh Piper's Pickled Peppers placed in every lunch room every morning. It was well known that employees were expected to eat those pickles. Frank Pistole would lean over slowly and creepily and sniff the breath of any employee he encountered to see if the employee had skipped the pickled peppers that day. Jerry hated the taste of the things, and they gave him heartburn. Each morning, he took one from the bowl. From time to time during the day, he forced himself to suck on the pickled pepper, hoping that that would do the trick if Frank checked him. He still got heartburn, but he knew it would be much worse if he swallowed the damned thing.

It did seem to do the trick, and Frank did check him often, because the detestable man had taken a strange shine to Jerry from the start, stopping by Jerry's cubicle during the day, calling him into the enormous presidential office to chat about inconsequentials, and promoting him regularly, all the way from the mail room up to senior editor, Jerry's current position. It made Jerry feel guilty about despising the man, but he couldn't help himself. Jerry's title was Senior Editor, but in fact he was the company's only editor, and seemingly the company's only literate employee, so he was swamped with work much of the time. His salary was shamefully large, far larger than he could hope to get at another company. He felt guilty about taking the money of a man he hated while pretending to like him, but the size of his biweekly paycheck was a powerful argument in favor of saying nothing and continuing to suck the pickle.

Even so, he had worried about the paycheck continuing. Not because he feared crossing Pistole—he seemed to be safe in that regard—but rather because he feared for the future of the company.

The great days of Piper's Pickled Peppers had come and gone before Jerry had started working there.

Frank Pistole had founded the company 35 years earlier. At the time, he was a newlywed, making a meager living working in an office-supply store. At night, he pickled peppers.

According to company legend, Pistole experimented with various pickling brines in his kitchen before coming up with the one that resulted in what he considered the perfect pickled pepper. The key lay in a secret ingredient, the details of which were known only to Frank Pistole. Thanks to modern food regulations, in later years he spent a huge amount of money every year keeping those details from appearing on the labels of his product's packaging. He was, of course, a firm—even fierce—supporter of Republican politicians. The more they lauded small—or better yet non-existent—government and deregulation, the fiercer his support.

His only child, a daughter, was born five weeks before Frank perfected his recipe. His wife skipped out a couple of days after giving birth, leaving a note saying that she hated Frank and she hated pickled peppers, but she was sure he'd give their child a better home than she could. The baby remained nameless during those five weeks. When Frank tasted that first perfect pickle, he named his daughter Piper. He founded his company on the same day. No one knew if he had named his company after his daughter or the other way around.

Frank himself came up with the company's motto: "Pick Piper's

Pickled Peppers!"

The company quickly became synonymous with gourmet pickled peppers of all kinds, prized worldwide by the kind of people who prize premier pickled peppers. Frank Pistole had not been satisfied with pickling the varieties of peppers everyone else pickled. He searched the world for odd plants that were technically peppers, including those that grew only in some tiny plot of earth hidden from the view of everyone except for the eagle–eyed pepper detectives in Frank's employ. Then he bred those plants on his own big farms and pickled them in his secret brine and bottled them and distributed them and grew ever wealthier and more famous.

Inevitably, in time others got into the game. Frank Pistole refused to change anything, from his management style to his marketing methods to the company's motto. Despite the secret ingredient, Piper's Pickled Peppers started to lose ground. In time, it lost its preeminent position. Now it was just one gourmet pickled pepper company among many, and not even the biggest of them. There were many empty cubicles and offices in the three floors the company occupied, and layoffs were a regular event. When he dropped dead from a severe attack of bile, Frank had been trying to bully the building's owners into letting him break his lease and downsize to one floor.

That was six months ago.

Fortunately, when Frank Pistole died, control of the company passed to Piper, his equally intimidating but extraordinarily beautiful daughter.

A couple of years earlier, Piper had persuaded her father to hire her husband, George Gordon. George subsequently spent his days in the marketing department, jumping at sudden noises and keeping out of his father–in–law's way. Everyone pushed George around. Even the stupid kid in the mailroom did it.

Jerry liked George, who had a sweet disposition and was pleasant company when he wasn't terrified. He also envied George for being married to Piper and often wondered how such a match had come about.

To everyone's surprise, upon her father's death, Piper put George in control of the company. To everyone's even greater surprise, George flowered in the role, and he did so without losing his good nature. He brought new energy and new ideas to the company. More important, he forged new and better relationships with customers and retail outlets. Six months later, the company was growing again instead of shrinking, employees were smiling, and there was a buzz of optimism in the air. George also got rid of the bowls of pickled peppers in the lunchroom, which made Jerry adore him.

On this bright and cheerful morning, on his first day back after his Florida trip, Jerry rode the elevator to the fourteenth floor and headed for his cubicle, whistling. After a few seconds, he realized that the place was unusually quiet, so he stopped whistling.

He passed a couple of occupied cubicles and called out a cheery "Good morning!"

No one replied.

He turned back and looked at the two people he had just greeted. A horrible fear had washed over him. To his relief, they looked like normal human beings, not zombies. However, they looked like normal human beings who had just received some awful news. They stared back at him mutely, their eyes wide and their faces pale.

Oh, crap, he thought. Some major customer must have just gone bankrupt.

He hurried on to his cubicle.

George Gordon was there, waiting for him, staring into space and bouncing up and down on his toes. All of him jiggled up and down as he did so. George was tall and wide and soft, and he jiggled much of the time.

"Morning, George. Who died?"

"Jerry! Thank God! No one died. He's back."

Before Florida, Jerry would have had no idea what George meant. Now, he knew immediately.

"He un–died," George added.

"Frank."

"Mr. Pistole. The boss."

"You're the boss, George. Frank died, and Piper made you the boss."

George shook his head. "Not any more. Mr. Pistole's back in his office. I guess I'll go back to marketing."

"He's dead, George. He's not real. Just ignore him. Think of him as a ghost." Even as he said those things to try to instill some spine into perennially spineless George, Jerry remembered his own behavior in Florida, and he knew that his efforts were pointless.

"Could you go and talk to him, Jerry? He always liked you. He won't talk to me or to anyone else. He'll talk to you. Ask him what his plans are for me."

To eat your brains, Jerry thought. "Yeah, okay. I guess I'm the guy who talks to zombies."

"What?"

"I've had experience. By the way, are there any jars of those pickled peppers in the office?"

"I think so. Why?"

"Put some bowls of them in the lunchrooms."

George looked around quickly and then leaned close to Jerry. "Do I have to?" he whispered. "I hate the damned things."

"I think it would be wise."

Jerry put his briefcase under the shelf that served as a desk inside his cubicle and headed for the staircase. He climbed the stairs to the fifteenth floor, feeling disturbingly alone and isolated inside the empty stairwell. He told himself that he should have taken the elevator.

There were no cubicles on the fifteenth floor. It was given over to large offices and conference rooms. The largest of the offices was reserved for the president. For decades, Frank Pistole had occupied that big office. For six months, George Gordon had sat there, visibly happy and ill at ease at the same time.

When Frank Pistole was in that office—or so it had seemed to Jerry—darkness had emanated from it, pouring through the doorway to fill the entire floor. For six months, the fifteenth floor had instead seemed filled with light. Now, as he opened the door from the stairwell and stepped into the big open space at the center of the fifteenth floor, the darkness had returned.

You have an overactive imagination, he told himself.

No, I don't, he replied. I didn't imagine the zombies in Florida.

As he stood in the doorway of the president's office, he saw that George hadn't imagined the return of Frank Pistole from the dead, either.

The man in the office wasn't sitting at the big desk. Instead, he stood by the window, bathed in sunlight, his eyes closed, his face turned to the sun.

Jerry shuddered at the sight. Then he looked more carefully and saw that Pistole looked surprisingly good—much better than Jerry's parents. The expensive embalming job mandated in Pistole's will was paying dividends.

There was a radio in the office. During George's six-month tenure, it had always been tuned to the local NPR classical station. Now it emitted the nasal droning of Big Jim Tweddle, Frank Pistole's favorite right-wing radio ranter.

Jerry took a deep breath, knocked on the door, and said, "Welcome back, Mr. Pistole."

Pistole opened his eyes and turned away from the sun slowly, reluctantly. For a moment, he seemed not to recognize Jerry. Then he moved out of the glare, toward his desk, and his face lit up with a smile. "Jerry! I'm relieved to see you." The voice, which had been strong and commanding in life, was weak and muffled. "I was afraid that you might have left the company out of grief. Never fear. I'm back. I had to walk all the way home from the cemetery. That fool George didn't think to put money for a taxi in my suit."

"The suit looks good, sir. Um, surprisingly good."

"Oh, it's not the one I was wearing when I woke up." His voice seemed to be getting stronger and clearer as he spoke. "That one was split down the back. Absurd. This one belonged to one of the servants at the house. They were surprised to see me. They didn't want to let me in. Fools. Brainless idiots." Pistole smiled. "Especially after I got inside."

Jerry fought against the urge to run. "We're all very surprised to see you, sir. And happy, of course," he said.

"Of course you are. I understand that my daughter put her fool of a husband in charge. The company must have gone to the dogs while I was away."

"Actually, sir, it's been good. Sales are up. We've added a lot of new outlets. Profits are very good."

Pistole frowned. The embalmed skin of his forehead cracked audibly and something white gleamed in the crack. "That's because of what I was doing when I left. How long was I gone?"

"Six months, sir."

Pistole nodded—carefully, as though he were afraid his neck would break. "Six months. Exactly. That's how long it takes for a president's policies to take effect."

"I've read that," Jerry said.

"Of course you have. You were always one of the few people in this place with brains." He stared intently at Jerry. "Brains."

"I'll get back to work now, sir," Jerry said quickly. "I just wanted welcome you back." He turned to go.

"Wait." Pistole's voice was suddenly strong and commanding again. It was a voice that had always undermined Jerry's confidence, and it did so even more now. "I have a mission for you."

Pistole reached down and picked up a small piece of paper from his desk. He held it out to Jerry. "Take this over to Foxtrot's headquarters. They'll be expecting you."

Jerry approached hesitantly and reached out across the desk. He tried to come no closer to the zombie than necessary. He snatched the paper from the embalmed hand and stepped back again quickly. He glanced at what he was holding. It was a company check for fifty thousand dollars, written to the reelection campaign of Senator Fred Foxtrot.

"I don't think this is legal, sir."

"You're a smart young man. Sometimes it's not good to be too smart. To have a lot of brains." He walked around his desk and stepped toward Jerry."

Jerry stepped back to the doorway, ready to bolt to the staircase. "I'm leaving right now, sir."

"Send in a pickle," Pistole said. "Tell my idiot son–in–law to bring me one of my pickled peppers. I love my pickled peppers."

"Everyone loves them, sir."

Jerry backed through the doorway. It occurred to him suddenly that Pistole might not be the only zombie on the fifteenth floor. He whirled around, but he was alone in the central space. Sweating, he rushed to the door into the stairwell and ran down one flight of stairs.

George was still waiting at Jerry's cubicle.

"What did he say?"

"He wants a pickle."

"What? Fuck those damned pickles. What did he say about me?"

"He said he wants you to bring him a pickle."

"I'm not going in there."

"Send someone else. Someone without brains."

"But what did he say when you asked him about me?"

"Oh, hell, I forgot, George. I was too scared to remember. I'm sorry. But he did specify that you were to procure the pickle. So I guess you're still working here."

"I'm the pickle fetcher," George said. "That's great."

"I'm the deliverer of illegal campaign donations." Jerry held the check out for George to see.

"Shit. He's always had a thing about Foxtrot. He always wanted to give money to that slimeball. That preacher, too. You know—the televangelist, what's his name, Flexman."

"Brother Steve. Another slimeball."

"Yeah, that's the guy. I used to be able to talk Frank out of doing it. He's going to destroy the company."

"Talk to him. Go in there."

"Hell, no. I'm going to send someone stupid in there with a pickle."

The local headquarters of Arapahoe's senior senator were in downtown Piketon, less than a mile away from the building containing the headquarters of Piper's Pickled Peppers.

It was still morning, the sun was shining brightly, and the people on the sidewalks looked normal. Despite that seeming normality, Jerry walked quickly, looking behind him frequently.

After a zombie-free trip, he walked through the front door of

Foxtrot headquarters. The building was a simple store front, the windows of which were filled with big color photographs of Fred Foxtrot and American flags and a sign saying FOXTROT FOR AMERICA. Jerry felt dirty just entering the place.

He expected a buzzing hive of activity, all of it sleazy, rightwing, and reprehensible. Instead, he found himself in a large, almost empty room. There were a few desks with no one sitting behind them. There were a few chairs scattered around. Jerry had been thinking of venting his intense dislike of Foxtrot and his politics on the first smirking Republican he encountered in the Foxtrot headquarters. He looked around for a target.

There was one occupied desk, facing the entrance. A young woman sat behind it, her attention focused on a paperback book she held. Jerry assumed she was the receptionist, and he decided to vent his anger on her. His gorge rose in preparation.

"Hello," he said.

She looked up, and his heart skipped a beat and his anger faded. She was breathtakingly beautiful. Jerry smiled at her. He thought his smile was charming and made him look interesting.

"Yeah?" she asked. "What?"

"Senator Foxtrot is expecting me." That makes me sound important, he thought.

She gestured over her shoulder with her thumb. "Upstairs." She returned to the paperback.

"Do I need to sign in?" He wanted her to look up again. He wanted to gaze at her face forever.

She shook her head, her attention still on the book.

"Are you sure?"

"Go away."

Jerry sighed and went away. Some things were as terrifying as zombies, he thought. Or almost. Such as Piper Pistole Gordon,

George's wife, Frank's daughter, a woman he lusted after and feared in equal measure. He would always wonder why she had married George, and how George had managed to survive this long. It occurred to Jerry that, when he wasn't looking frightened, George smiled a lot.

The beautiful thumb had indicated an internal staircase at the back of the room. As he started up it, Jerry could hear two men talking. One of the voices was the familiar loud, unpleasant nasal whine of Foxtrot. The other was lower in both pitch and volume.

Jerry couldn't make out the words, but as he reached the top of the stairs and found himself looking into an office and at Foxtrot's back, he heard the senator say, "You're sure it's working now? No more exploding cows or corpses?"

"That was only at the beginning," the other man said. "Now they're taking their old places back and integrating nicely." He lowered his voice and said something that Jerry couldn't hear.

Jerry stepped forward, hoping to hear the rest of the conversation. He had no idea what they were talking about, of course, but since they didn't know he was there, he hoped it was something that an opponent could use against Foxtrot in the next election.

Maybe me, Jerry thought. I could run for office. Then I'd have my own beautiful receptionist. There are supposed to be a lot of beautiful girls in politics.

On the other hand, if he won, he'd have to spend much of his time in Washington. He dismissed the idea and listened again.

The second man's back was toward him, and Foxtrot was facing him. Suddenly the senator noticed him standing there and scowled. "Who the fuck are you?" he snarled.

"Pickle delivery," Jerry said. He stepped into the office and held up the check so that Foxtrot could see it.

The senator snatched the check from his hand and glanced at it.

A smile spread over his face, and his whole demeanor changed. His voice dropped in pitch and increased in volume. He ratcheted up the smarm level. "Why, this is excellent, young man. I see that Frank Pistole signed this. My dear friend, Frank. He's back in the office, is he?"

Jerry nodded. He was looking at the other man in the office, trying to remember why he looked familiar.

The man noticed Jerry's look and turned away, suddenly becoming interested in a framed photograph of a mountain vista that hung on one wall.

"Please tell Frank how grateful I am," Foxtrot boomed.

When Jerry, looking at the back of the third man's head and still trying to remember who he was, didn't respond, Foxtrot said, "You can leave now."

"What? Oh, right."

Downstairs, the beautiful receptionist was still engrossed in her book. Jerry said loudly, "Hi, again! I'm leaving now! Bye!"

For all the attention she paid to him, she might have been one of the zombies he had seen in Florida with their faces turned toward the sun.

He sighed and headed for the front door.

Someone else was coming in. The person was a silhouette against the bright sunlight outside, and Jerry couldn't make out the face. He thought it was a woman, but he wasn't even sure of that.

Then the silhouette entered the room and became the person Jerry hated most in the world.

"What the hell are you doing here?" Wendy Kline, his ex-wife, asked him.

"I have to be somewhere."

"No, you don't. You shouldn't be anywhere."

They had actually loved each other, once. Or so they both had claimed. They had dated for six months, and then they had married impulsively. Two weeks later, they were both saying, "I hate you," loudly and frequently. Foolishly, they had put off getting divorced for another two years. Comparing those two years to his time at Piper's Pickled Peppers while Frank Pistole was alive and to his recent experience in Florida, Jerry wasn't sure which of those periods he would rank as the worst.

"You should be in Florida, visiting your dead parents," Wendy said. "If you know what I mean."

"Funny you should mention that."

"Awful chatting with you," Wendy said. "Good bye. I'm here to have lunch with a friend." She turned and waved at the receptionist, who smiled at her radiantly.

Jerry staggered.

Wendy snickered. "She's out of your league."

"You remind me so much of Lily."

"You know, your sister is the only member of your family I ever liked. How is she?"

"Eaten."

"What?"

"Up with grief."

Wendy looked surprised. "If you say so. Tell her to give me a call."

Jerry heard steps on the staircase. He turned to look and saw the oddly familiar man from Foxtrot's office creeping down the stairs as though trying to avoid detection. When the man realized that Jerry was watching him, he straightened and walked normally the rest of the way down the stairs and then across the room toward the exit. He kept his face averted from Jerry as he passed by.

"Yeah, I'll tell her," Jerry said. He followed the man through the door to the sidewalk outside.

"Excuse me," Jerry said. "Sir."

The man walked away quickly.

"Sir!"

The man walked faster. Halfway down the block, he got into a car parked at the curb, started the engine, and pulled out of the parking spot quickly and drove away.

Jerry watched him drive past and made a mental note of the license plate: BT STUD.

Walking back to the office, Jerry felt guilty that he hadn't thought of Lily since making his escape from Florida.

Surely he had succumbed to an overactive imagination, he told himself. Surely his parents hadn't killed their own daughter and eaten her brains. She had just been out for a while when he stopped by the elder Morgensterns' condo to say goodbye. By now, she was probably back home in New York and being her normal, unpleasant self.

He should have called her to check.

I'll call her today, he thought. She'll be at work now. I'll call her this evening. I'm her older brother. I'm supposed to protect her.

Memories of Lily as a little girl came back to him. She had been a nasty, treacherous little creature, stealing or destroying his belongings when she wasn't ratting on him to their parents.

I'm glad I never protected her, he thought. But I'll call her, anyway.

When he got back to the building housing the offices of Piper's Pickled Peppers, Jerry steeled himself and took the elevator to the top floor. There were still no zombies in sight as he walked across the open space to the president's office. He paused, breathed deeply a couple of times, then knocked on the door and walked in.

George Gordon was sitting behind the president's desk.

"This is a surprise," Jerry said. He closed the office door and came inside. "Is everything back to normal again?"

"Hell, no. The dead man left for the day. He said he wanted to get out while the sun was still shining and soak up some rays. That's what he said: 'Soak up some rays.' I thought the sun was supposed to destroy them."

"That's vampires. Frank's a zombie. They seem to like the sun. Did you get him his pickle?"

"I did. I sent Joey in with it. You know him? That stupid kid from the mailroom?"

"Yeah. Good choice."

"He went in, but he didn't come out again. I looked around in here after Frank left for the day. There's something red on the carpet over there." He nodded toward a corner of the room. "It looks like a smear of blood, but how the hell would I know? That's all I found. This isn't real, is it?"

"I've got something to tell you," Jerry said. He sat down in the chair beside the desk and told George everything that had happened to him in Florida.

George sat shaking his head back and forth the whole time. "This doesn't make any sense," he said. "I don't believe it."

"You've seen it. Frank Pistole was dead, and now he's back again. He's a zombie. I guess it's not limited to Florida."

"Let's say I believe you," George said. "What am I supposed to do? Put silver all over the place? Have everyone wear crosses?"

"I'm not going to wear a cross, George. Anyway, that's vampires again, not zombies. Didn't you ever watch horror movies?"

"No. They always scared me too much. What do you do about zombies?"

"I think you're supposed to shoot them in the head. Right

through their brains."

George shivered. "Not me. Although..." He looked wistful. "No. Piper would kill me. Help me, Jerry."

"I'll see what I can come up with. I think I'll go back to my desk and try to get caught up. The work probably piled up while I was away. Maybe not focusing directly on our problem will help. I'll focus on work instead and let my unconscious have free rein."

He was right that work had piled up in his absence, but when he skimmed a few of the white papers, marketing announcements, and internal software documents waiting for him to turn them into English, he moaned in despair and turned away from his monitor.

He couldn't deal with it all. He'd find something else productive to do and hope that his unconscious would do its job anyway.

Lily!

He remembered her again, and again he felt guilty about not calling her sooner. Maybe she wasn't at work. Maybe she was at her apartment, unpacking or doing her laundry. Or maybe she was grocery shopping. He'd try her apartment and then her cell phone.

He left the office and went down to the building lobby. Only a few people were walking through it at that time of day. He settled down in one of the couches that were scattered around the lobby and called Lily's apartment on his cell phone.

Almost to his surprise, she answered.

"Lily Morgenstern. Make it quick."

What a relief! She was there, and she was her normal abrasive, fast–talking New York self. "It's me. Jerry. I was just checking to make sure you got home okay."

"Jerry!" she shouted. "I hurt my head somehow in Florida!"

He held the phone away from his ear. "What?"

"And then I got home and I started to think about Florida and earthquakes and tsunamis! And my head hurts! I've got a big scab!"

"What?"

"Mother Earth is screaming, Jerry! We have to help her! Goodbye!" She disconnected.

Oh, God, he thought. They did eat her brains.

What was worse was that it had made so little difference.

CHAPTER THREE

Jerry left work early. When he got back to his apartment, he Googled *arapahoe license plate bt stud*. License plate information was publicly available in Arapahoe, so he assumed that this search would give him at least the name of the driver of the car he had seen.

Instead, his search returned endless sites offering to sell him the information he wanted, including many that claimed that they would give him the information for free but that turned out to require payment after a click or two, along with a few sites warning him that any sites offering to give him the details about a license plate for free were scams. His search results also included sites offering to hook him up with studs living in Arapahoe.

Fortunately, among the list of sites returned by Google, he spotted an article from a local business blog about someone named Walter Zing, mentioning that his personalized license plate was BT STUD.

Walter Zing, Jerry said to himself. He repeated the name a few times. Walter Zing. Walter Zing. Walter Zing.

And then he remembered.

Twenty-five years earlier, when Jerry was 12, Walter Zing had had a science program for kids on local television.

Jerry sat back and smiled in fond reminiscence. He had never been particularly interested in science, but Zing—Doctor Walter, as he had called himself on the show—had made it interesting.

Doctor Walter's Superscience Show.

Jerry chuckled at the remembered name.

Zing had been young, slender, and filled with enthusiasm for his subject. Enthusiasm and love. Jerry remembered being aware of the man's love of everything he talked about, and he talked about everything, every area of science he had time for.

About the time he turned 13, Jerry stopped watching the show. He hadn't thought of it since.

It was hard to connect the energetic young lecturer Jerry remembered with the round, furtive man he had seen in Foxtrot's office, but he was sure it was the same man. In his mind's eye, he applied Photoshop to the face, trimming away the jowls, removing the wrinkles and the shadows under the eyes, and making the hair thicker. He imagined the man standing straighter and grinning. Yes, it was definitely the same man.

What had happened to Walter Zing in the intervening years?

Jerry clicked through to the online article.

Zing had been working for BioTyne, a huge pharmaceutical company headquartered in Piketon, for the last 20 years, the article said. He was now Chief Scientist at BT and in charge of a number of projects, none of which he could talk about to the reporter because they involved proprietary information. He did tell the reporter, proudly, that he had had his personalized license plate since shortly after he had started at BT.

Jerry knew little about BioTyne other than they produced a number of expensive prescription drugs that they advertised heavily on television. Ask your doctor if Blixodene is right for you. Known side effects include acne, sinus congestion, elevated blood pressure, blindness, suicidal thoughts, appearing naked in public, and, in rare cases, agonizing death.

Sad, Jerry thought. The enthusiastic young scientist had sold his soul and turned into the man Jerry had seen that morning, a man no one in his right mind would call a stud now.

What had Zing been doing at Foxtrot's office?

Maybe there was nothing unusual in that. Foxtrot was notorious for his slavish support of Big Pharma in general and BioTyne in particular. When the industry or just BioTyne wanted legislation that would benefit them, Foxtrot could be relied on to introduce it in the Senate. When regulations needed to be blocked or watered down, Foxtrot was the man for the job. His enemies sneeringly referred to him as the Senator from BioTyne. That seemed to bother him not one whit. His election campaign fund was always immense, and his retirement fund was probably immense as well.

So Zing was probably just there to deliver a check and the latest instructions, Jerry thought.

But in that case, what was all that about exploding cows and corpses? Jerry couldn't shake the feeling that it was important and that something was going on beyond the usual licking of the corporate shoe by the senatorial cur.

I have to find out more, Jerry thought.

How was he to do that, though? It was easy in movies. If Jerry were a movie character, he would walk in through the front door of BioTyne, easily defeat the human and technological security barriers, and make his way to Zing's office, where he would know just what to say to make the man spill the beans. In the movie version, Jerry would also be taller and better looking.

Or he would hide in the back seat of Zing's car and then terrify the scientist after the latter had entered his car. Apparently, movie characters never lock the doors of their cars.

I bet Zing locks his doors when he leaves his car, Jerry thought.

Even if Jerry could get inside Zing's car, how long would he have to wait? In movies, the person hiding in the car knows when the character who is to be terrified plans to get in the car. I might have to wait for hours, Jerry thought. Days, even. I could get really cold and hungry. I could die in the back seat of Zing's car. That inconsiderate bastard! What if I had to shit in there? The smell would give me away.

It occurred to Jerry that the only creature that could handle a long wait in the back of someone's car was a zombie. The cold wouldn't bother a zombie. Also, Jerry presumed that zombies didn't have to shit or pee.

Had he locked his own car? Suddenly he wasn't sure.

There could be a zombie waiting patiently right now in the back seat of my car! Jerry thought.

I wish you hadn't thought of that, he told himself.

Wrenching his mind away from the image of a silent zombie in the seat behind him, Jerry considered trying to approach Foxtrot, instead.

I could drop by his campaign headquarters a few times during the day, he thought. Chat with the receptionist. Get to know her.

He thought of the beautiful receptionist's manner toward him and her friendship with his ex–wife.

Forget that idea, he told himself.

For the first time, Jerry wondered what the situation was at the Pistole mansion. Frank had mentioned going back to the house and the servants being surprised to see him. Frank had been referring to the Pistole mansion, of course, where he had lived until his death and where George and Piper now lived.

After their marriage, George and Piper had lived in a succession of apartments and rented houses. Money hadn't been a problem for them, thanks to George's salary and the investments Frank had set up for his daughter. Piper had loved the mansion and had planned to move back there with her husband as soon as her father died. She hadn't wanted to be encumbered with any other properties.

Jerry had once pointed out to her that she could buy a house while waiting and then sell it for a profit once her father died. House prices always rose in Piketon, at least in the long run.

Piper had replied, "My money buys me and George freedom and happiness. If I have to worry about managing my money, I won't be able to enjoy it."

Where were George and Piper now? Jerry upbraided himself for not having asked George at the office where they were living, now that Frank had returned from the place where everyone assumed and hoped he had gone for good.

Piper must have been at home when Frank showed up at the mansion. Was she all right? What Frank had said implied that he had killed the servant whose suit he was wearing, and he hadn't even mentioned Piper. Surely he wouldn't harm his own daughter! Remembering Florida and his own parents, Jerry didn't feel too sure about that.

George tended to turn his cell phone off when he got home from work, and Jerry didn't know Piper's cell number. Alas, he had never had any reason to know it. So the only way he could try to contact them was to call the Pistole mansion and see what happened. At the very worst, Frank Pistole would answer. Which would be pretty damned bad.

Fortunately, George answered.

At first, Jerry wasn't sure who it was on the other end of the line. The hello was low and tentative and the voice trembled.

"Hello," Jerry said, "this is Jerry Morgenstern. Who—"

"Jerry! Thank God!" George sounded more like his normal self—tentative and fearful, but recognizable.

"I wasn't sure if you'd be there," Jerry said. "Is Frank in the house with you?"

"Yes, he is. It's awful, Jerry."

"Why don't the two of you get out? Go to a hotel or something and look for a new place?"

"We wanted to, but he ordered us to stay. He glared at us, and one of his eyes popped out. Popped right out. It looked like a pickled egg. Then he shoved it back in place. I promised him we'd stay."

"At least avoid him, George. Let the servants deal with him."

"They're all gone. I guess they quit. I don't blame them."

"So you guys are alone with him? Christ!"

"I know. Can you come over? You could move in. We've got lots of extra bedrooms."

Jerry shivered at the thought. He had escaped from Florida, and now Florida had come after him. "No. Absolutely not."

"Maybe just for this evening, then? Help me adjust? I've got lots of whisky on the table right here in front of me. There's beer in the fridge. We could order pizza."

"That sounds homey. Maybe Frank could join us."

"Actually, he's busy right now. Thank God. He's upstairs in my office—I mean, his office—with Senator Foxtrot and some guy from BioTyne."

"BioTyne! Describe him."

"You know what he's like. All weaselly and bombastic and completely insincere."

"That sounds just like Foxtrot."

"That's who I'm talking about."

"No, George. I mean, describe the guy from BioTyne."

"Oh, him. I didn't really notice him all that much. He kind of faded into the background. Sort of average height, a bit overweight, somewhere in his fifties. Sandy hair. Looked down at the floor a lot."

That could have been Walter Zing. The description was far from definitive, but it would be hard to describe Walter Zing definitively. Still, the chance was too good to pass up.

"I'm coming over," he said. "Order a pizza. Whatever topping you like, so long as there are no peppers on it."

Jerry left his apartment and went out into the parking lot, walking toward his car. The lot was well lighted and he saw no one else as he walked. Nonetheless, he kept looking to left and right and turning around to look behind him. He hated to think of living the rest of his life this way. On the other hand, he wanted to live a long life.

The sun had set, but it was still hot. Usually, even in the middle of summer, the temperature started dropping before sunset, but this summer seemed to be different. He wondered if would cool down at all during the night.

It's a dry heat, he reminded himself.

If zombies needed energy from the sun, how much did they slow down at night? The heat in the air after sundown was still heat from the sun, so did that mean they would slow down less on nights like this, when the air remained warm?

He shivered and looked around quickly.

When he reached his car, he unlocked the trunk and looked inside it. There was nothing there that should not have been there. Then he tried the driver's door. Locked. Good, he thought. I did remember. Even so, he opened it cautiously, just enough to cause the interior dome light to turn on, and then he peered in through the side window behind the driver to assure himself that no zombies were hiding in the back seat.

At last, he got in, locked the door, and drove off. He felt safe inside the car, with the engine humming smoothly. He almost wished he could stay inside his car indefinitely.

It was a fairly long drive from his part of town to Redland Heights, but tonight the streets and freeways were almost empty and he made good time.

In Redland Heights, the garages were bigger than Jerry's apartment building, and the mansions were bigger than the building he worked in. Or so it seemed to him. For the last six months, he had envied George and Piper the home they had inherited when Frank Pistole died. But the thought of them cooped up in the place with a zombie, no matter how big the building, put a different light on the matter.

Still, he thought, as he drove up the long driveway toward the immense building, its front lighted by spotlights, this is a pretty damned great place to live.

Jerry had been a frequent dinner guest at the mansion in the six months since Frank's death. He was used to being met at the front door by a servant dressed like a character in a BBC costume drama—a butler or a footman or whatever the proper term was. Now, as Jerry came up the steps, George opened the door himself.

"Oh, man, am I glad to see you," George said, putting a heavy, beefy arm around Jerry's shoulder and hugging him.

"Back off, George, unless you're going to give me one hell of a raise."

George backed off. "You know jokes like that embarrass me."

"Everything embarrasses you."

George thought for a moment. "You're right. Come on in. The pizza should be here any minute. We're using the table in the small kitchen."

"We? You, me, and the zombie?"

George shuddered. "No, no. Frank's still up in his office with Foxtrot and the BioTyne guy. It's you, me, and Piper. We're way ahead of you on the alcohol."

They walked together across the mansion's ground floor toward the small kitchen, which was at least three times the size of the kitchen in Jerry's apartment.

"Piper?" Jerry said. "I've never seen her drink alcohol."

"She just started tonight."

They reached the small kitchen. Piper was slouching in a chair next to the table in the center of the room. She looked blearily at Jerry and waved. In her other hand, she held a kitchen tumbler half full of what looked like whisky and ice. Her eyes, normally piercing, looked unfocused. Her back, normally ramrod straight, was rounded. Her hard, gym–toned body slouched and looked soft. Her mouth, normally so firm and so ready to issue a cutting remark, sagged partially open. She said, "Jer. Hi."

"Piper. You're looking...You look like shit."

"Feel like shit. Why do you drink this stuff?" She put the glass to her lips and swallowed noisily.

"It makes me feel good."

She stared at him. "You feel like this when you feel good?"

"When I feel good, I probably don't feel the way you do now."

The doorbell rang.

"Pizza!" George said. "I'll go get it." He looked nervously toward the empty expanse he would have to walk through to reach the front door. "Would you like to come with me, Jerry?"

"No. I'd like to stay here and guzzle alcohol and keep Piper from falling off her chair."

"Oh. Okay. I'll just...I guess I'll just go by myself, then." He dithered for a while. When Jerry went to the refrigerator, got out a beer, opened it, and then sat down at the table next to Piper, George sighed and went to the front door.

He returned a few minutes later carrying a big pizza box. The sides were greasy. George had opened the lid along the way. He balanced the box in one hand and held a slice of pizza in the other. Half of the pointed end of the slice was gone, and he was chewing noisily. "Mmph!" he said enthusiastically.

The box tilted. Jerry could see the pizza starting to slide out. He jumped from his chair and caught the pizza against his chest. The topping spread over his shirt. His beer bottle toppled over on the table and splashed foaming beer across the table and onto the floor. He said, “Shit.”

George said, “Oh, man, I’m sorry.”

Piper put her mouth against the table and slurped the beer. “Tastes good. What is it?”

“You should never drink again,” Jerry said.

“She just needs some solid food inside her,” George said. “Honey, have some pizza.” He put his slice down on the table, in the beer, scraped the rest of the pizza back into the box, and put the box on the table. “I feel better already.”

Jerry picked up the almost empty beer bottle and swallowed what was left. With all the servants gone, he wondered who would clean up the spilled beer. Maybe no one would. It would start to stink fairly soon.

He went to the fridge for a fresh bottle. Tomato sauce was dripping down his front. He noticed a piece of pepperoni on the front of his shirt. He picked it off and ate it.

Normally, what had just happened would have upset him. Now he told himself that compared to the ongoing zombie invasion, spilled beer and a dirty shirt were fairly minor matters.

The conversation was disjointed and rambling, especially on Piper’s part. George ate most of the pizza by himself, accompanied by a fair amount of whisky. Leaning against the sink, Jerry nibbled a slice of pizza, sipped his second beer, watched the other two deteriorating before his eyes, and felt depressed. He wished he had stayed at home.

He heard voices from somewhere nearby.

“Oh, golly, they’re finished,” George said. “He’s downstairs.”

Both George and Piper looked very sober very suddenly. They began trying futilely to clean up the mess on the table.

Piper looked at Jerry. “Your shirt!” she said. “That won’t do at all.

Father is such a proper person."

"Your father is a fucking zombie," Jerry said. "He eats people's brains. He'll probably like my shirt."

"That's disrespectful," Piper said. She started to cry. George pulled his chair over next to hers and put his arm over her shoulder. She leaned against him, weeping loudly.

"What is this?" Frank Pistole stood in the doorway glaring at them.

Piper stopped crying. She and George leaped to their feet.

"Father!"

"Sir!"

Jerry gestured with his beer. "Hi, Frank." He had decided that it was inappropriate to be respectful toward zombies.

The zombie's dark expression lightened a bit. "Jerry! I didn't know you were here. How nice." Suddenly distracted, he sniffed the air. He smiled widely. "Something smells good! What have you guys have been cooking? Well, never mind that. Jerry, I'd like to introduce you to my visitors. Come on out here." He turned and left the kitchen.

"Don't go!" George hissed. "You'll be alone out there with him."

"And his visitors."

"He's probably made them into zombies already."

Jerry wondered if George were right. The idea of being alone in some empty part of the huge house with Frank Pistole was terrifying.

But Piper was watching him, so he straightened up, laughed carelessly, and sauntered from the room.

Behind him, Piper, who had actually been staring into space, threw up.

Jerry's bravado evaporated as he passed through the door. Fortunately, ahead of him, he saw Pistole standing with two other men, Fred Foxtrot and Walter Zing, and neither seemed to be a zombie.

"Ah, here you are," Frank said expansively. He seemed quite

normal—scarcely a zombie at all if one ignored the crack in his forehead. Jerry wondered if he should suggest Gorilla Glue but decided not to.

Then Jerry noticed masking tape on the top of Frank's head. He stared. Frank had repaired himself with wood putty covered with masking tape. Jerry tried not to stare.

"Guys, this is Jerry Morgenstern," Frank said. "He's one of our best and brightest employees. Don't mind his shirt. Geniuses are eccentric. I have great plans for this young man. I think he could be useful in, er, in our project."

"You trust him?" Foxtrot asked. He had looked at Jerry without interest or any sign of recognition.

Frank smiled frighteningly and stared intently at Jerry. "I think he understands the consequences of not being trustworthy. Right, Jerry?" The illusion of normality disappeared.

"Oh, yes, sir." Jerry realized that he was still holding his beer. He lifted it to his mouth and swallowed a few mouthfuls gratefully. I'll soak my brain in alcohol, you evil old bastard, he thought. See how you like the taste of it then.

"Good, good," Foxtrot said. He held out his hand. False bonhomie suffused his being. "Delighted to meet you, young man."

Jerry couldn't ignore the outstretched hand, so he grasped it and then quickly released it. "We've met before."

"Oh? At a campaign appearance?"

"Sort of." Jerry turned to Walter Zing. Zing was frowning slightly, as though trying to recall why Jerry looked familiar. Jerry said, "Doctor Walter's Superscience Show."

Zing's face lit up. He laughed. "Good God! You're familiar with that?"

"I never missed an episode when I was a kid. I idolized you." Actually, much as he had liked the show and Zing, he had also thought the scientist an embarrassing dork. But the business world had taught Jerry well.

The smile remained on Zing's face. "I loved doing that show. I'm a poor choice for an idol, though. It's Jerry, right?"

"Right."

"What was your favorite episode, Jerry?"

"Oh, for God's sake," Foxtrot said. "Can it, Zing."

"That's Doctor Zing, Senator," Jerry said sternly. He could feel Zing's gratitude oozing toward him. Damn, he thought, this manipulation stuff is easy. Why didn't I ever try it before?

Frank was looking at him with an approving, knowing smile. Frank was also licking his lips, which caused Jerry's initial self-congratulation to be replaced by nervousness.

George and Piper entered the room from the direction of the small kitchen.

"Oh, yes," Frank said. "My daughter, Piper."

"And her husband, George," Jerry said. "George did a wonderful job of managing Piper's Pickled Peppers during Frank's recent absence." He wasn't sure himself what role the beer was playing in his behavior and how much of it was due to a sudden lack of concern for the future. If the world was about to end in a zombie apocalypse, why shouldn't he go out with flair?

Frank repeated, "And her husband, George."

"Well, hello," Fred Foxtrot said, and this time the smile was genuine. "Last time I saw you, you were a child. My, how you've grown."

George was getting that subservient, beaten-down, cast-into-irrelevance expression that Jerry always hated to see on George's face. It distressed Jerry even more that Piper seemed to responding to Foxtrot's ersatz charm. But then, she was drunk.

"Senator," Jerry said, trying to distract him, "you made a speech recently about voting rights for some dispossessed minority. I didn't quite catch which minority you were talking about. I wonder if you could explain."

Foxtrot glanced at Frank Pistole quickly. "It's complicated," he said.

Pistole said, "Jerry, I've always liked your intellectual curiosity, but this is not the time or the place."

"Jerry," Walter Zing said, "which episode of my show did you like the best?"

"Oh, er, bacteria. That one." There must have been a show about bacteria. Jerry was almost sure of that.

"Why, that's my own favorite!" Zing said. "We're doing some wonderful stuff with bacteria right now. Maybe you'd like to come over to BioTyne and see?"

Foxtrot cleared his throat in a meaningful manner.

"Oh, what's the harm?" Frank Pistole said. "I want him involved in the project, and this is a good way to get him started."

"Great!" Zing said. "Come over to BT tomorrow morning. Tell the guys at the front gate that you're there to see me."

Foxtrot and Zing left. The Pistole zombie muttered something about having work to do and returned to the upstairs office. George swayed slightly and looked frightened. Piper grabbed Jerry's arm and begged him to stay the night.

Piper hanging onto his arm and begging him to stay the night had long been one of Jerry's favorite fantasies, but she mentioned a guest bedroom, and he would never stab George in the back, and the smell of vomit on her breath turned his stomach, and there was a zombie in the house, so he said no and went home.

CHAPTER FOUR

Jerry woke up to the sound of the alarm feeling better than he had expected to. The sun was shining, the world was young, and Mr. Coffee was doing his job in the stolid, unthinking way that household gadgets do their jobs.

Kind of like zombies, Jerry thought. His good mood evaporated. He looked at Mr. Coffee and Mrs. Toaster with suspicion. Then he called himself a fool and poured a cup of coffee and made toast.

He scrounged around the kitchen, microwaved an egg and two strips of bacon, and ate it all with a second cup of coffee. He went to the bathroom and shaved and showered. He knew he was dawdling, delaying going to BioTyne. He told himself that his reluctance stemmed from his belief that nothing would come of the trip, but in truth something else underlay that, a feeling of unease with no logical basis.

After he had dressed, he decided that he should call his sister again.

It was two hours later in New York, so she'd be at work. He called her work number, and after some odd clicks and buzzes, a receptionist answered.

That's odd, he thought. "I was trying to reach Lily Flicker," he said. "I dialed her number."

"Ms. Flicker is no longer with the company. Can I direct your call elsewhere?"

"What? When did this happen?"

"I am not allowed to divulge that information, sir. How may I direct your call?"

"To her new place of employment. Where is she working now?"

"I'm afraid I can't tell you that, sir. Can someone else help you?"

"Are you a zombie?"

"I beg your pardon, sir?"

"Never mind." He hung up and tried Lily's home number.

She answered with a new greeting. "Woo Zen Fabrics and Fitness. We provide fitness classes, earth-friendly clothing, acupuncture, yoga, and meditation rooms."

"You know," Jerry said, "I never did understand why you worked. Mom said that you got a great settlement when you divorced Flicker."

"The money stopped when that bastard offed himself."

"Sorry. I didn't know. So you quit that other place?"

"It was corrupt. Anyway, I wanted more connection with the earth."

"How's your head?" Jerry asked.

"Oh, it's fine. It hardly hurts at all."

"Have you seen a doctor about it? I mean, a head injury. You shouldn't ignore that."

"I'm fine," she repeated, sounding vaguer and further away. "I'm busy."

Trying to hold onto her, he said, "I saw Wendy recently. She said she'd like you to call her."

"Wendy!" For a moment, Lily sounded like her old self. "I always liked Wendy. She was the best thing that ever happened to you, you know. You didn't deserve her. She was way out of your league."

"Yeah, I play in the human league, and she plays in the Emasculating Bitch League."

He had expected Lily to rise to the bait. But that was the old Lily. The new one, operating without brains, said, "I have to get back to work. Mother Earth needs me. 'Bye."

"'Bye," he said to the dead phone line.

He left for BioTyne.

BioTyne was at the far eastern edge of the metro area, out in what had been flat farmland 20 years earlier. Now it was an area of office parks, spreading suburbs, and malls. It was also an area Jerry avoided when possible, except when he had to drive through it on the way to Florida or some other abominable part of the United States. If he had his way, he would never drive out of Piketon in any direction other than west, but he rarely had his way.

He took Interstate 25 south to the South Street exit. He headed east on South Street, squinting into and cursing the morning sun. Even though most of the traffic was on the other side of the street, heading into downtown, the drive still seemed interminable. He kept glancing at the hurrying crowds on the sidewalk, relieved each time to see no silent, unmoving zombies with their faces turned to the sun.

Maybe Frank Pistole was the only one outside Florida. But why would that be the case?

Jerry shook his head in annoyance. It was all an endless mystery. All he knew was that the dead were walking—when they weren't sunbathing—and it gave him the creeps.

"It creeps me out," he said aloud, because he had the air conditioning on and the car's windows were closed. "It creeps me out!" he said louder. "Do you hear that?" He glanced over his shoulder, but the back seat remained empty of lurking zombies.

After he had passed Lifeway Center and then the river, the traffic became light and the stop lights further apart. The speed limit rose from 30 mph to 40. Jerry drove along at a good, steady speed.

This isn't bad, he thought. It's pleasant. A lot nicer than spending the day at Piper's Pickled Peppers, now that Frank Pistole's back from the dead.

A sign warned him that BioTyne Boulevard was coming up on his left. He slowed down, waited for an opening in traffic, and turned left into the wide boulevard. A complex of buildings sprawled ahead of him.

At a guard hut, a man in uniform gestured Jerry to a stop. Another guard stepped to the other side of his car. Both men rested their right hands on the pistols holstered at their belts and frowned suspiciously at him.

Jerry rolled his window down. "Walter Zing is expecting me," he said. "I'm Jerry Morgenstern."

Both guards looked skeptical. One of them requested his driver's license, went inside the guard hut with it, and spoke to someone on a telephone. His attitude changed suddenly. He came back out smiling. "Yes, sir," he said, his tone deferential. He handed Jerry's license back. "Doctor Zing is waiting for you in his office." He pointed. "It's the main building, the tall one in the center. You can park anywhere you want to, sir. The guard in the lobby will direct you." He stepped back and saluted smartly. So did the other guard.

This is kinda cool, Jerry thought as he drove away.

The guard in the lobby of the main building was waiting for Jerry. He saluted and said, "Mr. Morgenstern. Welcome to BioTyne. This way, please."

Jerry decided he that could get used to this kind of treatment. Piper's Pickled Peppers didn't even have guards. There was the secret ingredient in the brine that made Piper's Pickled Peppers so different and so special, but that was all kept in the factory, not the office building. Jerry thought about suggesting more protection when he got back to the office. He'd make up some reason for it. He loved the idea of uniformed guards saluting him every morning and clearing the way for him through crowds of peasants.

The guard took him to an elevator, up to the third floor, and down a hallway to a large office, the door to which had a metal plaque engraved with

Walter Zing, PhD
Number One

Zing was waiting for him inside the office and came forward with his hand held out and a smile on his face. "Jerry! Delighted to see you!"

"Doctor Zing." He shook Zing's hand.

"Walter, please. You're on the inside, now."

Zing nodded to the guard and said, "Thank you."

Knowing his place, the guard left.

"Besides," Zing said, "you're the only fan of my old program I've met in...well, years."

"I'm surprised. There must be a lot of them around."

"I'd like to think so, but given that the show was cancelled because of low ratings, probably not."

"I always wanted to ask you about the show's name," Jerry said. "I loved the name when I was a kid, but when I got a bit older, I started to wonder how you chose it."

Zing smiled. "When the show started, I was engaged to a wonderful girl who used to call me..." He paused, then laughed shyly and said, "Her super science stud."

Jerry stared at him in amazement.

"Honest," Zing said. "She did."

"I guess that explains your license plate, too."

Zing nodded. He was still smiling. He seemed to have drifted into another time and place.

"So, Walter, what happened to the girl? Did you marry her?"

"No." Zing sighed. "She married someone else."

"I'm sorry."

"It was a long time ago." He straightened, and the smile returned. "Let me give you a tour."

They walked for hours.

They went up staircases and down hallways and down other staircases. Sometimes they took elevators. They walked through great empty spaces and narrow, claustrophobic ones. They looked at lots of strange equipment and people in white coats doing mysterious things, and they encountered colorful vapors and bizarre smells. Every now and then, Walter Zing would turn to Jerry with a broad smile and say, "Isn't science grand? Yes, science is super!"

Jerry's feet started to hurt. Then his back started to hurt. This was the sort of tour a company would give to a visiting bunch of schoolkids. He had expected to be let in on some kind of secret.

"I thought I was supposed to be getting involved in some kind of big project, Walter."

"Oh, don't be cranky. There's something down here that you'll really love. It involves your favorite—bacteria." He walked down the hallway, whistling.

Jerry had no idea where in the immense complex he was. The idea of being left on his own panicked him suddenly. In zombie movies, zombies popped out of doorways in places like this. He hurried along after Zing.

When he had caught up with the scientist, Jerry said, "I'm surprised you're still working with bacteria. I thought microscopic machines were the hot thing now. Our military's working on them.

Probably everyone else's military is, too. Maybe World War Three is going on right now all around is, in the air, or down there on the floor, and we can't even see it."

The two men stopped and stared at each other. They stared up and down the hallway. They stared down at the floor. For a moment, Jerry's skin crawled at what he had suggested, and he forgot about zombies.

Then Zing said, "No. They're a long way from that. Now, bacteria..." His wide smile returned. "They've been making themselves more and more complex for billions of years. They're way ahead of any little machines we can make. Bacteria are wonderful. They're amazing. They're super. Come along. Don't dawdle."

He took off again. Jerry tried to keep up with him, although he was panting by now.

They passed a door on either side of which stood an armed guard. Both of the guards glared warningly at Jerry. The door was huge—floor to ceiling and twice normal width—and shiny gray, as though it were made of steel. It was blank, with no sign of any kind on it. There was a numeric keypad set into the wall beside it.

Jerry caught up with Zing and grabbed his shoulder. Zing stopped. Jerry pointed back at the huge door. "What's in there?" he asked.

"Secret stuff. Secret science stuff. Super secret super science stuff." Zing shook off Jerry's hand and continued, walking even faster.

Jerry followed him.

Zing stopped before a long window on one side of the hallway. He looked at Jerry and then pointed at the window. "BioTyne Bacterial Butchershop," he said proudly. "You'll be seeing our product in grocery stores by the end of the week."

Jerry looked through the window and saw a large room crammed with conveyer belts. Long, red, rectangular objects lay on the belts, moving at a steady and fairly rapid rate. At the belt nearest the window, on the other side of the belt, stood a man in white butcher's clothing, complete with white hat. He watched the belt and the moving objects intently. On the left breast of his suit were green script letters spelling the initials BTBB. The front of his suit was spotted with red. As the objects moved beyond his station, they passed under a shiny metal overhead object. Knives flashed down, slicing the objects into identical squares of about four inches on a side."

"Come quickly!" Zing said excitedly. He hurried along the window.

Jerry followed tiredly.

Zing stopped after a few feet. "Look!"

From their new location, they could see the next step in the journey of the mysterious red objects. Slender metal arms were picking them up, placing them on white plastic trays, wrapping them quickly in plastic wrap, and affixing labels. Then the arms replaced them on the conveyor belt, which carried them out of sight.

Jerry turned to Zing for an explanation. The scientist was watching the process with a dreamy look. "BioTyne Bacterial Butchershop," he said again. "Feeding the world. Cheaply. With bacteria. Technology is so great."

"You're feeding people bacteria? That's what those red things were, bacteria?"

Zing turned to him with a hurt expression. "Bacteria aren't that big, Jerry. And they don't look like that. Weren't you paying attention when you watched my show? Wow, it's a good thing I didn't give tests, right?" He laughed, and Jerry wondered why he had found Doctor Walter amusing back then.

"No, no," Zing said. "We use a special strain of bacteria that we developed right here to produce meat. It feeds on, er, well, waste products of various types. Don't worry about that part. You wouldn't like it. Anyway, it consumes the waste and converts it, producing real meat. You could say that the meat is the bacteria's waste product. Ha, ha! Muscle and fat and blood and everything. Texture's still a bit of a problem, but we're working on that."

"Waste, huh?" Jerry grimaced. "Well, at least you're not feeding it pickles."

"Why did you say that?" Zing seemed bigger suddenly, threatening. He spoke loudly and angrily. "I would never feed Studley pickles! Don't even suggest such a thing. Pickles!"

Jerry stepped back from the suddenly very mad scientist. "Sorry. I have pickles on my mind. Studley, you said?"

Zing smiled sheepishly, harmless again. "That's my nickname for our bacteria. I did most of the development work. It feels like my child. It has a formal, scientific name, but I always call it Studley. The name really fits the little guy. We figure that one batch of Studleys can produce close to a hundred pounds of meat before it runs out of steams and conks out."

"What do you do with it then? When it conks out? Do you feed it more waste to get it going again?"

"Oh, no. Once he's shot his wad, we kill him with bleach and flush him down the drain. Come on." He set off again, intent on showing Jerry more wonders of super science.

It's like some kind of metaphor for life, Jerry thought. Poor Studley.

He realized that exhaustion was interfering with his ability to think straight. "Walter!" he called out. "Please, stop."

Zing trotted back to him, looking concerned. "Are you all right? Are you tired? Hungry?"

"Tired, yes. I mean, this is all very wonderful. It's, er, super."

"Yes! It is! Isn't it?"

"It is. But I *am* tired and hungry and thirsty. I'd love to sit down somewhere and have a beer and have you finally tell me about the project I'm supposed to be included in."

"You mean you really do want to know about the project? I thought you were using that as an excuse to get a tour of the place."

"I loved the tour, but I think you're using the tour as an excuse to avoid telling me about the project."

Zing sighed. "Frank said you were one of his brightest employees. All right. Let's go back to my office. I'm a bit hungry, too. I'll have someone bring us some food, and then I'll tell you all about it."

Back in Zing's office, the scientist asked Jerry, "Did you really want a beer?"

"I'd love one."

"Well...We do have beer, but it's produced in-house by a cousin of Studley's. I didn't work on that strain of bacteria, and I don't trust the result. We're just starting human trials of the beer. Before that, we fed it to rats. Most of the rats died. The survivors begged us to kill them."

"I'll have a Coke."

Zing phoned in their order to the restaurant in the company cafeteria. While they waited for their food to arrive, he asked Jerry about his family.

Jerry was annoyed at what struck him as yet another delaying tactic. He also didn't know what to say about his family. He finally settled for, "My parents are dead, and my sister is brain dead."

"Oh, how unfortunate! Was it some kind of accident?"

"Old age, in my parents' case. My sister...That was carelessness on her part. I warned her."

Zing shook his head. "Young people. Drinking and texting and driving." He sighed. "Very tragic. Did she watch my show, too?"

"Not that I remember."

Zing shrugged. "Oh, well, in that case..."

"Were you ever married, Dr. Zing? Any kids?"

Zing shook his head. "No," he said sadly. "I had one true love in my life. When G left, that was it for me. I was a useless, worthless bacterium. I was ready to kill myself with bleach and flush myself down the toilet."

"I'm glad you didn't. I would never have seen your show."

"That show saved my life. But you know, Jerry, the fact is, I'd be smiling and making jokes for the camera, and then I'd go backstage and think about G and cry my eyes out. Then I'd go back in front of the camera, and I was okay again. Show biz, huh?"

"She was named G?"

"That was my nickname for her. Well, well. Science saved my life. It has saved so many lives, Jerry." Zing was very serious now. He looked at Jerry intently. "And it will save many, many more."

Their food arrived, brought in on a tray carried by an attractive young woman in a waitress outfit.

Jerry tried to catch her eye and smile charmingly at her.

She ignored him, deposited the tray on Zing's desk, and left. Jerry could almost hear his sister saying that the waitress was out of his league.

"You have *that* in your cafeteria?" Jerry asked. "I should come to work here."

"It's a good cafeteria," Zing said absent-mindedly. He unwrapped one of the sandwiches, lifted up the top slice of bread, and said, "Oh, good. They left out the pickles."

They ate in silence for a few minutes. Jerry's impatience was on hold while he satisfied his hunger and thirst. When those pangs had subsided, though, his eagerness to be informed and be gone returned.

"So," he said. "Walter."

"How's your sandwich?"

"It's great. I mean, it really is great. But aren't you supposed to be telling me about this secret project?"

Zing put down his sandwich and sighed. "Yes. All right." He stared into space for a while, thinking, and then began. "You know what a bacterial ghost is, don't you?"

Jerry shook his head.

"You don't?" Zing looked disappointed. "I thought you would, since bacteria are your favorite science subject. Oh, well. So. You start with a gram–negative bacterium. Okay?"

"Gram negative," Jerry repeated, wondering what that meant, and nodding because he guessed that he was supposed to nod.

"Exactly!" Zing said happily. "I see you're with me. Then you remove the cytoplasm. The result is pretty much just the cell envelope. That's what we call the bacterial ghost. You can then fill it with various substances you want to deliver to the subject. Okay so far?"

"Wow, that's really fascinating," Jerry said, because he assumed it was.

"Yes! Now, we have been working with a very special line of bacterial ghosts. Ours contain gunk—"

"Gunk?"

"That's how we refer to it in house. Anyway, gunk from a very special..." Zing's attention drifted, and he stared at the ceiling for a while. He sighed. "Oh, so special." He shook himself. "What? Oh, right. It's gunk from a very specific human cell culture derived from a cadaver. So we call our bacteria bacterial zombies. Clever, eh?"

"Oh, yeah." Jerry shivered. He hadn't expected the conversation to take a turn toward the creepy.

"Hold that thought. Now, many years ago—actually decades ago, not long after I helped found this company—I was experimenting with tissue from the cadaver I mentioned. I was subjecting it to various substances for reasons that don't concern you. Something happened, and the cells in the tissue came back to life. What's more, in life..." He trailed off for a moment again, lost in thought. "When she was alive—the cadaver person, I mean—she suffered from a serious genetic illness. The revived cells didn't show that. Then I deliberately induced DNA damage in the cells, and they healed themselves."

"That's wonderful. It sounds like you found a cure for a lot of diseases."

"That was my hope" Zing said. "The next step was to administer to human subjects the formula that had had such a beneficial effect on the cadaver's tissues."

"You went straight to human trials? Is that legal?"

"They were all volunteers," Zing said, not quite answering Jerry's question.

"I guess that's okay, then. It's not like you kidnapped them," Jerry laughed, "and imprisoned them in your secret underground laboratory. Right?"

"Of course not. They were all prisoners at one of the state prisons. They get some benefits for volunteering."

"That's not really entirely voluntary, then, is it?"

"Moral issues and choices abound in life, young man, and they're often difficult and fuzzy around the edges. There are few absolutes. You'll understand that when you're older."

Jerry was feeling older by the second. "I hope your formula cured everything that was wrong with them, at any rate."

Zing shook his head. "There were no significant effects. There's something about that cadaver tissue." His voice trailed off, and he stared into space.

And there's something about that cadaver, Jerry thought, that really seems to get to you, Doctor Walter.

"Did you know," Zing said, "that there are a lot of very old men in prison? Sentenced to very long terms, or even life, when they were still young. I didn't know that before this experiment."

"I've heard that."

"The old prisoners in our study were the only ones who showed any effect at all. They developed a craving for Piper's Pickled Peppers."

"They really liked those pickled peppers, huh?"

"Much more than just liked. There was a riot in one prison when the supply of Piper's Pickled Peppers ran out. Fortunately, all of the rioters were very old and quite infirm, so no harm was done. But that incident showed Frank the way to make his pickled peppers the most sought after of all pickled peppers."

"That is so disturbing."

"It certainly disturbed me."

"Of course Frank Pistole didn't mind profiting from something disturbing, right?"

Zing said, "Frank Pistole is a great humanitarian." He looked away. There was a long pause, and then Zing said, "Well. After that failure, I decided to step back from human trials and to try a different delivery system. After some years, I decided to create bacterial zombies containing gunk from the cadaver's cells. I injected the bacterial zombies into rats. I was hoping that the gunk would be integrated into the rat's cells, and the rats would acquire the same ability to repair their own DNA damage that I had previously observed in the cadaver tissue. Unfortunately, I didn't see any effect in the rats. Well, no positive effect."

"Poor rats," Jerry said.

"They're martyrs to the cause."

"Jeez, it's not like they volunteered. Did anything happen to them? Were there negative effects?"

Zing frowned. "In a few cases."

"How negative? What happened to them?"

"They became voracious cannibals. It was extremely unpleasant. I don't think I should tell you more. It might give you nightmares."

"Oh, come on, Dr. Walter! Please!"

"After I had sacrificed the rats and studied them extensively," Zing said, ignoring Jerry's pouting and foot stamping, "I came to think that their body size was the problem, so I gave up on more rat tests."

"And all the surviving rats cheered."

"I don't think rats can cheer," Zing said. "I decided to test the zombies on cows."

"Why cows?"

"Why not?"

"Could you call them something other than zombies? That really bothers me."

"Oh. Um, how about happy cells?"

"Yes! I like that!"

"All right. So. I decided to apply the, um, happy cells to cows. As it happens, I'm afraid of cows. So is everyone on my team. So we ended up spraying the happy cells from the air onto a herd of cows."

"I didn't see any cows around here."

"They weren't ours. We, um..." Zing looked from side to side, as though afraid of being heard. He lowered his voice. "We found a herd nearby. We did it at night."

"Is that legal?"

"Possibly not. Did you know that cows produce methane?"

"Vaguely."

"Well, they do. A lot of it. It's quite combustible. Our happy cells...This is embarrassing. I believe that our happy cells really liked the methane. They followed the methane trail down through the air and entered the cows through their, well, you know, their elimination ends."

"Their shitholes?"

Zing grimaced. "All right. Yes. Their shitholes. The happy cells traveled through the cows' digestive systems, consuming methane and concentrating it. And then somehow they combusted. Methane is very combustible."

"They burned?"

"Exploded."

"That story about exploding cows!"

Zing nodded. "Yes. I discontinued that avenue of research."

"Yeah, those cows created a big mess, as I remember. One cow makes a lot of cow parts." Jerry thought that the joke was clever enough to repeat. Maybe Zing would appreciate it more than Lily had.

Zing looked puzzled. "Well, no. One cow makes exactly one cow's worth of parts. Actually, slightly less than that, because some of the parts are vaporized in the explosion. See?"

"Okay, okay. So you gave up on the whole idea, then?"

"Oh, no. I just gave up on cows. Bacteria were too small, and cows were too big. Also too methaney. Remember that I hadn't tried my happy cells on those prisoners. I thought it was time to let the little guys have a go at human beings."

"This sounds illegal to me. I mean, even if they volunteer, if you inject science-fictional bacteria into human beings, how can that be legal?"

"It's no problem so long as they're dead before you start. I experimented on cadavers."

"Exploding cadavers," Jerry said, remembering the short-lived TV news sensation that had followed closely on the short-lived exploding-cows TV news sensation.

"Unfortunately so. Apparently my happy cells react to the gases of decomposition the same way they do to methane. They love that stuff. Eat it up."

Jerry closed his eyes and by a great effort of will managed not to vomit. "Please."

"This is *science*, Jerry! Bacteria! Your favorite subject."

"It's a horror story. It's like being stuck in Florida in August with no way out and no air conditioning. Is there more?"

Zing was clearly hurt. "Nothing more," he said stiffly. "I've hit a brick wall. I'm afraid to try my happy cells on living human beings."

"Maybe you could try them on Frank Pistole. He's not living."

"What? Of course he is."

"He's a zombie. He returned from the dead."

"Nonsense. He was just away for a while."

"You don't think he's changed? You must not have known him for very long."

"I've known him since college. He's always been very supportive of my work. He's a great humanitarian," Zing repeated.

"Since college? Then you must have known his wife, Piper's mother. There's a picture of her in Piper and George's house. She was beautiful."

"Oh, so very beautiful." Zing sighed and stared into space and the past.

"Piper looks a lot like her."

"Yes, she does."

Jerry thought that if he said, "It's sunny outside," Zing would reply, "Yes, it certainly is."

"Do you know why she left Frank?" Jerry asked. "Piper was a baby at the time, I think."

"Yes," Zing said, still staring into space. "Piper was still a baby when Zelda disappeared."

"Zelda? That was her name?"

"Yes," Zing said. "Her name was Zelda." He repeated it softly. "Zelda."

This meeting is a bust, Jerry thought. Why was I even asked to come here? "So this is the secret project you were supposed to tell me about? Some medical research that isn't going anywhere? What's the connection to Frank Pistole?"

"Frank Pistole is a great humanitarian."

You haven't worked for him, Jerry thought.

"He's funded part of my work," Zing said.

"You said you were one of the founders of BioTyne. Why would you need funding from Frank Pistole?"

"This isn't a BT project. It's a pet project of my very own. I just use the facilities here. BT has nothing to do with it."

"And it costs so much that you need money from Pistole?"

"Money and other input. I couldn't have done this without him."

"What does he get out of it?"

"The knowledge that he's helping mankind. He's a great humanitarian."

Jerry noticed that Zing's jaws were clenched. The scientist's grimace contradicted his words. "But—"

"Oh, dear," Zing said, glancing at his watch. "I see our time is up. Thanks for watching, children."

The office door opened and an enormous man in a guard uniform stepped in. "You buzzed, Dr. Zing?"

"Yes, I did. Mr. Morgenstern was just leaving. Could you please escort him to the front door? All the way to the door?"

"Of course, Doctor." The guard looked down at Jerry. The guard frowned.

Jerry jumped to his feet. "I was just leaving," he said.

CHAPTER FIVE

The guards at the main gate waved goodbye to him in a friendly way, and Jerry waved back, feeling silly.

I should go to the office, he thought.

Instead he set his course toward Redland Heights. He should check up on Piper and George, he told himself. Make sure they were okay. Frank Pistole would surely be at the office. Or—Jerry shivered—out somewhere catching some rays. Charging up his zombie battery.

He assured himself that George would be at the house even though he knew that George would almost surely be at the office. Jerry felt guilty. He drove toward the Pistole mansion anyway.

However, when he got there, George opened the door. "Oh, man, am I glad to see you!" George said loudly.

Jerry felt even guiltier. "Still no replacement servants?"

George shook his head. "I guess the word's gone out. The original ones are all gone." He leaned close to Jerry and whispered loudly, "Eaten!" His breath stank, but it was the stink of being up all night and drinking too little water and not brushing his teeth, not the stink of zombie corruption. Or so Jerry hoped. "And we can't get any new ones," George said, drawing back. "There's a servant grapevine, you know."

Jerry breathed again. "I didn't know." The ways of servants were not included in his experience of the world.

"Come in, come in." George pulled Jerry into the hallway. Then he stepped back to the doorway, looked nervously outside, and closed and locked the door. "No sign of him," he said. "Thank God."

"Frank? He's not here, then."

"No. He went to work bright and early. Told me not to bother coming in if I didn't want to. That's fine with me." He turned and led the way to the small kitchen.

Piper was sitting at the table in the small kitchen. By Piper standards, she looked awful. There was an empty pizza box on the table and a lingering smell of vomit in the air.

"Have you guys been here all night?" Jerry asked.

"That's a different pizza," George said.

Piper said, "How do you treat a hangover? I know you get those all the time."

"I do not!" Jerry said.

"Sure you do. You drink all the time."

"No, I don't. I have one drink a day, maximum. Except when I'm stressed."

"You must be stressed a lot, then," said Piper, reminding Jerry unpleasantly of his sister before her brain was eaten.

He tried to calm the waters. "Not during the last six months, thanks to George being in charge of PPP."

Piper looked up at her husband and smiled blearily. "George is the best."

Jerry sighed. Zombies had taken over Florida. Republicans, little different from zombies, had taken over Washington. And Piper would be always be unattainable. That was the way the world was. He didn't like reality, but he had to accept it.

"Are you hungry?" George asked. "We could order another pizza."

"I ate a little while ago." He realized suddenly that he hadn't thought to ask if the sandwich he'd had at BioTyne had been made with meat from actual animals and not something from Studley.

"So what do we do now?" George asked.

"You could move out while Frank's away," Jerry said. "This is your chance."

"Let's watch television," Piper said. She got up and walked carefully from the kitchen, grimacing with pain.

"Is this your first hangover?" Jerry asked her.

"First and last."

She led the way to a room about the size of Jerry's living room. A huge television screen occupied most of one wall, and chairs and small couches were arranged to view it. And this, Jerry thought in amazement, was the small television room. It was an astonishing house, and it had been built entirely by pickles.

Piper said, "On!"

The screen turned on.

George said, "News!"

The television tuned itself to Fixed News, the fake news network that was the only news network Frank Pistole allowed in his house or his company offices.

The news network that eats your brain, Jerry thought. I bet it appeals to all the zombies.

George threw himself into one of the couches. "I guess we could move out," he said, "but it would be hard to leave all of this."

"You could watch whatever news station you wanted," Jerry pointed out.

"If we moved out," Piper said, "Dad would fire George and disown me, and we wouldn't be able to afford a television set. Look. It's Fred."

On the screen, Fred Foxtrot was preparing to make a speech in the Senate.

"I didn't know you were on a first–name basis with that jerk," Jerry said.

"He dandled me on his knee when I was a little girl. So he says, anyway."

Jerry experienced a wave of revulsion. From George's expression, he was experiencing the same thing. Jerry felt even warmer toward George.

"What's wrong with the jerk's face?" George asked.

"Oh, my God," Piper said, "he's a zombie!"

Jerry stared at the screen, his eyes narrowed in concentration. "No, I don't think so. I think he's wearing zombie makeup."

"Why would he do that?" Piper asked.

"Ssh," George said. "What's the jerk saying?"

"He's not a jerk," Piper said.

"Ssshh!" Jerry and George said simultaneously.

"...congratulate my colleagues on passing my bill," Foxtrot was saying, "the Restoration of Voting Rights to Interrupted Existence Compatriots Act. I urge the House to act quickly, and I'm sure the President will sign the bill into law without delay. Then at last our great silent majority will be silent no longer. Too long deprived, they will come into their own and join the ranks of their fellow Americans. America is the greatest nation in the history of the world. We are the ultimate democracy. Now we will be even greater and...er...more ultimate. Thank you, and good night. God bless you, and may God bless the United States of America."

The camera panned over the handful of senators present to listen to Foxtrot. Jerry was astonished to see that most of them were also wearing makeup that made them look like zombies. They applauded Foxtrot vigorously and whistled and cheered.

"These kids today," Jerry said. "No decorum. I wonder what that bill of his is about."

"Something vile, I'm sure," George said. "Did you hear the way he ended his little speech? He thinks he's the president."

"That's always been his goal," Piper said. "That's what he told me, anyway."

Jerry and George stared at her.

The camera switched to one of Fixed News's interchangeable commentators, a beautiful woman who had little to fear from zombies.

Jerry and George switched their attention to the TV screen.

"That was Senator Fred Foxtrot addressing the United States Senate just a few minutes ago," the beautiful woman said, "right after the Senate passed his bill, the..." She concentrated hard on her teleprompter. "The R...V...R...T...I...E...C Act. Which restores voting rights to..." She frowned winningly. "To a bunch of people."

She turned to her right and said to her handsome and equally vacuous male colleague, "We'll be hearing more about this, won't we?"

"Where'd he come from?" Jerry asked.

"He's been there all along," Piper said. "Ssh."

"We sure will," he said, displaying as many of his expensively straightened, capped, and artificially whitened teeth for the camera as he could. "Long term, the Foxtrot Restoration Act, as it's being called, will have a big effect on the next election. Before this, Senator Foxtrot's own reelection bid was expected to be in political trouble, but once this act takes effect, he'll be in good shape, thanks to the IEC vote."

His coanchor was staring at him blankly.

"The Interrupted Existence Compatriots," he said to her.

"Huh?" she said.

He ignored her and faced the camera again. "Once the bill passes the House and is signed by the president, which should happen before the end of the week, we'll be looking at some debate over how to pay for one of its major provisions, the installation of powerful sunlamps throughout the entire Capitol building, starting with the Senate visitors' gallery."

The beautiful woman smiled even broadly than her coanchor. "Great!" she said. "I love sunlamps!"

The man nodded. "Yes, it's good news for everyone. Folks, stay tuned after this news program for a special edition of Fixed Money, when we'll examine portfolio strategies that will enable you to take full advantage of the new opportunities offered by the Foxtrot Recovery Act."

"That's right," the woman said. "Stay tuned to Fixed News for all the information you need to help you think the *right* way. Now let's have a look at the day's sports action."

The screen turned itself off.

"I set it to do that as soon as it hears the word *sports*," Georg said proudly.

"Good man," Jerry said.

"He's the best," Piper said.

"I still don't know what the hell all that was about, though," George said.

"Probably nothing important," Jerry said. "I think we wasted our time."

"Yeah," George said. "I'm hungry. I'm going to order a pizza. Come on back to kitchen and grab yourself a beer."

Jerry sighed and followed him. He always ended up drinking too much when he was at the Pistole house. Something to do with stress, he supposed.

George used the telephone in the small kitchen to order a pizza. He got two beers from the fridge and offered one to Piper. She made a face and shook her head. He handed it to Jerry instead.

Jerry twisted off the cap and said, "You've got so much money. Why do you always buy such cheap beers?"

George shrugged. "After the first one, you can't tell the difference, anyway."

"I can."

Piper smirked. "That's because you have such an experienced and well trained palate."

"You always used to be nice to me," Jerry said to her. "What's changed?"

"No, I always used to ignore you. There's a difference."

"Please don't fight," George said.

"He started it."

"You don't know my sister, do you?" Jerry asked.

"No. Why?" Piper said.

"Just wondering. So, anyway, to change the subject, I was meeting with Walter Zing this morning, before I came over here."

"Eew," Piper said. "He gives me the creeps."

"*He* gives you the creeps but Foxtrot doesn't?"

"Did you ever watch his TV program when you were a kid?" George asked, also trying to change the subject.

"I never missed it."

"Wasn't it great? Doctor Walter's Superscience Show." George shook his head and then put his beer bottle to his mouth and tilted it up. He swallowed noisily. He lowered the bottle again and said, "You know what my favorite part was? When he talked about bacteria. Man, that was the best. I wanted so much to be a scientist when I grew up."

"What happened?"

George looked at the floor. "I got sidetracked," he said sadly.

That's like a summary of life, Jerry thought. I got sidetracked. At least it's better than being killed with bleach and flushed down the drain.

"Oh, George," Piper said. She looked at Jerry. "Why'd you have to bring up the creepy scientist?"

"Because I think he knows something about this whole problem. He talked a lot, but he kept avoiding the real subject."

"What problem?" Piper asked. "What subject?"

"The zombie apocalypse."

Piper rolled her eyes. "Zombie apocalypse. All that alcohol has fried your brain."

"It's real." Jerry told her about Florida.

"That doesn't mean those old people were zombies," Piper said.

"Oh, yeah, they're zombies. Just like your father."

"He ate a kid at work," George said.

"What?" Piper said. "Oh, come on."

"He was capable of it even before he died and came back as a zombie," Jerry said. "You know it. Think about what happened to your servants."

"They left for better jobs," Piper said, with a note of uncertainty in her voice.

"Your father ate them."

"That's just stupid."

"No, really," George said. "Jerry's right. Like I said, he ate a kid at work." He told her about the dumb kid who had delivered the pickle to Frank Pistole and had vanished.

Piper looked slightly less doubtful. "Was it someone you liked? Someone important?"

"Well, no. He wasn't important, and he was stupid and lazy and no one liked him."

"There! You see? Dad was helping you out. I bet it was someone you should have gotten rid of long ago. You're too soft–hearted."

"Well, maybe, but not by eating him."

Jerry said, "Piper, you can't see what's happening because you're suffering from *dementius primus alcoholicus*. It happens to some people when they drink heavily for the first time. It completely distorts your perception of reality."

Piper looked at him. She frowned. "Is that real?"

"George?" Jerry said.

"Oh, absolutely, honey. Jerry's right. I've seen it happen to guys in bars."

"I didn't know you ever went to bars."

"Very rarely. Right, Jerry?"

"You bet. I've almost never seen you in a bar."

"And you'd have seen him, whatever bar he was in," Piper said. She stood up. She stared into space. "Where's the bathroom? Oh, yeah." She wavered out of the room.

"You are simultaneously very creative and very full of shit," George said.

"Maybe I should switch to the marketing department."

"I think you should stay away from the office completely. It's not safe."

"I need the paycheck, George. Anyway, I think we need to stop avoiding the problem and try to solve it."

"You mean—" George lowered his voice. "You mean, kill Frank? Make him dead again?"

"That's an idea, but it's not what I was thinking about."

Piper came back into the kitchen. "The bathroom's not there," she said. "They moved it." She sat down at the table, looking confused.

George moved behind her chair and placed a comforting hand on her shoulder. "We'll find it, honey. So, Jerry, you were talking about Doctor Walter."

"I was. Frank said I was to go over to BioTyne and be told about some important project."

"That's right. That was last night. We were there."

"I wasn't sure you'd remember. Especially Piper."

"Why not?" Piper said, sounding annoyed.

"Because you were pickled."

George winced. "Please."

"Okay, soused. You were soused. I bet you don't remember anything that happened last night."

"I remember everything," Piper said. "You were sucking up to Dad."

"I was not. I was sucking up to Doctor Walter."

"Eeew!" Piper said.

"This isn't getting us anywhere," George said. "Kids," he added.

"You're right," Jerry said. "Okay. I went over to BT this morning to meet with Doctor Walter so that he could tell me all about the big project. I was there for quite a while."

"Well? What's the big project?" George asked. "I hope it's not something that requires more big checks from Piper's Pickled Peppers. The old man's going to undo all the good I did during the last six months."

"I don't know what the big project is. Doctor Walter talked a lot, but he didn't really say anything. He took me on a tour of BioTyne. We walked for miles. I saw all kinds of stuff I didn't understand."

Piper snickered. "That's not saying much."

George said dreamily, "Oh, man, I envy you."

"You wouldn't have envied me when I was watching chunks of bacteria-produced meat being chopped up. There was bacteria-made blood everywhere."

Piper's face took on a greenish tinge. "That's disgusting," she said.

"It *was* disgusting."

"Sounds really cool," George said.

"You won't think so when it shows up on your table. They'll be selling it in stores soon."

"I won't touch it," Piper said. "People with money will always be able to get meat cut from real cows. Or steers, or whatever."

Jerry said, "Now that your father's back in charge of Piper's Pickled Peppers, you won't be one of the people with money for much longer."

"No! George?"

"I'm afraid he's right, honey. Your father's going to run the company into the ground, and we'll end up living in a cardboard box."

"Yeah, and try defending that against the starving zombie hordes," Jerry said.

"Why would they be starving?" George asked. "I mean, why are zombies in movies always starving? Don't they reach a point where they just couldn't swallow another brain? No, thank you, no more brains for me. I'm full."

"That's a good question," Jerry said. "I never thought about that. However, I think we should assume they'd be starving, just to be on the safe side."

"You're probably right."

"George," Piper said, "he's turning you into an idiot. You're spending too much time with him."

"That's not fair, honey," George said. "Sometimes, Jerry says some clever things. For example, he says he knows how to solve our problem."

"Right," Jerry said. "At any rate, I know where we should start looking."

"That's good," George said encouragingly. "Keep going."

"On the tour this morning, Doctor Walter was eager to show me everything in the place, with one exception." Jerry described the massive door and the two massive guards standing beside it. "He tried to walk right by it as though it wasn't there," Jerry said. "When I asked him what was behind the door, all he would say was 'super secret super science stuff,' and then he hurried me away."

"Super secret super science stuff," George repeated, staring dreamily into space. "Wow."

"By process of elimination," Jerry said, "the big, secret project must be behind that door. Because it's not anywhere else."

"Anywhere else at BioTyne," Piper pointed out. "It could be anywhere else in the world."

"I guess," Jerry said grudgingly. "But probably not. Doctor Walter's involved with the project, whatever it is, and I was told to go to BT to be told about it. So the odds are it's there."

"Okay," George said thoughtfully. "I'll go along with that. But why do you think that this secret project is the answer to our problem? Maybe it's something else entirely."

"Because he was talking about cadavers and healing DNA damage and bringing tissues back to life. It just makes sense." Now that he said it aloud, it didn't make sense at all. Maybe it's the alcohol that made it make sense, he thought. Maybe I do drink too much.

"Well," said George, who had far more alcohol in him than Jerry did. "I guess. Maybe. You've more or less convinced me that we need to see what's behind that door. I see two problems. Second: getting past those guards and through that door. And first: getting into BioTyne."

And first and a half, thought Jerry, remembering the long and confusing tramp through corridors and up and down staircases, finding our way from the front entrance to the door.

"I'll take care of that stuff," Piper said.

"You're delusional," Jerry said. "Drunk and delusional. You should stay here and sleep it off."

"You won't get in without me."

"I got in this morning."

"That's only because they were expecting you."

Jerry remembered his reception at BioTyne and thought she had a point. "What makes you different from me?"

"You'll see."

Jerry looked at George and raised his eyebrows questioningly. George, however, was looking at Piper worshipfully. "Great, honey," George said. "Thanks."

Jerry sighed. "Okay. Let's go, then."

"Hold on," Piper said. "I still need to pee."

She left the kitchen. Ten minutes later, she was back, smiling happily. "They put the bathroom back! Thank God! Okay, I'm ready."

They went in Jerry's car because he didn't trust either of the other two to drive. On the way, Piper kept up a bizarre running commentary. "Look, George. There's that park. Do you remember when we screwed there? There's that motel where we spent the night. That was a great night! You're the best." And so on.

George looked embarrassed. Jerry felt like shooting himself. "Look, George," he said, "there's that alley where we set that cat's tail on fire when we were boys."

"We didn't know each other when we were boys, Jerry."

"Right."

"Look, George," Piper said, "there's that gutter where Jerry puked his inebriated guts out Saturday night."

This is the longest drive of my life, Jerry thought.

It ended at last, and they drove up to the guard shack at BioTyne.

"What do we do now?" George asked.

"I have no idea," Jerry admitted.

He pulled to a stop.

A scowling guard approached the car, one hand on the handle of the pistol holstered on his hip. He leaned down and peered into the car. Suddenly, his face brightened! "Hey, MG!" he said. He straightened and waved to the other guards. "It's okay," he called. "It's MG."

Cheers erupted from the guard shack. The guard saluted smartly and waved them through.

"Toldja you needed me," Piper said. "They always let MG in."

"MG?" Jerry said.

"Money Girl. I used to deliver checks for my father. He insists on paper. He doesn't trust electronic transfers."

George said, "I never heard anything about this."

"Of course not, honey. We didn't think you'd deal well with it."

"Well, hell," George said.

"So you're a money launderer for a drug company," Jerry said. "You're a woman of mystery."

"I bet all women are a mystery to you," Piper said.

They parked in front of the main building, where Jerry had parked that morning.

"Now what?" George asked.

"I don't know," Jerry said. "Let's try just marching in as if we belonged here and knew what we were doing."

"That's the story of Jerry's career," Piper said.

"We've got Money Girl with us," Jerry said. "Maybe that will do the job."

"I am the one who counts," Piper said. She got out of the car and walked toward the main entrance.

Jerry and George got out and stood for a moment watching her uncertainly.

George said, "I'm glad my wife and my best friend like each other so much. It would be really unpleasant, otherwise."

"Are you kidding?" Jerry said. "Piper obviously hates me."

"Oh, no, not at all. She's very attracted to you. Insults are her style of courtship. That's how she courted me. Golly, it was fun!"

"*She* courted *you*?"

"You don't think I had the guts to court her, do you? Anyway, it's a good thing I trust you so completely. Otherwise I'd be worried."

Jerry felt guiltier than ever—guilty for his past lust for Piper and for the even greater future lust that he knew George's revelation would give rise to.

Piper turned around and beckoned them impatiently, and they hurried after her.

The main entrance of the building presented no more problems than the guard shack had. They were greeted with cries of "MG!" and snappy salutes. Piper smiled graciously at everyone and floated serenely through the lobby. Jerry and George followed in her wake, both of them looking nervously at the floor and hoping not to draw any attention.

Piper walked down a hallway and up some stairs and then into an elevator. When George and Jerry were in the elevator, she punched the button for the third floor. On the third floor, she walked down another hallway and down a flight of stairs. She turned corners and went up stairs and down stairs. She took elevators up and down.

George said, "Wow, you know just where to go! You're wonderful!"

Jerry said, "She's just stumbling around at random. We're lost."

Piper stopped and pointed. The big metal door and the two monstrous guards were directly ahead.

"How did you do that?" Jerry asked.

"I just asked myself, What Would Jerry Do? And then I did the opposite."

"Hmph," Jerry said. "We still have the two biggest guards in the history of the world to deal with. I don't think those guys are gonna shout 'MG!' and wave you through that doorway."

"They don't look familiar to me," Piper said. "It could be a problem. I wonder What Jerry Would Do?"

While Jerry was trying to come up with a sarcastic answer, hidden speakers somewhere in the ceiling crackled to life.

"All–employee meeting begins in five minutes in the auditorium. It's about your 401k, people. Be there, or be screwed."

The two monstrous guards left their posts immediately and hurried away.

"Jerry would have run way like a scared rabbit," Piper said. "That's What Jerry Would Do. It's a good thing we didn't do that."

"Okay," George said. "Now, how do we get through that steel door?"

"Force!" Jerry said. He was filled with anger. He screamed and ran full–tilt at the door. He bounced off and landed in a sitting position on the floor of the hallway. "Ouch," he said.

Piper laughed sarcastically. "I'll be kind to it." She stepped up to the door. "Hi, door. How are you?" She stroked the shiny surface slowly and sensuously. "Wouldn't you like to open up for me?"

Watching her, Jerry felt electric tingles running through his body, with the exception of his chest, which had collided with the door and still hurt, and his rear end, which had collided with the floor and also still hurt.

The door slid silently to the right. The opening was black. Piper turned around and flashed a smug smile at George and Jerry. Then she turned back and walked through the dark opening.

"Isn't she wonderful?" George asked. "Come on, Jerry." He followed her through the opening.

That's not what Jerry would do, Jerry thought. Nonetheless, he pushed himself to his feet and staggered after the other two.

The light from the hallway didn't penetrate far. It illuminated a patch of gray floor in front of him, but it faded away within a few feet. Jerry could see nothing beyond that, although he sensed that he was in a large space.

Then the door slid shut again, and he was standing in pitch blackness.

CHAPTER SIX

"I hate the dark," Jerry said.

"Pussy." It was Piper's voice. It seemed to come from Jerry's immediate right.

"Piper?" Jerry tried to make his voice sound panicked, which was quite easy under the circumstances. "Where are you? I can't see anything!" He reached out toward Piper's voice, hoping he'd get a chance to touch her.

Bright lights turned on. Jerry discovered that he was about to cop a George feel. He pulled back quickly.

His companions hadn't noticed his reaching hands. Piper was in front of George. She and George and Piper were staring at something ahead of them.

"What is that?" George asked.

"It's a woman," Piper said. "Sort of."

Jerry looked in the direction of their gaze. Ahead of them, a human figure sat behind a desk. It was female but huge—about eight feet tall if it were to stand up, Jerry estimated. When the light went on, it raised its head and stared at the newcomers. "Hello," it said.

The sound was mellifluous. It could have been the voice of an operatic soprano, although, considering the white gleam of bone in the almost skeletal face, it would have been a soprano with no hope of getting roles on any major opera stage. The bones were delicate, and a few locks of black hair hung from what was left of the scalp, and the creature held itself in a way that told Jerry it considered itself attractive.

"Thanks for turning on the lights," it said. "The motion sensors only react to living beings."

"That's interesting," George said, stepping forward.

"George!" Piper grabbed his arm and prevented him from getting close to the thing behind the desk.

"So," Jerry said. "I'm not sure how we should open this conversation."

"Considering that you're a disgusting, rotting zombie," Piper said.

"I wasn't going to say that," Jerry said.

"Of course not. You're a pussy."

The creature lowered its gaze to the surface of the desk. "I know that I've changed," it said. "I used to be young and beautiful."

"Yeah, right," Piper said.

"But that's no reason to be cruel," the creature continued. It raised its huge head and stared directly at Piper. "There was a time when I looked a lot like you. In fact, a great deal like you. Come closer."

"Not on your—"

Piper stared into the creature's sunken eyes and her voice faded away. Slowly, using very small steps, she moved toward the desk.

The creature rose, shoving back the chair it had been sitting in. "Yes, that's right," she said.

What a beautiful voice, Jerry thought. In fact, she's really a beautiful woman. You just have to ignore that cracked, leathery skin and the bones showing through. I think I could ignore those.

What the fuck's the matter with you? he asked himself.

Look at her, he told himself. She's lovely.

You're right, he answered.

He realized that, without having thought about it, he was walking toward the creature. Out of the corner of his eye, he could see George doing the same.

This isn't wise, Jerry thought. I should probably stop moving.

But he couldn't stop himself. With an effort, he tore his glance away from the creature and looked at George. George was smiling, but other than that, his expression was vacant.

Jerry tried to talk, but he could say nothing. He gave in to the pull he felt and let his eyes turn back toward the creature standing on the other side of the table.

Her sunken eyes gleamed with eagerness. She reached her skeletal hands toward him.

"You look familiar," Piper said, her voice sounding as though it had been forced through a layer of molasses.

The creature focused on Piper.

Jerry stopped walking. He was frozen in place. George was frozen beside him.

The creature stared at Piper. It leaned forward, fascinated. "We'll talk after I eat the brains of these two," it said.

"Oh," Piper said. "Okay."

The creature turned back toward Jerry and George. Uncontrollably, they started moving toward it again.

"It's so nice to eat you," the creature said.

It stared into Jerry's eyes. He couldn't look away.

The creature said, "No, st—!"

The lights went out.

Jerry was engulfed in blackness. He could feel it pressing in on him from all sides. He couldn't breathe.

But he was no longer under a compulsion to move forward. He stood still, able to move but afraid to do so. He was disoriented and feared that if he moved, it would be in the wrong direction and he'd end up in the creature's clutches.

If I don't move, he reasoned, I'll be safe.

Then a terrible thought struck him. Maybe it's creeping up on me in the dark!

He mustn't move. He mustn't make a sound that would attract its attention. Maybe it could hear him breathe. Maybe it could smell his breath! Did I brush my teeth this morning? he asked himself. He couldn't remember. He held his breath, just to be safe.

Then another even more terrible thought struck him: What if it can see in the dark?

He squeezed his eyes shut. He didn't know how that could help, but it made him feel ever so slightly better.

A hand grabbed Jerry's shoulder.

He screamed.

"Oh, hush." It was the voice of Dr. Walter Zing, super science guy. "You kids are so noisy."

"Walter! She's going to eat us!" Jerry whispered.

"Just your brains," Zing said, speaking in a normal voice. "Don't worry. She can't do anything when the lights are off."

Zing turned the lights off, Jerry thought. The creature saw him and was telling him to stop. Good thing she didn't get a chance to lock eyes with him first.

" Hold still now," Zing said. He put something on Jerry's face. "Good boy," Zing said. "You were very brave."

Suddenly Jerry could see again.

The room was still dark but not pitch black. The floor glowed faintly with a purple light. A few feet away from him, George and Piper were lit up in shades of purple and blue. George looked silly and Piper looked exotic and painfully desirable. Walter Zing stood in front of Jerry, smiling broadly. His teeth were a mixture of blue and purple patches with black speckles. He wore heavy glasses that looked like miniature binoculars.

Jerry touched his own face. He was wearing similar glasses. "Your teeth look really weird, Doctor Zing."

Zing sighed. "You must learn to focus on what's essential, Jerry. Like that." He pointed.

He was pointing at the creature that had menaced them. Now purple—a brilliant purple where its bones were exposed—it stood behind its desk, unmoving, staring into space.

"Cool," Jerry said. "How did you do that? And can it hear us?"

"I don't think she can hear us. She's in a quiescent state now. There are ultraviolet lights installed in this room. Those are special UV glasses I put on you. UV light doesn't activate her."

"So they *are* feeding on sunlight!" Jerry said. "I thought so."

"Very good," Zing said, smiling approvingly.

"That's why she started to say, 'No, stop!' when she saw you turning off the lights."

"That must have been it," Zing said.

"You know a lot about the zombies, don't you?"

"I'm still blind," Piper said.

"Me, too," George said.

"Sorry," Zing said. "I only have two pairs of the magic glasses."

"So turn the lights on," George said.

"Weren't you paying attention to what I was telling Jerry?" Zing said impatiently.

George looked down at the purple floor and shuffled his purple feet. "Sorry. I only pay attention when it's about bacteria."

"Oh, well," Zing said. "In that case, all right. The lights are on. You just can't see them. You have to be wearing the magic glasses. Jerry, I haven't really told you absolutely everything."

"Obviously."

"Let's go to my office. Now that you've seen what's in this room, I guess I might as well tell you more."

"Tell me everything."

"I'll tell you more than I have so far."

"Well, don't leave us in the dark," Piper said.

"That's funny," Zing said. "Hold on." He walked over to George, put his hand on George's upper arm, and led him to the door. Then he did the same to Piper. She shrank from his touch but then mastered herself. Jerry couldn't tell if Zing had noticed.

Zing beckoned Jerry. When Jerry had joined the others at the door, Zing placed his hand on the door, and it slid open. Zing stepped out into the lighted corridor. "Come on!" he said urgently. "The light will awaken her!"

The three of them rushed out after him. For a moment, they got stuck in the doorway. Then George pushed Piper through ahead of him, and the blockage was cleared. The door slid shut again behind them.

Jerry pulled the UV glasses from his head and breathed a sigh of relief.

Zing leaned close to the door and peered at it. Satisfied, he stepped away and expelled a breath. "Whew! There. That seems to be okay. I hate to think what could happen if she got ou—" He broke off and looked at the three of them looking at him. He laughed nervously and unconvincingly. "I was referring to a movie I was watching on TV last night. Nothing to do with the real world."

Piper narrowed her eyes. "You're lying."

Jerry pointed at the door. "Is she the super secret super science stuff you referred to?"

Zing wouldn't meet his gaze. He looked down at the floor and nodded. Suddenly he raised his head and looked around carefully. He grabbed the UV glasses from Jerry's hands. Then he put his finger to his lips and gave a "follow me" gesture with his head. He took off at a rapid walk, with Jerry, George, and Piper close behind him.

Once again, Zing walked quickly through a confusing sequence of corridors and staircases and elevators. At one point, they passed the window showing Studley Bacterium at work, but this time Zing didn't seem interested in watching.

At last they were in Zing's office. He closed the door behind them. Then he said with forced cheerfulness, "Is anyone hungry? I could order—"

Piper cut him off. "Oh, stop. You have something to tell us, so tell it."

Zing sighed. "Oh, all right." He sat down behind his desk. "It's so hard to know where to begin. Let me think...Well, let's see. I was a dreamer when I was a child. I used to dream about helping humanity. I've always been interested in science. Why, I can remember when I was only five years old—"

"Save that for your memoir," Piper said. "Fast forward."

"Jeez," Zing muttered. "All right. When I was in college—" He held his hand up quickly to keep Piper from interrupting again. "It's relevant. You know, you look just like your mother. Looking at you is like seeing her again. You also act like your mother. She used to push me around, too."

Piper leaned over toward Jerry and whispered, "He's even creepier than you."

"I guess that's why I loved her so much," Zing said. He sighed.

"What?" Piper shouted. "You loved my mother?"

"And she loved me." Zing chuckled. "If it had lasted one month more, I'd have been your father."

"Oh, my God," Piper said. She looked ill. "You're making this up."

"Oh, no," Zing said, shaking his head rapidly. "Oh, no, no, no, no, no. I never make things up."

"You just don't tell everything," Jerry said.

"Of course," Zing said. "That's okay. That's just protecting people."

"So you were in college and you loved Piper's mother," George said. "Then what?"

"Then she left me for Frank. Piper's father," Zing added.

"Why?" George asked. "You knew all that stuff about science!"

"He knew all that stuff about money."

"Ah," George said.

"Not that he had all that much at first," Zing said. "That came later. But I guess Grizzy could see that he'd be rich some day. She just couldn't foresee—" He stopped suddenly and looked at Piper. "You won't want to hear the next part," he said. "Maybe you should wait outside and rejoin the class later."

"Don't be ridiculous," Piper snapped. "What could be worse than what you've already said? Go on."

Jerry said, "I thought Piper's mother's name was Zelda."

"Griselda," Zing said. He repeated the name slowly, lingeringly. "Griiiseeellldaaa." He wrapped his tongue and mouth around the word, fondling it sloppily.

"That was obscene," Jerry said.

"Don't be silly," Zing said. "It's just a name. Griselda. It means 'dark battle.' Very appropriate, actually. Her friends called her Zelda, but *I* called her Grizzy."

Jerry said, "And she called you—"

"That's private!" Zing shouted. "Keep that to yourself. Some data should not be made widely available."

George and Piper looked at Jerry with their eyebrows raised in question. Jerry shook his head. "He's right. That's private." Stud, he thought. That's what she called him. Her super science stud. She wasn't saying, No, stop! She was saying, No, Stud! The older generation is so weird. And sometimes kind of nauseating, even when they're not zombies. He thought of telling Piper later what her mother had once called Zing but decided against it.

"Well, okay," George said. "This is a curious almost connection, but what does it have to do with zombies and the creature you have locked away in that room?"

"And why did you make the door of the room open for us?" Jerry asked.

"I didn't make it open," Zing said. "I didn't even know you were there. The guards should have kept you away from it."

"The guards got distracted and left," Jerry said.

Zing shook his head sadly. "Ordinary people are like that."

"So who did open the door? Not that creature?"

"No, no. She was dormant until you moved and made the lights turn on. Tell me how it happened. What were you doing when the door opened?"

Piper snickered. "Jerry threw himself at it like a real manly man."

"And it opened?" Zing asked, looked surprised.

"Hell, no. Jerry bounced off it and landed on his butt, looking like an idiot."

"Piper spoke to it," George said.

"That wasn't it," Piper said. "It didn't open till I touched it."

"Ah!" Zing said. "Of course." He stared into space, nodding thoughtfully.

Jerry let him do that for a few seconds and then asked, "Why 'of course'?"

Zing waved his hand. "Oh, DNA, DNA. The door is keyed to my DNA and a couple of other people's. It only opens to my touch and theirs. One of us just happens to be closely enough related to Piper that the DNA sensor thought the match was close enough. Everyone in the world is your cousin, you know."

"Fascinating!" George said. "I'd love to know more about that

DNA sensor."

Zing brightened. "It's very cool!"

Jerry said, "You mean I'm related to Fred Foxtrot? That's horrifying."

"Well, yes, it would be, wouldn't it?" Zing said. "But I'm sure that you and he are very, very distant cousins."

"I don't know about this," George said. "Doctor Walter, I don't know much about DNA and cousins, but this doesn't seem right to me. If your system will open the door for someone who happens to be your cousin, then it's not very secure, is it?"

Piper said, "Who's the other person the door is keyed to? Something tells me that's the important part, and you're avoiding it."

Zing sighed. "I suppose I have to go ahead and reveal a bit more data."

"Jesus Christ," Piper said. "This is like squeezing blood from a fucking turnip."

"Your mother would have strongly disapproved of your language," Zing said disapprovingly.

"Yeah, well, my mother is dead, isn't she? She died when I was a kid."

"Well," Zing said. "Sort of. Actually, well, she didn't really exactly entirely quite die."

"She's alive?" Piper asked.

"Not really exactly entirely quite alive, either."

Piper, George, and Jerry said simultaneously, "She's a zombie!"

"She's *the* zombie," Zing said. "The original one." There was a note of pride in his voice. "She's the best zombie of them all."

"Oh, hell," Piper said.

"So, where is she?" George asked.

"She's in that room," Jerry said, hit by a sudden realization. "She's that creature."

"Well, yes," Zing said.

"I felt it," Piper said. "I felt a connection. She felt it, too. She wanted to talk to me."

"You're crazy," George said. "Darling," he added.

"She didn't want to talk to you," Jerry said. "She wanted to eat your brains. That's what parents do, especially when they're zombies."

"No. She's my mother. I want to go back there and talk to her."

"Oh, please don't," Zing said. "Jerry's right. She's not really your mother anymore. She's dangerous."

"But you go in there."

"That's different. I'm a scientist."

"That doesn't make any sense at all."

"Of course it does. I'm studying her. It's research. I'm utterly detached and impartial and unemotional."

"About Grizzy?" Jerry said.

"Grizzy," Zing murmured, lost in a dream.

"What kind of research are you doing regarding her?" Jerry asked.

" Secret stuff. Super secret super science stuff. Sorry. Can't say more."

"Who's the other person the door is keyed to, Dr. Walter?" George asked.

Zing sighed. "Grizzy. I mean, her. Grizzy's DNA."

"Why would you do that?" Jerry said. "Jesus, you mean she can just leave whenever she wants to? Anytime the lights are on and she's energized?" He remembered the zombies in Florida staring at the sun. With the lights in that room, they wouldn't need the sun. They could be walking around and eating people's brains day and night. He shivered.

"Oh, no. She can't get out. Her touch only opens the door from the outside. You see, I was always afraid that despite all of my precautions, Grizzy would manage to leave the room somehow."

"Escape, you mean," George said.

"Leave the room somehow," Zing repeated. "If that ever happened, she would be in great danger. People would be frightened of her."

"No shit," Jerry muttered.

Zing continued. "At the very least, they'd run from her. At the worst, they'd try to harm her. I'm quite sure that she'd want to be back in the only safe place she knows, that room. So I made sure the door would only open to her touch from the outside."

Piper squinted at him. "If you were a safe, I'd keep all my money in you."

"Why, thank you!"

"That wasn't a compliment. How many other people is the door keyed to?" When Zing didn't answer, she leaned forward and raised her voice. "How many others?"

"I hope you don't talk to your teachers in school this way," Zing said. "Only one other person. Your father. Frank Pistole. That's why the door worked for you—because your DNA is a combination of your parents', and the door is keyed to both of them."

"Man!" George said. "I really want to learn about that DNA sensor!"

"Stuff it, George," Piper said. "Why my father?"

"He paid for my research. He said it was his right to be able to see the subject whenever he wanted, especially considering that he was married to her. Once," he added, a tone of bitterness creeping into his voice. "When she was still alive. Death dissolves that, of course. I'm sure the law doesn't take return from death into account. They're not married now in the eyes of the law, you know. She's available again."

"She's a zombie, Walter," Jerry said. "She's not available to anyone. She's not Griselda any more. You said that yourself."

"Hmph. I was in love with her before Frank even met her."

"Yeah, well, you don't get any points for that in life. Or after life, I suppose."

"I don't care!" Zing said. "She still loves me! I can tell!"

"So she has human feelings for you?" Piper asked.

"Why, of course she does."

"In that case, she must still have human feelings for me."

"That's diff—My, you are clever! Just like your mother."

Piper stood up. "Let's go."

"Go where?" George asked.

"Back to that room," Jerry said.

"Oh, shit," George said.

Zing rose slowly to his feet. "I never could stand up to your mother, either. Well, let's go, then. But you'll have to be really careful and do exactly what I say at every moment."

"Fat chance," Piper said.

"Oh, all right." Zing led the way out of the office.

They returned to the secret super science room by a different but no less confusing route. Jerry tried to keep track of the corners they turned and the staircases they went up and down and the elevators they took in both directions—or possibly sideways in some cases; he couldn't be sure—but he soon gave up. He trudged along after Zing and let his mind drift into a reverie in which he lived in a world with no zombies but lots of Piper Pistole.

His adolescent fantasies were interrupted when they passed the doorway to the large auditorium where the employee meeting was being held.

Jerry heard the amplified voice of the speaker saying that the 401k plan had been cancelled. "None of the money is vested," the speaker said, "so it will all be transferred to the corporate general fund. BioTyme wants you to know that we're grateful for the past and future use of what used to be your money." There was an angry muttering from the audience, growing in volume and then fading away as Zing led the group down the hallway.

So BioTyme is just another zombie company, Jerry thought. Eating its employees' life force. Or would that make it a vampire company?

He couldn't decide. He drifted back into fantasies about Piper.

This time, his fantasy ended when Zing said, "We're here." They were standing in front of the steel door.

Zing had brought the two pairs of UV glasses with him. He handed one to Piper. "Since she is your mother," he said, "you should have these." He waited till Piper had put them on. Then he nodded in satisfaction and put on his own pair.

"What about me and George?" Jerry asked.

"You'll be blind," Zing said. "You'll be free to imagine things creeping up on you in the dark."

"Oh, great," George said.

"I'm sorry," Zing said quickly. "I shouldn't have said that. I hope it won't give you nightmares."

"Don't worry, honey," Piper said. "I'll be able to see. I'll protect you."

"And Jerry," George said.

"I'll protect you," Piper repeated.

Zing reached out to the door. "When it opens," he said, "we must all get inside quickly. The door will close behind us and the lights will come on. I'll go right to the switch and turn the visible lights off and the UV lights on. It should only take a few seconds. It won't be enough time for Griselda to grab anyone."

"Are you sure about that?" Jerry asked.

"Fairly sure."

"But George and I won't be able to see! We won't know how close we are to her, or if she's trying to grab us."

"That's quite true," Zing said. "Isn't science exciting? Now, then." He placed the fingers of his right hand gently on the surface of the door.

The door slid to the right.

"Quickly, now!" Zing said. He rushed through the door.

Piper followed him quickly.

George followed her a bit less quickly.

Jerry dawdled in the corridor, wondering if anyone would notice if he stayed there. Then he imagined Piper saying something sarcastic about his cowardice, and he took a deep breath and stepped into the darkness.

The door slid shut behind him.

Jerry could almost feel teeth crunching into his skull.

Bright lights came on.

The four of them were alone in the room. The desk was still there, but the chair behind it was overturned. The terrifying monster that had once been Piper's mother was nowhere to be seen.

"This is extremely worrisome," Zing said.

CHAPTER SEVEN

"No shit!" Jerry said. "Where is she? Where'd she go? What happened?"

"I have absolutely no idea," Zing said.

Watching his face, Jerry was sure that he did have some idea. Piper was right about blood and a turnip. "You used to be so eager to impart information, back when I was a kid watching you on TV, Dr. Walter."

"Things happen, Jerry," Zing said. "Say, why don't you kids all go home and get a good night's sleep? I have some ideas I want to look into. I'll call you when I know something."

They grumbled, but in the end they agreed.

Piper said in a low voice, "I want my mom."

George put his arm around her shoulders comfortingly, and she clung to him.

Jerry sighed hopelessly.

Piper removed George's arm. "Come on," she said. "I know the way."

She led them unerringly through the building and out to the parking lot.

Damn, Jerry thought. She has absolutely no faults at all, other than the fact that she hates me.

They climbed into Jerry's car, and he drove them back to the Pistole mansion. He intended to drop them off there and then go home, but George insisted that he come in with them.

"I need a pizza," George said. "I bet you do, too."

"I need a beer," Jerry said.

"Of course you do," Piper said.

"On second thought," Jerry said, "I'm going home. "Call me if Zing calls you."

The next day was Saturday. Jerry woke late trying to grasp the wisps of fading nightmares and then, when he remembered them, trying to push them away. He staggered into the kitchen, started a pot of coffee dripping, and stared out the window, wishing he had a better view than a parking lot.

He puttered around the kitchen, grabbing random foods from the refrigerator for breakfast. He realized that he was waiting for a telephone call from Zing, or from George saying that Zing had called. When no call came, he finished the coffee, showered, dressed, and went out to do his weekly grocery shopping.

He had been planning to buy a lot of meat. He had been feeling like eating a steak a day for a week. But when he stood in front of the butcher section in the supermarket, looking at fine cuts of meat that once would have made his mouth water, all he could see was slices of dead animals.

They're just unsuccessful zombies, he thought.

What about the Studley stuff? he asked himself. When that hits the market, won't that be okay?

Hell no, he answered.

He loaded his cart with fruits and vegetables. Later, he'd try to find a vegetarian cookbook.

Feeling morally superior and a bit less queasy, he paid for his groceries, loaded everything into the trunk of his car, and drove home.

When he entered his apartment, the telephone was ringing. It was George. "There you are, at last," George said. "This is the third time I've called."

"Why didn't you call my cell phone?"

"Because you always answered your home phone before. And you did again. See?"

"That almost makes sense. What's happened?"

George lowered his voice and said something Jerry couldn't understand.

"What? Speak up. Why are you whispering?"

"Sorry. It seemed appropriate. Zing called. He's coming over here. How soon can you be here?"

"Maybe you don't need me. I've got groceries to put away. I have to water the plants on my balcony. And then I was going to take a nap."

"Do I have to put Piper on the line?"

"I'll be there. Thirty or 45 minutes."

When Jerry got to the Pistole house, Zing was already there.

But this was a different Zing than the one he had known before. This Zing stood straighter and looked taller. There was a fierce light in his eye and a manic aspect to his behavior. He was dressed in black and had a rifle slung across his back. He was no longer Dr. Walter, Super Science Guy. He was Walter Zing, Super Science Stud. Or possibly Walter Zing, Super Dangerous Psycho.

"Hi, Dr. Walter," Jerry said. "I see you're planning something."

"Yes, young Gerald, I am." The voice was deeper and louder than before.

Jerry noticed that Piper seemed to no longer be repelled by Zing. Instead, she was looking at him with interest. Black clothing and a gun? Jerry thought. Is that the secret? No, probably not. After all, look at George.

"Is it something involving violence and bloodshed?" Jerry asked.

"Quite probably, Gerald." The voice grew even deeper and louder. Piper looked even more interested.

"Then we should probably let the police handle it," Jerry said.

"Ha, ha, ha!" Zing laughed. It was a very loud and very grating laugh. "Those flatfoot bozos? Not a chance. All right, men. Gather round. And woman," he added.

"That's all right," Piper said. "I'm one of the guys." She didn't seem insulted at all.

"Here's the sit," Zing said. "Well, actually, this was the sit as of yesterday."

"Wouldn't that make it the sat?" Jerry asked, but everyone ignored him.

"What's a sit?" George asked.

"Situation," Piper said. She hugged George. "It's okay that you didn't know that."

"Yesterday," Zing continued, "when we discovered that Grizzy was missing, I immediately suspected that she had been taken by Frank Pistole. Your father." He nodded to Piper.

"Grizzy's husband," Jerry said.

"Death dissolves marriage," Zing said.

"Yeah, maybe, but still, doesn't he have some kind of rights?"

"He signed them away. Sort of. Mostly. Pretty much. Anyway, as I told you, he's the other person to whose DNA the door is keyed. Hence, I deduced that Frank had kidnapped her."

"Or liberated her," Jerry said, but once again he was ignored.

"Then I checked the surveillance video to make sure, and there he was. The scoundrel! He must have been there at the same time we were, hiding, waiting for his chance. After we left, he took advantage of the absence of the guards and wheeled her away."

"Wheeled?" Piper asked.

"He would hardly take the chance of leading her by the hand, would he?"

"She'd probably have bitten his hand off," Jerry said. "And then various other parts."

"Exactly," Zing said. "In the video, you can clearly see that he he's wearing UV glasses when he enters the room. He has a dolly with him. When he comes out, he doesn't have the glasses, but he does have Grizzy blindfolded and securely strapped to the dolly."

"He had the dolly on the dolly!" Jerry said.

Zing glared at him. "Levity is out of place, Gerald. Then he wheeled her away, out of sight of the camera."

"No one stopped him?" George asked. "He took her out of the building that way, and presumably into a waiting vehicle, and no one did anything about it?"

"He's poured a lot of money into BioTyne," Zing said. "Everyone who works there wants that money to continue pouring in."

"Ah," Jerry said, "money. The force that rules the world. Some people can't imagine living without it." He stared meaningfully at Piper.

"You try it," she said.

"Focus, children!" Zing said, very loudly. "Now, then. We must rescue Grizzy. I won't tell you Frank's purpose in stealing her. It would give you nightmares. However, it's urgent. We can't waste time."

"First we have to know where he's taken her," George said.

"The pickle factory. I'm quite certain of that. He took her to the pickle factory. We must go there and rescue her and return her to the safety of the room at BioTyne. I will change the access permissions so that Frank's DNA will no longer open the door. I'm ready." He reached over his shoulder and tapped the rifle slung across his back.

"That's why I brought this."

"I'm surprised you own a rifle," Jerry said.

"There's more to me than you know," Zing said smugly.

"I don't think we'll need a rifle," George said. "The factory's closed on the weekend."

"Oh." Zing looked disappointed. "Well, it never hurts to be sure. Better safe than sorry. A stitch in time saves nine. You should all put on black clothing. And blacken your faces. I have black shoe polish with me. We'll all apply it before we infiltrate the factory. Bring flashlights. Do you all have guns?"

They all shook their heads.

"No? Well, that's a shame. I only have this one." He reached back over his shoulder and tapped the rifle again. Then he stroked the barrel lightly. "Don't you have any weapons here? Swords? Big knives?"

"Ordinary kitchen knives," George said. "You know—the kind you eat with."

"What about big knives that the cooks use? Big, sharp knives with terrible points and thick, heavy handles?"

"Er, no. The cooks took all of those with them when they quit."

Zing sighed and shook his head. "I'm quite disappointed in you."

"We have steak knives," George said. "They have points. And serrated blades. I cut myself badly with one, once."

Piper hugged him again. "Yes, you did. I remember."

"I suppose that will have to do."

"It does seem odd to go into battle with steak knives," Jerry said. "I mean, the heroes in action movies—"

"This isn't a movie, you dumb shit," Piper said.

George leaned toward Jerry and whispered, "Boy, she *really* likes you!"

Jerry said, "I'll take one of those steak knives, George."

"I'll go change into black clothing," Piper said. "George?"

George said, "I don't have any black clothes. The closest thing I have is that old navy blue suit."

"That'll have to do," Piper said. "Come on. I'll pick you out a nice tie to go with it."

After they had left, Jerry said, "A suit will constrict his movements."

"Perhaps," Zing said. "But it will make him feel more professional."

"Oh, God," Jerry said. "Well, I'm going like this." He was wearing a red t–shirt, blue jeans, and white running shoes.

"I don't really approve, Gerald."

"I could stay behind."

Zing shook his head. "We're going to need every soldier on this mission."

Mission, Jerry thought. Soldier. Oh, God.

They waited silently until George returned. He looked uncomfortable in his navy blue suit. "I hate wearing ties," he said.

"Why the hell are you wearing one now?" Jerry asked.

"Because, you know," George waved his hands, "a suit."

"Suits don't suit you," Jerry said.

"Thanks."

"And you should be wearing running shoes, not those leather ones."

"If Frank's there, I don't want to make him mad at me."

Piper entered. She wore a skintight black leather cat suit, complete with a tail and cat's ears.

The three men stared at her wordlessly for a long time.

When Jerry was finally able to breathe again, he asked, "Why do you own that?"

George, smiling and looking into space, said, "We sometimes

have occasion to use it."

Jerry stared at the floor, feeling immensely sorry for himself.

Zing said, "Let's get going!"

They formed a caravan. Zing was in the lead. Jerry came behind, driving alone, staring at Zing's BT STUD license plate and trying to expel from his mind images of a young Zing having sex with a young, zombified Griselda and parallel images of Piper pulling off her cat suit in order to have sex with George. He kept glancing in the rearview mirror to make sure that George and Piper were following him and also in hopes of seeing Piper, but all he could see was the sunlight reflecting on their windshield.

Zombies eat your brains, Jerry thought, but Piper devours my heart. Which is worse? After a moment's reflection, he decided that zombies were worse.

They headed for East Drive and drove north along it, still in a tight caravan. The pickle factory was in an old industrial area to the northwest of downtown. It was the only factory the company owned.

During the height of the company's prosperity, the factory had run 24 hours a day, seven days a week, taking in truckloads of peppers and ingredients for the brine and sending out truckloads of finished product to eager customers. Underground, a huge basement storage area held the jars of peppers while they pickled. In the factory proper, long assembly lines carried the raw peppers past workers who graded and washed and trimmed them, on to other workers who put them in jars, then past spouts that poured in salty water and vinegar and various seasonings, and then past sensors and guards who made sure that the moving belt carried only uncapped jars, through an opening in a wall and into a guarded room. The belt emerged through an opening in the wall at the far end of the guarded room carrying the jars with their tops screwed on. The capped jars then went into another open area where workers packed the jars into boxes and stacked the full boxes on pallets. The pallets were then moved down to the basement to wait while the peppers pickled properly.

What happened in that closed, guarded room? The only entrances were one highly secured door that opened only to a few authorized personnel and the tightly guarded and heavily sensored opening through which the conveyor belt carried open jars of fresh pickles in brine into the room. The only exits were the same door and the opening through which the conveyor belt carried the capped jars from the room, and there were sensors and guards on the other side of that opening. Ah, this was the heart of Piper's Pickled Peppers! This was the room that set Piper's Pickled Peppers apart from all other pickled peppers, or indeed from other pickles of any sort. This was the place that made Piper's Pickled Peppers so irresistible to so many old people throughout the sunny parts of these blessed United States.

This was where the secret ingredient was added.

What was this amazing secret ingredient? Can't tell you. It's a secret.

It was a secret that Frank Pistole was willing to go to great lengths and financial expenditure to protect. If he had to commit murder to protect the secret, he would. Perhaps he already had. It wasn't the pickles that were the foundation of the Pistole fortune. Not really. It was the secret ingredient.

Even the few workers who were allowed into that room to oversee the addition of the secret ingredient to the jars before a machine near the exit capped the jars didn't know what the secret ingredient was. They just knew that they were required to watch while a machine dropped a single tiny droplet of a clear liquid into each open jar. They didn't even get to do this themselves. They just watched to make sure the mechanized dropper and the movement of the jars remained synchronized so that not a drop of the precious secret ingredient was wasted. The caps were screwed onto the jars by another machine. The humans didn't do that, either.

Once those workers entered the room, they couldn't leave it till the end of their shift. They couldn't take cell phones or any other electronic devices into the room with them. Once inside, they were isolated from the world. A meal was delivered in the middle of the shift. Coffee was available. The room contained a single small lavatory which they were allowed to use at measured intervals. Every second of their working day within that room was monitored by video cameras and microphones, the output of which was in turn monitored in another room by extraordinarily alert and eagle-eyed guards with super-sensitive hearing. When the workers left the secret-ingredient room at the end of their shift, they walked past super-secret super-science gadgets that could detect even a few molecules of the secret ingredient. Rival pickle companies would have paid a fortune to any employee who managed to smuggle a drop or two of the stuff out, but that had never happened and never would.

Unknown to them, their homes were thoroughly bugged. Security personnel from Piper's Pickled Peppers listened to every word they said or that was said to them and watched everything they did, from the most hum drum to the most intimate and/or embarrassing. Those who spoke incautiously found, on the next work day, that they were no longer employed by Piper's Pickled Peppers.

On the bright side, their paychecks were enormous.

During the good times, the single factory had been unable to keep up with the demand for the company's pickles. Underlings such as George Gordon had urged Frank Pistole to open factories elsewhere, or at the very least to expand the existing one. Frank had always refused. When pressed by George, he had said that he could only obtain limited amounts of the secret ingredient at a time. The current production, at its current level, was all that was possible.

When the company began to lose market share and the factory's operating hours were reduced, the existing facility was more than enough to keep up with the fading demand.

Then Frank Pistole died. When the reluctant guards finally recognized George's authority and let him into the secret room, he discovered that the entire current supply of the secret ingredient was contained in a large plastic jug that had been upended into the top of the machine that delivered drops of the stuff to the pickle jars and in a half-dozen similar sealed plastic jugs standing on the floor in a corner of the room. The upended jug was half empty. Questioning of the terrified workers—terrified because of the enormous guards standing over them while George questioned them—revealed that Frank Pistole himself had showed up from time to time with a new sealed jug, and that no one but Frank Pistole was allowed to replace the upended jug, when it was empty, with a full one and to take the empty jug away.

From what he could gather, George estimated that the existing supply of secret ingredient would last for about a year. Later, when, thanks to his good management, the market for the company's pickles improved and the factory added a second shift, he lowered that estimate to six months. He had no idea what would happen then, once the secret ingredient was used up. He would have to find out somehow what it was and where Frank had been getting it from.

In the meantime, George authorized the people who worked in the room to replace the empty jug themselves. He told them to leave the empties in the corner for later pickup. Then he immersed himself in running the company and forgot about the sealed room and the secret ingredient.

The industrial area the caravan of cars was headed to had been set up after World War Two by a cabal of businessmen. Promised big paychecks after they left office, the then-mayor of Piketon and the then-governor of Arapahoe had acquiesced immediately. The Business Council of Greater Piketon, the official name of the cabal, had chosen the location partly because, at the time, it was well outside the city. The smoke billowing from the smokestacks of the factories they planned to locate there, and the ugly factories themselves, would be invisible from the city proper. In addition, much of the unused farmland in the area, which would be bought for the new development at inflated prices with state government money, was owned by members of the cabal. Finally, the prevailing winds in Piketon blow from west to east, and so the factory smokestacks' great billowing clouds of yellow and green poison would be carried away over farms and ranches out in Nowhereseville, much of it not even in the state. The farmers and ranchers and small town residents of those area had no political pull, but they would have enough brains to say nothing and slaughter the six-legged steers and five-eyed chickens and sell the meat and milk and eggs to stores in Piketon. People would get sick in Piketon, but people were always getting sick in Piketon, and they wouldn't know why, and the members of the cabal would keep getting richer. The workers in the factories would either commute from Piketon or they'd live in new housing areas near the factories, and they'd be so happy to have jobs that they wouldn't complain. It was all gravy—just not the kind you ate if you were in the know.

The Business Council of Greater Piketon had named the area Steelville, which sounded nifty and industrial and macho to them. As the city grew and surrounded Steelville, locals took to calling it Smogville. Some called it Hell.

Jerry normally avoided that part of the city. The miles of

factories, the green air, the rows of small, dilapidated houses all looked like the aftermath of a war that had destroyed civilization.

He had once said as much to George. George had responded with surprise. George had disagreed. Steelville, he had said, made him think of progress. It symbolized the future.

"*That's* our future?" Jerry had said.

"If we're lucky."

Unlike the other factories in Steelville, the Piper's Pickled Peppers factory had no tall smokestacks belching poison. It was a long, rambling building with short chimneys from which came only occasional puffs of white smoke—emissions far less harmful to the world than, say, the white puff of smoke from the Vatican announcing the election of a new Pope. Hidden from view were the pipes where toxic byproducts of the washing and pickling processes, along with minute quantities of the secret ingredient, were flushed into an underground sewer system, installed when Steelville was first built, which emptied into the nearby Pike River.

The three cars pulled into the empty parking lot and stopped. George emerged from one of them with a smile on his face. He looked up at the poisonous sky and beamed. He breathed deeply. "Mmm," he said.

Jerry climbed out his car, and George said, "That's the smell of jobs, Jerry. Soon we'll be able to run the factory on weekends, too."

"It's a good thing for us that it's closed on Saturdays, isn't it?"

"Oh. I guess so." George examined his key ring and selected a key. "Good thing I've got this, too. Frank didn't ask for it back. If he hasn't had the locks changed, we can go in through the front door."

"And if that key doesn't work?"

"In that case," Piper said, pointing to a row of small windows two stories up, "you'll have to climb up there, Jerry, and go in and open the door for us."

"I could fall and get killed!"

"Yeah, you could."

Zing, who had just joined them, said, "Isn't this exciting? I do wish you all had guns or swords, though."

"Good God," Piper said.

They trooped across the empty parking lot, glowing an alien yellow–green thanks to the harsh morning sun shining through the smog, and ended up at the wide glass double doors.

George's key turned smoothly in the lock, and he pulled one of the doors open.

"You're in luck," Piper said to Jerry.

That depends on your definition of luck, Jerry thought as he followed the others inside.

CHAPTER EIGHT

The huge space was silent. No artificial lights were on. Sunlight coming through the small row of windows high up on one wall, the windows Piper had said Jerry would have to crawl through, was the only illumination. Dust motes danced in the beams of sunlight. Huge machines hulked in the dimness. A motionless conveyor belt snaked through the view, appearing from the darkness on the left and disappearing again into the darkness on the right. It was much spookier than Jerry had anticipated.

To Jerry's relief, the place felt empty. He had been sure there'd be a watchman of some sort, but there didn't seem to be. He wanted to ask George why there wasn't one. It seemed irresponsible, and that surprised him, given how responsible George always was.

Maybe we're being watched on surveillance cameras, Jerry thought. Giant armed thugs are about to descend upon us.

"George," Jerry said, "why aren't there—"

"Watchmen," Piper finished.

"I should have asked you about that before," Zing said.

"I laid them off," George said. "Saved money. I mean, really, who's going to break into a pickle factory and steal ancient bottling machinery?"

"Isn't there some kind of secret ingredient?" Jerry asked. "That's what I always heard."

"Oh, shit," George muttered, suddenly remembering his earlier calculations. "You know," he said loudly, "let's go check on that first."

He led the way to the center of the factory floor. A closed steel box stood there, about thirty feet on a side. As they approached the box, Jerry could see that the conveyor belt ran into an opening in the side of the box.

"I've never been here before," Jerry said. "What is this?"

"This is where the secret ingredient is added," George said.

"Oh, dear," Zing said.

"There's a door on this side," George said, pointing.

They all followed him to the door. It was made of steel, like the rest of the box, and barely distinguishable from it. The door had no handle. A numeric keypad was set into the wall beside it.

George said, "It's a highly secure room. You have to enter the right sequence of numbers with just the right pauses in certain places. You only get two tries."

"What happens if you fail both times?" Jerry asked.

"In the old days, the system would alert the Triple Pees."

"The what?"

"The Pistole Pickle Police. Frank hired a bunch of huge thugs with no sense of right and wrong. He dressed them in green uniforms and had them patrolling the factory, watching for workers who tried to steal jars of pickles. Or single pickles, I guess. When the factory was closed, they watched things through surveillance cameras, and they showed up if someone tried to break in. I got rid of them after Frank died. Now, if you fail to enter the code properly, the system alerts the big boss. That's still very bad."

"But you're the big boss."

"Well, I used to be. Okay, now, everyone be quiet." He frowned and stared intently at the keypad. "I have to concentrate on this."

Piper looked at Jerry and mouthed the words *he's wonderful.*

Oh, God, Jerry thought.

Wondering what the polished steel of the door felt like, he put his hand on it. Without a sound, it swung open inwards very slightly.

"I guess you did the numbers correctly," Jerry said.

"I didn't even start," George said. "The door was unlocked. That's never supposed to happen."

"Someone must have left it open."

"Anyone who did that would be in big trouble."

"With the big boss?" Jerry pushed on the door. It swung open the rest of the way. The room beyond was dark. "This looks familiar," he said, "and I don't like it."

"Wimp," Piper said. She pushed him aside and entered the room. Bright overhead lights came on. She turned and said to Jerry, "There. Now it's not scary."

The other three entered the room. Jerry, Zing, and Piper looked around with interest.

"So this is where the secret thing happens, whatever it is," Jerry said.

"Mm hmm." George was distracted. Against one wall was a line of empty jugs. As he had feared, the secret ingredient was all used up. He looked up at the machine that dropped the ingredient into the pickle jars, at the top, where an upended jug should have been. There was no jug there. Instead, a plastic tube ran into the machine. "That's new," he muttered, looking at the tube.

The tube was attached to the ceiling above the machine. His eyes followed it back from the ceiling to a corner of the room, where it disappeared behind a lumpy pile of black cloth about as tall as he was.

"This is really weird," George said. "Are there more jugs behind there?" He walked over to the pile of cloth and tugged at it.

The cloth slipped to the floor, revealing Griselda. The bright lights glistened on the exposed bones of her face. She was sitting in an oversized metal chair. Her wrists were tied to the arms of the chair and her ankles to the legs. Her chin rested on her bony chest and her eyes were closed. The end of the tube was taped against the side of her neck.

She opened her eyes. “Cat’s out of the bag,” she said in that lovely voice.

They stared at her in astonishment.

She looked at Piper. “Dear, would you please pull this tube out? It’s uncomfortable.”

“Tube?”

“This tube. It goes into my neck. It has a little suction device that draws fluid from me.”

“And drops it into the pickles,” Jerry said. “That’s the secret ingredient!” He looked George, who looked as nauseated as Jerry felt.

“You shouldn’t have said that, Grizzy,” Zing said.

“It’s your fault,” the creature said, staring intently at Zing.

He froze in place, unable to move or speak.

She switched her attention to Piper, but now her gaze was softer. “Please, dear.”

“Of course, Mother.” Gently, Piper removed the tape that held the tube to the creature’s neck. “Oh, my, that looks painful!”

“It is.”

“Tsk, tsk.” Piper shook her head. “Who did this to you? Was it him?” She pointed at Zing.

“Oh, no. Not this time. It was…I’m sorry to have to tell you this, dear. It was your father.”

Piper hissed angrily. She tugged at the tube. Nothing happened.

“Pull it!” the creature said. Her voice was loud and not so mellifluous now.

Piper yanked. A couple of inches of tube emerged from the creature’s neck and fell to the floor.

"Thank you, dear. That's better." The voice was soft and beautiful again. "Now untie me."

"Honey," George said, "I don't think that would be a good—" His voice choked off as the creature stared into his eyes.

"Who's he?" she asked.

"My husband," Piper said. "He's wonderful. Really."

"Untie me. Now."

Piper pulled at the wide plastic bands holding the creature in place. She could do nothing with them. "I can't. I..."

"NOW!"

Piper looked around the room, a desperate and fearful expression on her face. Finally she thought of something. "George, did you bring a steak knife with you?"

His face blank, George reached inside his suit and brought out a steak knife. He handed it to Piper.

She set to work sawing at the creature's bonds. The creature looked down approvingly at what she was doing.

Jerry struggled to say something, to shout at her to stop. As if she sensed what he was trying to do, the creature switched her attention to Jerry. Her huge, dull, dead eyes bored into his. His mind froze. He couldn't even think, let alone speak.

Satisfied, the creature looked back at the knife sawing away at the plastic band around her left wrist.

The knife cut far enough for the band to snap. The left arm was free. The creature raised it in the air and flexed her hand. Then she took the steak knife from Piper, who let go of it docilely.

With the creature's great strength behind it, the knife cut through the remaining restraints quickly. She put her hands on the chair arms and pushed herself to her feet. The chair bent as she did so.

She towered over the three of them.

"Stud," she crooned.

Zing shivered violently from head to foot.

The creature laughed and looked at Jerry. She stared at his forehead as though evaluating his brains. Then she shook her head in dismissal.

She moved in a blur. She grabbed George's head, one hand on each cheek, and lifted him off his feet. She lowered her head to the top of his head. Her mouth opened horribly wide. Some of the teeth were missing. Jawbone showed. Her jaws closed on George's head with a crunching, splintering sound.

Jerry was looking at George's face. He wanted to look away, but he couldn't control himself. He couldn't turn his head or close his eyes. He wanted to scream. He wanted to help George. He wanted to run away. He wanted to shut out the look of terror on George's face.

Then the creature sucked powerfully, an awful slurping sound, and George's face went slack and expressionless. His arms and legs quivered slightly and then hung limp.

The creature dropped his body to the floor. Her mouth was covered with red. She wiped her mouth with her left forearm. "Yum," she said. "He *was* wonderful. Piper, you have good taste in men."

Piper moaned and sank down onto George's body and hugged it.

"Oh, come now," the creature said angrily. She reached toward Piper.

Jerry could move again. He pulled Piper away from George and out of the creature's reach.

The creature glared at Jerry. "You shouldn't get between a mother and her young," she said. Once again, Jerry couldn't move. The creature stepped toward him, her hands reaching for his head.

It looked like it didn't hurt George when she killed him, he told himself reassuringly. In any case, it was quick.

He kept trying to move, to run away, but without success. The creature's big hands were getting closer to his head. She was grinning nastily at him, as though she was feeding on his fear in advance of feeding on his brain, and he was afraid that he was about to exit life with urine running down his legs.

Somewhere outside, someone yelled. Lights came on in the factory. There was the sound of tramping feet, approaching rapidly.

The creature stopped moving toward Jerry, turned her face to the doorway, and listened.

"Inconvenient," she said.

The spell was broken. Jerry grabbed Piper with one hand, Zing with the other, and dragged them both out of the room and into the factory proper.

Outside, the huge space was now brilliantly lit by artificial light. The shafts of sunlight coming through the high windows were drowned out.

The sound of feet had stopped. Blinded by the light, Jerry squeezed his eyes shut and then opened them a fraction.

A group of large, armed men dressed in green uniforms and nibbling pickled peppers stood in front of him. And in front of them stood Frank Pistole, chewing steadily.

Pistole glared at each of them in turn. He growled like a hungry predator. He finished chewing and swallowed. Then he said, "What are you doing here?"

"Daddy!" Piper said. "George is dead! Mommy killed him."

"Good," Pistole said. "He was interfering with me. This frees you up for Foxtrot."

"Foxtrot?"

"I made a deal with him for you. I was planning to get rid of George myself."

"No!" Piper shrank back against Jerry, who enjoyed the contact despite being filled with terror.

"Frank," Zing said, "what's going on here? I know you took Grizzy from BT. I saw it on the security videos. Why is she here?"

"Because you were objecting to supplying me with the you-know-what."

"The secret ingredient," Zing said.

"Idiot," Frank said. "If you talk about it, it's not a secret. No wonder Zelda preferred me."

"It was just your money she preferred. I was the one she really loved."

"Oh, yeah?" Frank stepped forward, raising his half-decayed right hand threateningly.

"Yeah!" Zing responded in kind. The aging scientist and the zombified ancient faced each other, glaring, very macho, ready to go at it tooth and nail for the favors of a long-dead giantess.

"Guys," Jerry said, "this is kinda silly."

The man and the zombie lowered their fists and stepped back from each other with ill-disguised relief. They grumbled and muttered and moved their shoulders in a manly way to show the world that they weren't afraid, just stepping back from the brink before being forced to annihilate their opponent.

"He started it," they said simultaneously.

"Stop that!" Jerry said. It felt strange to be in control for once. "Look, here's the situation. The zombie that used to be Griselda Pistole is in that room. Frank, you stole her from Dr. Zing's lab at BioTyne and stuck a tube in her vein. You're putting something from her into your pickles." At his own words, his stomach lurched and he had to stop talking until he was sure he wasn't going to vomit. "You need to return her to BioTyne so that Walter can continue his research—What *is* that research, Walter?"

"It's super-secret—"

"Stop saying that!"

"I told you that you were too smart for your own good, Jerry," Pistole said. "The same applies to Walter, here. Fortunately, I don't need him any more. Hell, Walter, I never did need you. I just let you carry on your research on Zelda because I felt sorry for you, and as long as you kept supplying the secret pickle ingredient, it didn't matter. But the current setup is simpler. I should have done it that way from the beginning."

The beautiful, hypnotic voice interrupted him. "What was that, my darling husband?" Monster Griselda stood in the doorway of the inner room. She leaned comfortably against the side of the opening. The exposed bones of the top of her skull pressed against the top of the doorway.

"You set her free!" Pistole said. "You idiots!"

"Oh, don't blame them, my little love pistol. Once they took off the black cloth you had covered me with, the lights woke me up. Then they were helpless. Just like you." She stared intently into his eyes.

"I'm a zombie, Zelda," Frank said. "That doesn't work on me. Obviously, death hasn't made you any more intelligent."

Griselda growled.

Zing whispered to Jerry, "I think we should leave while they're preoccupied."

"What about your rifle? Take control of the situation."

"It doesn't have any bullets in it."

I could have been watering the plants on my balcony and napping, Jerry thought.

"And now," Frank said, "my guards are going to put you back in the chair, tie you down, and cover you up with that black cloth again. My enormous love strudel," he added.

The monster laughed monstrously. She stepped out of the doorway, straightening up. She towered over her late husband. The group of guards stared at her with little apparent interest. She stared back at them. “Hello, boys,” she said, pouring her charm into her amazing voice. “Grab this little man for me.”

“Won’t work,” Frank said. “They’re all zombies, too.”

“You’re right,” Jerry said to Zing. “Let’s leave. Come on, Piper.”

“She killed George,” Piper said. “I hate her.”

“Poor George,” Zing said. “He was a good boy. He loved bacteria, you know.”

The two zombie Pistoles were engaged with glaring at each other. The zombie guards stood watching them dully. The three living people edged backward slowly. Jerry wanted to get them out of the invigorating lights so that they could turn and run.

Suddenly, the two late Pistoles noticed their movements.

Griselda’s stare froze them in place. “You’re still my daughter, Piper,” she said. “And those two are food.” She began to walk toward them.

Frank pulled a few of the guards aside and issued an order to the rest of them. They threw themselves on Griselda and tried to wrestle her back toward the interior room.

Griselda yelled angrily. She went down with a mass of zombie guards on top of her. They were silent, but she kept yelling. Zombie body parts began to fly out of the writhing mass. The parts were too small to be from Griselda’s body.

The three humans took off running toward the front entrance. Behind them, Frank yelled orders, and the guards he had pulled aside a few moments earlier started after the escapees.

Fortunately, the zombie guards moved more slowly than humans. Unfortunately, Zing couldn’t move very fast and, to Jerry’s surprise, neither could Piper.

“Come on!” Jerry said to her. “What’s the problem?”

“It’s this damned cat suit. I can’t move in it. I told George that.”

She was panting with effort.

"What did he say?"

"He said I moved just fine in it." She started crying.

Guilt and self-pity mingled with Jerry's fear of the zombie guards chasing them. "Maybe he's not really permanently gone. Maybe he'll come back. Your father did."

"As a zombie?" Piper cried harder. She was hardly moving at all.

Zing was moving slowly, too. He was breathing heavily.

Jerry glanced over his shoulder. The zombies were getting closer. The door seemed infinitely far away.

Fortunately, the three of them were now out of the brightest part of the lit-up factory floor. Jerry thought the guards were moving more slowly. But they seemed to still be moving faster than Piper or Zing.

Okay, Jerry told himself. Time to be a hero.

He scooped Piper up from the floor, his right arm across her back and his left under her knees, and he began walking as fast as he could toward the exit. It was easier than he had feared, and he felt stronger than he had expected to. He also felt extremely manly and heroic.

"Walter!" Jerry said. "Keep up, or they'll catch you and eat you."

"Oh, dear," Zing said. He picked up the pace slightly.

It was enough. They reached the front door well ahead of the shuffling zombie guards.

When they reached the sunlight outside, Piper said, "You can put me down now."

"I don't want to." I've dreamed about carrying you away for years, he thought. Without pursuing zombies, though.

He made it to his car. By then, his arms were trembling with fatigue and he was afraid he'd drop her. He made a show of putting her down on her feet carefully.

"There," he said. "You'll be okay now. Leave your car. Let's go in mine." If I can still drive, he thought. He wasn't sure his arms would cooperate. "Walter, what about you?"

"Look!" Zing said. He pointed at the door of the factory.

The zombie guards were emerging into the sunlight. As they did so, they began to move faster.

"Goodbye," Zing said. He ran over to his own car, got in, started it, and zoomed away.

Jerry opened the passenger door of his car and pushed Piper in. He ran around to the other side, fishing the keys from his pocket as he ran. He got in, slammed the door shut, and pushed the button on the door that locked all four doors. He started the car and squealed out of the parking lot just as the lead guard was reaching for the handle of the driver's door.

"Stupid zombie," he said. "Doesn't even understand about locked doors."

"All your windows are rolled down," Piper said.

"Oh."

"Where are we going?"

"Away from there."

"Yes, but where are we going to?"

"Not your house. Frank would look for us there. I don't know. What do you want?

"I want George back." She began to cry again.

"Me, too." Jerry was surprised to realize how sincerely he meant that. He didn't think he'd ever forget George's face going from terror to slackness as Piper's dead mother sucked his brains out. He shivered at the memory.

He glanced over at Piper. She was curled up in the passenger seat, her feet on the seat in front of her, her face on her knees, her arms around her legs. He felt overwhelmed by the desire to pull her into his lap and comfort her. The first part of that desire was an old one, but the second part was new.

"We'll go to my apartment. Maybe we can figure out what to do next. Okay?"

"Okay. Just don't think you can take advantage of me because of my fragile emotional state."

"Right." She's recovering already, Jerry thought. Poor George. He deserves a longer mourning period than that. "Wouldn't dream of it."

"Of course you would."

Jerry sighed and concentrated on driving.

After a while, the tense silence began to bother him, so he turned on the radio. It was tuned to an oldies rock station that at that moment was playing a song he had hated for as long as he had been aware of it. He punched a button and switched to the local classical music station.

The opening bars of Tchaikovsky's agonizingly sad *Sérénade Mélancolique* poured from the speakers. Piper sobbed loudly.

Jerry punched a different button. This time he got an NPR station. Fred Foxtrot's creepy voice filled the car.

"Thanks to this bill, no longer will our patriotic returned senior citizens be oppressed by the tyranny of the dark. No longer will they have to wait for the morning sun to rise in order to fulfill their proper, God–given, American roles. The brilliant lights authorized by my bill, the Light Up the Nation Act, will give them dominion over the night. My fellow senators, I urge its immediate passage. Thank you, God bless you, and may God bless the United—"

Jerry turned the radio off. Blabber, blabber, he thought. What was he talking about? The guy never makes any sense.

They completed the trip in silence.

CHAPTER NINE

When Jerry unlocked the door to his apartment, the telephone was ringing. He locked the door carefully behind them before answering it.

It was his sister. "Jerry! Mother is screaming!"

"Mother is dead. Mom, I mean."

"No, not Mom. Anyway, she's alive. You know that. I mean Mother. The Mother. The great Mother."

"Oh, brother." When she didn't respond, he said, "Ha, ha."

"Why are you laughing? I need your help. Mother needs your help. It's the end of the world."

Despite no longer having a brain, she did have a point. "It does sort of look that way. But if we can find some way of fighting these zombies, then everything can get back to normal."

"Zombies? What are you talking about?"

"You know, like Mom and Dad."

"You're crazy. It's those stupid movies and books you waste your time on. That's what Dad always said about you."

"Yeah, he did always say that."

"Mom and Dad are just fine. Jerry, I'm talking about the end of the world. The actual world. The earth. The great mother."

"Great. We're back to that. Hold on." He looked around. Piper had disappeared. "Piper!" he called out. "Are you okay?"

She came in from the hallway. "That's a really dumb question, after what happened. Your bathroom is filthy."

Jerry turned his attention back to the telephone. "Okay, Lily, let's try to return to reality. Are you at home now?"

"Of course not. I'm here in Arapahoe, somewhere north of you. That's where the screaming was coming from."

"You're here? Where, exactly?"

"I don't know, exactly."

"Describe where you are. I'll come up there and get you, and we'll find you a nice, safe, cozy place to stay." With padded walls, he thought.

"I can see mountains."

"You're in the mountains?"

"No. I said that I can *see* mountains. I'm not in them."

"Describe the tallest mountain you can see. What does the top look like?"

"Like a mountaintop. They all look the same to me. Oh, it has snow on it."

"Great. What else?"

"Trees. I can see trees."

"Anything else?"

"A giant hole in the ground with some machines digging and that's where the screams are coming from and it's terrible and you have to help me stop it."

"How did you get there? Where you are, I mean. Wherever that is."

"By plane, of course. Like a sensible person."

"Okay. You came to Piketon by plane."

"Of course. Because that's where the screaming was coming from. Nearby."

"Then what?"

"Then I rented a car and drove toward the screaming. And here I am."

"You drove up the Interstate?"

"Right."

"What exit did you take?"

"The one the screaming was coming from."

The conversation continued in that vein for a while. Bit by bit, Jerry extracted from his sister the information that she was in the foothills west of the town of Bartle's Drop, and that when she turned off the state highway to get where she was she had passed a sign reading Bear Gulch.

"Okay," he said to Lily. "I can probably find that on Google Maps. Just stay there. I'll come to you."

"Hurry! The screaming is getting louder! It's really starting to freak me out!"

Jerry hung up. "Oh, God," he muttered. Everything was happening at once. He wished there were human colonies on the moon that he could escape to. Or Mars. Or further out.

"I need to go find my sister and commit her to an insane asylum," he told Piper. "Why don't you stay here and wait for me?"

Piper had been sitting listlessly on his couch. Now she sprang to her feet and threw her arms around him and pressed her face against his shoulder. "No! I don't want to be alone! I'm coming with you." She began to sob again.

Jerry put his arms around her and patted her back and said, "There, there. There, there." He felt himself getting aroused, which induced in him guilt and self-loathing and intense sexual desire.

He pushed Piper away gently. "Okay, come on. Let's go find that screaming mother."

They drove north on Interstate 25 in Jerry's car. He had his left hand on the wheel. Piper was gripping his right hand tightly with both of hers.

He wondered how often he had fantasized about Piper holding his hand while they drove out of the city together. More than he could count, he thought. Of course, in none of those fantasies had Piper been gripping so tightly that it hurt, and in none of them had she been whispering to herself, "Poor George. Wonderful George. Oh, George. I love George."

Jerry understood that Piper was just borrowing his hand because it was a convenient hand. To his surprise, he didn't mind. He rather liked it.

But even that came to an end.

"Look," he said, "that's the signpost up ahead. Our next stop, the screaming mother zone." He tugged until Piper let go of his right hand, and he took the exit for Bartle's Drop.

"Do you really think she's crazy? Your sister?" Piper asked.

"You've met her, haven't you?"

"Once. A few years ago. She seemed sane to me."

"She was, pretty much, but since then my parents have sucked out her brains."

"Isn't that what parents do?"

"I mean, literally. In Florida. My parents are zombies, just like yours."

"My parents aren't...I guess I can't deny it any longer, can I? But, wait a minute! They did the same thing to Lily that my mother did to George, and Lily's still alive. Then George must be okay, too!"

"I think maybe they only sucked out part of her brains. Maybe that made her halfway a zombie. I don't know. I know that she started acting even dumber than before, but she wasn't like George. I'm sorry, Piper. You saw what happened to him. He was gone."

Tears rolled down her cheeks. "He was gone," she repeated. She sighed. "You're right. George is gone."

Silence descended on them again.

The exit from the Interstate had taken them onto a winding, two–lane state highway. Their route was west, into the foothills of the Rockies. The ground was rising, there was little traffic, and the number of trees was increasing. If he had been making this drive just for pleasure, and with a happy Piper in the seat next to his, Jerry would have been in seventh heaven. On impulse, he turned on the radio and pressed the button for Piketon's classical station. A bubbly Viennese waltz danced from the speakers.

"That's nice," Piper said.

"Music to track down crazy sisters who're babbling about screaming mothers by," he said. He felt instantly annoyed at himself for saying that. Talk about babbling, he thought.

"Bear Gulch," he said, reading a sign. "Look for a small dirt road on the right."

"There." She pointed. "Do you think there're bears there?"

He turned off onto the dirt road. "There's probably not even a gulch. Some developer probably made up the name."

"I hope you're right. I'm scared of bears."

"Oh, they're not so bad. You just have to be careful." Jerry was terrified of bears, but he wasn't going to say so now. He was also terrified of mountain lions, rattlesnakes, bobcats, coyotes, and raccoons. He had once been frightened by the sudden, twitchy movements of a squirrel. However, this was the time to be the brave, protective male. He hoped he could pull it off.

Then it occurred to him to wonder if bears and mountain lions and the rest of them could become zombies. If humans could, then why not animals? The thought that there might be zombie coyotes lurking behind the trees beside the road made him shiver violently.

"Are you okay?" Piper asked.

"My back itches. I'm trying to scratch it against the seat."

"Lean forward a bit," she said. When he did so, she scratched his back through his shirt, from the base of his neck down as far as she could before the seatback interfered. "How's that?"

"Perfect. Thanks." Suddenly he felt very brave and manly and protective.

He drove slowly along the dirt road. Even so, his car bounced and the steering wheel kept turning by itself. Stones bounced against the body of the car and flew away. "My sister's gonna owe me for my suspension and alignment. And a new paint job."

"Expensive."

"She divorced well."

"I married well," Piper said. "I did, didn't I?"

"You certainly did."

A bit further along, he saw Lily standing by the side of the road. She had waited for him, just as he had told her to. He was surprised. He had half expected that there'd be no sign of her, and he would learn later that she had driven back to Piketon and flown back to the East Coast. Then he noticed that she was standing with her eyes closed and her face turned to the sun, and he shivered again.

Her rental car was parked under the trees just off the road. It was an SUV, which surprised Jerry. She had always favored small cars before. He pulled off the road and parked beside it. Before he unlocked the doors, he said to Piper, "Be careful. I think she's becoming one of them."

"Now you're being silly." She got out of the car and walked over to Lily, extending her right hand.

Jerry opened his door and ran to Piper's side. He pushed her hand down. "Lily. Here we are. Would you like us to take you someplace nice and safe?"

Lily looked down at Piper's right hand and then up at Jerry's face. She stared at him blankly for a while. Jerry examined her face, looking for evidence of exposed bones, but saw none. "Oh," Lily said. She paused for a long moment. Then she said, "Oh, no. I want you to come into the woods with me so that we can find the Great Mother because she's screaming and save her."

"Save her from what?" Piper asked.

Lily looked at her contemptuously. "From the thing that's making her scream, of course. Are you stupid? You must be, since you're Jerry's girlfriend."

"I'm not—Never mind."

Jerry felt relieved. This was more like the old Lily. Maybe she wasn't a zombie, after all. "That was nice, Lily. After we drove all the way up here to help you. Oh, and this is Piper. Her husband was just murdered in front of her."

Lily stared at the ground for a while. Finally, she muttered, "Sorry." In a more normal voice, she said, "It's hard for me to focus on anything other than the screaming. It's filling my mind."

"Lily, I can't hear any screaming."

Lily looked disgusted. "Then you can't help me."

Piper frowned and stared off into space. "Hold on, Jerry. I can sort of hear something. It's not screaming. More like a low moaning. It's right on the edge of being audible. It's all around us."

Lily beamed at her. "You're not stupid! Why are you with my brother? But it's not coming from all around us. It's coming from over there." She pointed up a nearby hillside.

Jerry looked at the hillside. It was covered with loose gravel that looked like it would be hell to climb up. Here and there, trees poked through the gravel—fairly large trees, with trunks that were wide enough to hide zombie coyotes.

"I think we should all go back to Piketon," he said. "Lily, you could stay with me for a while, relax, decompress." Get checked out by the craziness doctors. "You could get in touch with Wendy. She said she'd like to see you again."

"Who's Wendy?" Piper asked, squinting at Jerry.

"My ex-wife. Very ex."

"Oh, yeah. George mentioned her once." Her eyes filled with tears at the mention of her husband's name. Jerry could tell that she was fighting not to cry again. After a struggle, she succeeded. "You weren't married for very long, were you?"

Jerry shook his head. "We were engaged for longer than we were married. I should have known better. The engagement was bad."

"What were you engaged in?" Piper asked, trying to make a joke.

"Mutual self-destruction. Come on, Lily. You can follow us back."

"Coward," Lily said. "Are you afraid of a little climb? You're the one who lives here." She sneered. "Mr. Mountain Man."

Piper put her arm through Jerry's and squeezed his arm against her side. It was meant as a comforting gesture, he knew, but it made his heart leap. "Jerry's not a coward," Piper said. "You don't know him very well."

"Oh, please. I've known him all my life."

"You just thought you knew him. I really know him."

The two women glared at each other. Jerry felt his world shifting around him in strange ways.

One of those ways was that now he had to hide his cowardice.

There probably aren't really any zombie coyotes up there, he told himself. Or maybe only the slow kind, like movie zombies. They prey on slow zombie rabbits. They wouldn't be interested in me at all.

Those images didn't serve to stiffen his spine, so he tried another tack with himself.

Do it because Piper's watching you. Do it for your kid sister, who needs your help. We'll go wherever it is Lily wants to go, and she'll see that there's nothing there, no screaming Earth Mother, and then she'll calm down and go back to Piketon with us. Then she'll be normal again. A normal zombie kid sister, anyway.

Thus heartened, he pointed up the hill and said to Lily, "Okay, lead the way. Follow the screaming in your ears."

She bounded up the hillside, very fast and light on her feet for a zombie.

Jerry supposed it was due to the brilliant sunlight. Solar flux, he told himself. There's something to my theory, after all. He wondered again what solar flux was.

Piper squeezed his arm against her side again. "Good for you," she said. "You're a good brother." She released his arm and took his hand instead, lacing her fingers through his.

Jerry had no idea what was going on, but he did know that he felt happier than he had in years.

They climbed up the hill together after Lily, struggling a bit on the loose surface but helping each other, and Jerry didn't think about zombie coyotes at all.

It was a long, hot, sweaty way to the brow of the hill. Lily reached the top well ahead of them. She stopped and looked back down at them. "Come on!" she said impatiently. "Move it!"

"Are you sure she's a zombie?" Piper asked.

"Would anyone with a brain do this?"

"Hmm," Piper said. Then she concentrated on climbing.

When they reached the top of the hill, both of them were panting and sweating, but they were still holding hands.

Lily was looking down into a shallow valley beyond the hill. She pointed down. "That's where the screaming's coming from. Come on!"

She ran away from them, down the hillside, sometimes skidding on loose gravel, sometimes bounding from rock to rock, almost flying.

"Lily! Stop!" Piper yelled. "You're going to kill yourself!"

"Possibly," Jerry said, thinking that that would solve the problem of what to do about Lily. He felt guilty immediately for the thought.

Piper was staring at the diminishing figure of Jerry's sister. "Shouldn't we go after her?" she said.

"Possibly," Jerry repeated. "Look over there. That's what she was pointing to."

The valley was filled with giant yellow construction machinery, pickup trucks, milling humans, and a haze of dust. There was no noise, or at least none that reached them. The machinery wasn't moving.

In the center of the valley, surrounded by the machines and people, was a giant hole, circular, perhaps a hundred feet across. Because of the angle of the sun, only the rim of the hole and the first few feet of its inner wall on the northern side were illuminated. Below that, all was black. For a moment, Jerry thought he saw something white moving in that deep, dark shadow, but then that went away and he thought he must have imagined it.

"What is that?" Piper asked. "A strip mine?"

"I don't know. I've never seen a strip mine."

"A sink hole, then."

"A scream hole."

"Look!" Piper said. "There she is!" She pointed.

Jerry looked in that direction and saw a small human figure that might have been Lily hurrying toward the hole. He sighed. "I guess we'd better go down there."

They went down the hill much more slowly and cautiously than Lily. When they reached the valley floor, trees blocked from their view the machinery and people they had seen from above, but they could hear voices. Still holding hands, they headed in that direction.

They saw the yellow of the machines through the trees first.

Then they saw the backs of a few people.

Instinctively, Jerry and Piper slowed down and approached as quietly as they could. The crowd ahead of them was looking into the hole. No one noticed their approach.

Piper tugged Jerry to one side. With her free hand, she gestured at a low pile of boulders.

Jerry nodded. They climbed carefully onto the rocks and looked down at the crowd from their slight elevation.

They could see over the heads of the people standing silently in front of them. They were all facing toward the great hole in the ground. They weren't looking at the hole, though. They were looking up at the sun.

"Oh, man," Jerry muttered.

Piper gasped. Her mouth was open and her eyes wide. Jerry looked in the direction of her gaze and saw, a quarter of the way around the hole, Frank Pistole. Next to Frank was a tall, black thing that towered over him. Jerry realized that it was a human form wrapped in black cloth. And next to that was a bedraggled Walter Zing, sitting on a big rock, gagged and with his hands tied together in front of him. Zing's face was as white as the cloth next to him was black. A very large man in the uniform of a BioTyne guard stood on either side of Zing, holding his arms—not to keep him from running, Jerry guessed, but to keep him from falling off the rock. Next to Zing, being held in place by just one very large man in uniform, was Lily. She didn't seem to be in danger of collapse. Instead, she was trying ineffectually to pull away from the guard holding her.

Frank was staring right at Jerry and Piper. He pointed at them. His mouth moved, but Jerry couldn't hear what he was saying.

The crowd around the hole could, apparently. Moving as one, they turned around and stared at Jerry and Piper. Jerry was not surprised to see that their faces were like hard, dried leather or that they all held pickled peppers between their lips. Simultaneously, they spoke. A single voice, a loud hiss, rose from the mass of human figures. The words were distorted because of the peppers, but Jerry understood them. "Catching some rays."

"Weird," Piper said.

"Run!" Jerry said.

They jumped off the pile of boulders and ran. Jerry glanced over his shoulder and saw a horde of zombies gaining on them. Their ray–catching had made them better catchers. He ran faster. Piper was ahead of him and pulling further ahead. I should start going to the gym, too, he thought.

It occurred to him that this was the second time in as many days that he and Piper had run from a zombie army commanded by Frank Pistole. He hoped that it wouldn't become a habit.

A doglike shape with long legs stepped out from behind a tree ahead of them and stood staring at them.

"A zombie coyote!" Jerry gasped. He skidded to a halt, and so did Piper. The coyote stared at both of them, frowning, looking up from under its brows. He's wondering what seasonings to use on us, Jerry thought wildly.

Now he could see that the coyote wasn't a zombie. It was just a normal, everyday, run–of–the–mill, murderous coyote. The dangerous beast stared intently into Jerry's eyes. The gaze was as hypnotizing as that of Griselda the zombie, and the end result would be the same.

The coyote looked away from Jerry's eyes and over the man's shoulder at something behind him. The beast yelped in terror, turned, and dashed away, disappearing instantly among the trees.

A heavy hand fell on Jerry's shoulder. The pungent smell of pickled pepper combined with the stink of death filled his nostrils. A voice said, "Take you back now. Catch more rays."

Another zombie had captured Piper. Slowly but steadily, inexorably, the zombie army marched them back over the rough ground to the hole in the valley floor. Back to Frank Pistole, back to Walter Zing, back to Lily, and back to the eight–foot–tall thing bound in black concerning whose identity Jerry had no doubts.

CHAPTER TEN

Their zombie guards marched Piper and Jerry around the perimeter of the hole.

Jerry glanced down into it as they walked. The sun didn't penetrate far into it. Down in the shadows, he saw something white moving. He tried to stop, hoping to see what it was, but the zombies dragged him along toward Frank Pistole.

They stopped in front of Pistole.

Pistole glared at them. "Piper bad," he said. "Bad Piper. Jerry, too."

What could be worse, Jerry asked himself, than being held prisoner by a malevolent, power-hungry zombie? Answer: being held prisoner by a malevolent, power-hungry zombie with senile dementia.

Speaking in the most cheerful and least annoying tone he could produce, Jerry said, "Hi, Frank, it's us—the daughter you love and the employee you like and trust. How is everything? It sure is nice out here. Why don't we all go for a walk together?"

Pistole continued to glare at him. "Shut up," he said. "You interfere. Always interfere." He gestured with his chin toward the hole. "Like hole? I dig. Big machines go mrmm, mrmm. Big hole."

"It's a lovely hole," Jerry said. "But, um, Frank, why did you dig it?"

"Big mother."

"Yes, it is a big mother."

"In there. Big mother in there."

Griselda—for of course the big figure covered in black was Griselda—was struggling constantly to free herself. The cloth wrapping her had loosened, exposing part of her face to the light. Her beautiful voice crooned, "Stud!"

"He not stud!" Frank shouted. "I stud!" The ends of the masking tape on the top of his head curled up. He glared at Jerry, directing his anger at him, which was not rational, but which was also not surprising given what Frank was.

"I'm sure she meant you," Jerry said in what he hoped was a soothing tone. Distract him, he thought. "You were telling us about the big mother in the hole. How did a big mother get into that big hole?"

"Didn't get in," Frank said impatiently. "Grew there."

"And she's screaming!" Lily said.

Frank nodded. "Hungry. Just like me."

"*That's* why she's screaming?" Lily said. "I didn't know."

"Yes. Hungry. Like a newborn. Mother hungry."

"Then I *can* help her, after all!" Lily said. She pulled herself free of the guard's grip. She ran past Jerry, who was too startled to stop her, and leaped into the hole, disappearing into the darkness.

A scream came from the hole, a scream of delight. A slender column of blood shot high into the air. It blossomed, flowered into a thousand thin strands that rained down on the massed zombies and their human prisoners.

Griselda squirmed and struggled harder.

"Lily!" Jerry whispered. "Oh, no." His mind froze, filled with an image of Lily as a little girl.

Piper put her arm through his and squeezed it comfortingly. He realized that their guards had released them. The zombies were all crowded around the hole, standing on the very edge, looking into it in fascination.

"Better," Frank said. He was staring fixedly at the hole. He had dropped his pickle on the ground.

Slowly, Piper pulled Jerry toward Zing.

Jerry followed in a haze, scarcely able to think.

Zing's guards had left him. They had drifted over to the hole and now stood staring into it, like the rest of the zombies.

Piper set to work on the cord that bound Zing's wrists. Jerry came out of his fog and undid the gag.

Something made Jerry look to the side. He found himself staring up into Griselda's eyes. "Untie me, too," she said to him.

"Yes, ma'am." He reached for the rope that had been passed around her several times.

"Are you nuts?" It was Piper. She swatted his hand away from the rope.

"Huh?" He stared at her, not quite understanding what was going on. Griselda's hypnotic influence had combined with the earlier haze to make it almost impossible for him to think.

"Dear daughter," Griselda said gently, "he's useless. You do it."

"He's not useless," Piper said. "He's..." At that point, she made the mistake of looking into Griselda's eyes and came under her influence.

"That's enough, Grizzy," Zing said sharply.

The giant zombie smiled and looked down at him fondly. "Super science stud." She stared intently at him, as she had done at both Jerry and Piper.

"Don't do that, Grizzy," Zing said.

"Don't you still love me, triple-s?"

"Always."

"Release me, so that I can love you back properly."

Zing looked up at the giant zombie and thought for a moment. "It would be interesting," he said.

"Idiot," Piper said. She jumped onto Zing's rock, and with a quick flip of her hand, she threw the black cloth over Griselda's face. "Sorry, Mom, but I don't trust you. You murdered George."

"Ungrateful child," the zombie said.

All this time, Frank Pistole and his army of zombies had been standing at the rim of the hole he had had dug in the valley floor, staring into it as though bewitched.

"Dr. Walter, what are they so fascinated by?" Jerry asked.

"I don't know, but we should probably leave while they are."

"But my sister—"

"I'm sorry. She's gone. She's now part of the giant Studley earth mother screaming zombie."

"The what?"

"I'll explain once we're safe."

"He's right," Piper said. "Creepy, but right. We should go." She started walking away, watching her father and his zombies carefully as she did so.

Zing put an arm around the black-draped form of Griselda. "Come along, my love," he said. "I think you can walk."

"I'll kill you eventually, Walter," she said. She tottered along at his urging, despite the rope around her legs and ankles.

"Oh, dear," Zing said, shaking his head.

They moved slowly, but they put a steadily increasing distance between themselves and Pistole and his zombies, all of whom still seemed to be entranced by something in the hole.

"How are we going to get back up the hillside with her?" Jerry asked, gesturing toward the slowly hobbling giant female zombie.

"We don't need to," Zing said. "I have a pickup truck. It's parked just beyond those trees. We'll squeeze into the cab, and Grizzy can lie in the back of the truck."

"Bastard," Griselda said. "I'm going to suck your brains out very slowly."

"Yes, my dearest," Zing said.

"That's what my ex–wife did to me," Jerry said to Piper. "Sucked my brains out slowly, along with my manhood, my self–esteem, my money, and my will to live. George was so lucky to have you."

Piper nodded. "Yes. He was. And I was lucky to have him. But now he's gone and that's all over."

"That sounds cold–blooded and heartless."

"George would have wanted me to live."

"I suppose so," Jerry said, but he thought, Wouldn't he have wanted you to grieve, too? Just a bit longer?

They reached Zing's pickup truck. It was very big and bright red and decorated with decals of semi–naked women, men with enormous muscles, and pistols. The license plate read STUDLEE.

"This is not what I expected, Dr. Walter," Jerry said.

"It's my other side. Normally, I keep it hidden, but this was a special occasion." He walked around to the back and lowered the tailgate. "Now, Grizzy, we're going to have to load you in here. We could heave you in, but it would be better if you cooperated."

The zombie giantess said, "Before I suck your brains out slowly, I'm going to gnaw away your skull very slowly."

"Of course you will, my beloved. But not right now." His voice turned steely and manly and studly. "Cooperation or heaving?"

Griselda sighed heavily. "Cooperation."

"Good." Zing gestured to Jerry to help.

Between them, and with her reluctant cooperation, they managed to work the huge and very heavy creature onto the flat bed of the truck. Her feet stuck out over the tailgate. The two men shoved her feet simultaneously, and she slid in the rest of the way. Her head hit the back of the truck below the passenger cab with a loud clank. She growled but said nothing.

Zing nodded in satisfaction. He raised and secured the tailgate and climbed into the truck. Piper climbed in the passenger side and sat in the middle of the front seat. Jerry climbed in beside her.

Sitting pressed against Piper in the seat of a vehicle parked in a beautiful mountain valley, he thought. Why were all of his fantasies taking such weird and unpleasant forms in reality?

Zing started the truck and drove out of the shelter of the trees. He turned in a wide semicircle toward the right. Pine needles crunched under the tires. For a moment, the truck faced toward the crowd of zombies standing at the edge of the hole.

"Good Lord!" Zing said. He jammed on the brakes. "Look!"

Long, white strings were waving in the air above the heads of the zombie crowd.

"They're coming from the hole," Jerry said.

"They're pseudopods," Zing said. He was smiling in delight. "How wonderful!"

Suddenly, the pseudopods whipped downward and into the crowd. The zombies finally began to move, trying to back away, but they were too late. The pseudopods surrounded them and pulled them into the hole.

There was a loud babble of voices, the closest the zombies could come to screaming. Then they were all gone, except for Frank Pistole.

He had managed to back away in time. He was still backing away. He scuttled behind the rock Zing had been forced to sit on, and he crouched down, hiding.

The voices had stopped. Odd zombie body parts flew up into the air above the hole—arms, legs, heads, the occasional foot. They all fell back down into the hole. Then there was nothing—no sound, no movement.

"I wonder if that thing is still screaming," Piper said.

"I doubt it," Zing said. "I don't think she's hungry now. Or I should say, for now."

Piper and Jerry looked at him. "That sounds like a reason to get this truck moving quickly."

"True," Zing said. "But what about..." He gestured with his head toward Piper.

"Leave him," Piper said. "He's not my father anymore. And that thing in the back isn't my mother. You should have left her here."

Zing sighed. "I'm weak." He stepped on the accelerator, completed the turn he had been making before, and drove toward a dirt road that led up and out of the valley.

Griselda thrashed about in the back, trying to free herself. Jerry and Piper kept looking nervously over their shoulders through the window behind them.

"Oh, don't worry," Zing said. "She'll be okay."

After some blundering around, they found Jerry's car.

"Well, children," Zing said, "I think we should part now. And I think you two should go somewhere new. Start a new life together somewhere, perhaps."

"I think that's kind of premature, Walter," Jerry said.

"No kidding," Piper said.

"Together or separately," Zing said, "but somewhere else. Frank has lost his gang of zombies, but he'll be getting new ones, and then he'll come after you."

"What about you?" Jerry asked. "And Griselda? Won't Frank be coming after you, as well?"

"He will, but he won't find us," Zing said smugly. "I'll be taking Grizzy to a place Frank doesn't know about. No one knows about it."

"A secret lab inside a mountain?" Jerry asked. "Under the sea? On a floating platform in the air? On the moon?"

"You watch too many bad movies, Jerry."

"None of those, then. A cabin in the mountains?"

"Please stop guessing."

"I wish you wouldn't call her Grizzy," Piper said. "In front of me, anyway."

"What would you prefer?"

"How about Mrs. Pistole?"

"But she's no longer Mrs. Pistole. Death dissolves marriage."

"Good God," Jerry said. "My parents are living in sin. Well, not actually living."

"Call her Mrs. Pistole anyway. At least when I'm around."

Zing grimaced. "Do you have any idea how painful it is for me to call her that?"

"Do you have any idea how painful it is for me to hear you call her Grizzy? She's my mother!"

"She is no longer your—Oh, all right."

"I'm glad that's settled," Jerry said. "Before we go our separate ways, Walter, I wish you'd explain what just happened. Why did Frank have his zombies dig that hole? What was that thing inside it? Why did he have Griz—Mrs. Pistole there? Why does he want her? Why do you? Why were you there? In short, *what the fuck is going on?"*

"Oh, dear," Zing said. He looked at his watch. "I'll have to give you the short version."

"That would be best."

"Oh, all right, then."

CHAPTER ELEVEN

Zing drew a deep breath and began.

"I wasn't quite truthful when I told you that I killed the Studleys with bleach."

"You haven't been quite truthful about a lot of things, have you?"

"There is a degree of truth in that accusation," Zing admitted. "Well. Some of the Studleys survived." His face lit up. "They're very sturdy little fellows, my Studleys! Many of them survived my bleach treatment and ended up in the local groundwater, where they migrated hither and yon."

"Hither and yon," Jerry repeated. "What did they do in the ground? Make steaks?"

Zing laughed. "Make steaks! That's very clever, young Gerald. Well, no. Not exactly. Not by themselves. You remember the bacterial ghosts? Bacterial zombies?"

"Happy cells," Jerry said.

"Oh, right. I forgot. Happy cells. I didn't really stop that line of research."

"Of course you didn't. None of this ever ends, does it?"

"Science *never* ends. Anyway, the next step in my work with the happy cells was to spray them on cemeteries."

"Why? And don't answer, 'Why not?' Hey, wait a minute! Was that the secret project you kept managing not to tell me about?"

"It was. As to why I did it, any disastrous side effects would have remained hidden from view."

"Unlike the corpses in the funeral homes and those cows?"

"Well, yes. The plan was to exhume some of those bodies later and see what effect the happy cells had had on them."

"Which would be none, because they were already dead."

"You would think so, wouldn't you? In many cases, that was exactly what we found —unchanged dead bodies. In other cases, however, we found...Are you sure you want to hear this?"

"Of course I do!" Jerry said.

"I wouldn't want to be responsible for giving you nightmares."

"Spit it out!" Piper said.

"Well, then. In quite a few cases, we found empty graves."

"Zombies!" Jerry said.

"IECs"

"Zombies!"

"If you insist. I rather like the term IECs. It's catchy. Less insulting."

"Why shouldn't we insult zombies?" Piper asked.

"They have feelings, too." Zing said.

"Do they?" Jerry asked.

Zing frowned in thought. "Hmm. I'm not sure. Well. Back to my story. I was puzzled as to why some bodies came back to life as zombies and others didn't. Then I noticed a very strong correlation between the locations of the zombies and the places where Frank Pistole had once told me he sold the most pickled peppers. For years, Frank had been including a drop of Grizzy's vital fluids in every jar of Piper's Pickled Peppers. That was the secret ingredient that made Piper's Pickled Peppers so popular. Certain aged populations in certain parts of the country, such as Florida, seemed to be particularly addicted to those peppers."

"Yeah," Jerry said. "My parents couldn't live without them." Then he realized what unfortunate phrasing that was.

"A common addiction, apparently," Zing said. "I believe that the chemical changes in their bodies after death, interacting with the Grizzy fluids they had consumed while alive, and then later interacting with the happy cells sprayed on their graves, resulted in repair and revivification. Coincidentally, Frank himself was buried in one of those cemeteries, and as you know, he had been eating a lot of his own company's pickled peppers for many years. You've seen the result."

"You created all those damned zombies!"

"Yes!" Zing said happily. "It's Nobel–level work."

"You're destroying the world!"

"An unfortunate side–effect. I believe the military calls that collateral damage."

The noise from the back of Zing's pickup truck had been increasing. When Zing reached the part in his narrative about Griselda's bodily fluids, she began flinging herself back and forth violently, making such loud clanging sounds that Jerry wondered if she would manage to break through the side panels.

Zing finally paid attention. "I don't think that black cloth Frank put over her is sufficient," he said. "Help me put the cover over the bed. That should do the trick."

"Where's the cover?"

"It's in the back of the truck."

The two of them walked to the back of the truck. Zing stood on one side and Jerry on the other. They stared at the crumpled–up cover lying underneath Griselda, who was quiet and unmoving at the moment, and then they stared at each other.

Zing said, "Dearest, would you mind mov—"

She screamed and rolled toward him, raising her upper body. For a moment, it looked as though she would be able to fling herself from the truck and onto Zing.

As soon as she moved, Jerry reached in, grabbed the cover, and pulled it out. He began fastening it to the hooks along his side of the truck. He tried to be quiet, but Griselda stopped, tense, listening. Then she rolled in his direction.

Jerry moved quickly to the tailgate and fastened the cover there. He continued moving around the truck. Soon he had the cover tied down on three sides.

That seemed to be enough to do the job. Griselda stopped moving.

"Thank you!" Zing said. "I think you saved my life."

"That was very brave," Piper said.

"Oh, it was nothing," Jerry said, trying to look modest. He had acted without thinking. If he had thought, he wouldn't have acted. There was no need to talk about that.

"If you say so," Piper said. "Zing, what about the screaming mother in the hole?"

"That brings us back to the Studleys."

"The what?" Piper said.

Jerry said, "Those are the bacteria I told you about—the ones that produce steaks and chicken breasts. Walter made 'em."

"Oh, yeah. That disgusting story."

"They are extremely clever and sophisticated bacteria," Zing said. "As Jerry said, they have the ability to produce a variety of human foods. When they are no longer able to work, we kill them and throw them out."

"Because that's how big companies operate," Jerry said.

Zing ignored him and continued. "We were dumping them into an underground river beneath BioTyne. I recently discovered that the river empties into an aquifer underneath this valley."

"We have underground rivers?" Jerry said. "I never knew that."

"Sluggishly moving groundwater would probably be more accurate. Anyway, the Studleys that managed to survive the bleach treatment flourished in the aquifer. Groundwater from elsewhere in the area ends up in the same place. That includes some water that migrates through a cemetery where we sprayed the happy cells. Some happy cells and some decayed human tissue was carried to the aquifer, where it all combined with the Studleys."

"A witches' brew," Piper said.

Zing grimaced. "Witches and magic are fantasy. This is science. When the creative abilities of the Studleys combined with the reparative powers and astonishing vitality of the happy cells, the giant creature growing beneath the valley floor was the result."

"A giant screaming earth mother zombie," Jerry said.

"You could call it that," Zing said. "I discovered its existence when I traced the underground route of the Studleys."

"Which you did because...?"

"Oh, pure scientific curiosity. When I discovered that some of them were able to survive the bleach treatment, I began to wonder how my little friends were faring underground."

"Very well, apparently."

"Oh, yes. Aren't they wonderful little beings? But the resulting large creature struck me as dangerous. I uncovered it when I dug a small hole into the aquifer. I recall that when I first saw it moving, I lost control and shouted, 'It's alive! It's alive!' I'm quite ashamed of that.

"The creature was much smaller then. Even so, I knew that it would only grow and that it had to be destroyed. I enlisted the help of Piper's father. This was after he had returned as an IEC. Sorry, a zombie. He asked me to perform certain tests on the creature, which I foolishly did. To my surprise, I discovered that the creature manufactures the same fluids that Frank was extracting from

Griselda for use in his pickles. Perhaps that's not really surprising. At any rate, Frank wouldn't hear of destroying the creature. Instead, he started feeding zombies to it, thereby encouraging it to grow and produce more fluids. He wants to produce more and more pickled peppers containing the secret ingredient and thus produce endless zombies who will buy still more pickles. He'll get richer and richer. He's obsessed with the urge to become the richest man on earth. Or at the very least, the richest pickle manufacturer. When I insisted that the creature had to be destroyed, he threatened to feed me to it. He said he no longer needed my help, anyway. I drove up today to try to estimate how many gallons of bleach I would need. Unfortunately, Frank and his zombie army were already here. They took me prisoner and would have fed me to the beast if you hadn't shown up."

"And my mother?" Piper asked.

"He was planning to feed her to the beast, as well. He was convinced that combining her body with the beast's would result in a manifold increase in fluid production. Possibly the creature in the ground made him think that. You saw how dull he was back there. The creature seems to have that effect on zombies. It seems to control their minds, and its power to do so is growing as it grows."

"Why would the creature want to get rid of my mother?"

"I think it doesn't like competition."

"So now we have to stock up on bleach and find an opportunity to dump it in that hole," Jerry said. "End of problem."

"Well, no," Zing said. "Not quite exactly entirely. I believe the creature now extends quite far beyond the hole. I think it's extending pseudopodia along the courses of the groundwater in search of Studleys and happy cells and decayed human tissues."

"How far can it spread?" Jerry asked.

"Oh, I don't think there's any limit. Miles. Thousands of miles. Tens of thousands. Everywhere." He looked down at the ground a bit nervously. "Certainly this far."

"That thing's going to become the real screaming earth mother zombie," Jerry said.

"We're doomed!" Piper said.

"That does seem highly likely," Zing said.

"You're taking this very calmly," Jerry said. "You won't be getting your Nobel prize if that giant screaming earth mother zombie eats up Norway."

"Sweden. The Peace Prize is awarded in Norway. The others are awarded in Sweden."

"That is so irrelevant!"

"Precision is never irrelevant. Anyway, I have certain lines of research in mind pursuant to putting a halt to all of this. I'm concerned but not fatalistic."

"I'm terrified and convinced that we're all going to die," Jerry said.

"There's a lot you aren't telling us," Piper said.

"There always is, with Dr. Walter Zing," Jerry said. "Right, Walter?"

"I only withhold information for your own good," Zing said.

"Specifically," Piper said, "about my mother. She abandoned us when I was a child. And then it turns out she's a zombie and she's in your lab. How did that happen?"

"Well," Zing said. It seemed to be one of his favorite words. "I suspect that you haven't been given a complete picture of your family history."

"Who is?" Jerry asked. "Ever?"

Zing frowned and stared into space for a moment. "I know that I wasn't," he said. He shook himself. "Well. Back to the Pistole family. Thirty–five years ago, Piper, your father was a struggling young man with a wife and a newborn child. He was having trouble supporting his family. He had a good job and was earning a good salary, with fine prospects for advancement, but he was obsessed with becoming the pickle king, and he was sinking most of his income into pickled pepper research. Your mother was not supportive. After all, she had left me for your father in large part because she thought he would be rich and she was sure I never would be."

"In large part," Jerry repeated. "There were other reasons?"

"Well, yes. She told me that as much as she loved me, she didn't love me enough to go by the name of Zelda Zing."

There was an ominous noise from the back of the pickup truck.

"But never mind that," Zing said hastily. "Frank and Grizzy argued about his spending so much money on pickled pepper research while neglecting his job. The argument turned violent. Frank...murdered Grizzy."

Piper gasped. "Oh, my God!"

Her knees gave way and she grabbed onto Jerry for support. He put his arm around her waist and held her up.

"Why wasn't he arrested?" she asked. "How did he get away with it?"

"I'm afraid I had something to do with that," Zing said. "When he realized what he had done, he called me in a panic. He asked me to help for your sake, Piper—for the sake of the child of the woman he knew I still loved. For your sake, I couldn't let Frank be arrested and sent to jail or executed. I said I would take your mother's body away and cover up his crime so that Piper would grow up with a parent and a home."

"I did, anyway," Piper said. "Without a real parent, anyway."

Zing nodded. "I know, and I'm sorry. I often thought that I should have insisted on taking you away as well and bringing you up as my own daughter as part of the deal."

Piper shuddered. "That's okay."

"What did you do with Griselda's body?" Jerry asked.

"I took it to BioTyne. It was a small company back then. My partners and I had just founded it. I was already working on some ideas for revivification. If it worked with anyone, I wanted it to work for Grizzy."

"A second chance at love?" Jerry asked. He had meant it sarcastically, but it didn't come out that way.

"I suppose so. As you already know, my research bore fruit, but it didn't really bring Grizzy back to life. It made her what you see now." He gestured toward the covered bed of the pickup truck. A slight thump came from under the cover. "When I continued my work, the result was the eruption of zombies that we're now dealing with."

"Or not dealing with."

"Patience is a virtue in science, Jerry."

"Was she always that big? Back when she was alive?"

"She's alive now, in a sense. You mean, when she was first alive. No, she was about the same height as Piper. The natural vitality of her cells, augmented by the treatment I applied, seems to have resulted in her continued growth. I think it's similar to what's happening to the creature in the ground. As long as she's supplied with nutrients, Grizzy will continue to get larger."

There was a faint thump from the back of the truck.

"I think she likes that idea," Zing said.

"Nutrients?" Jerry said. "Brains? You're feeding her people?"

"Oh, heavens, no! Well, not live ones."

Piper made a gagging sound.

"It's all very sanitary and discreet," Zing said reassuringly. "The cadavers arrive in body bags. They don't even look like anything. Really. Scarcely."

"Where do you get them from?" Jerry asked.

"From Frank. Over the years, we expanded and formalized our arrangement. As his business grew, he supplied funding for my research. He also supplied cadavers."

"Where did he get the cadavers from?"

"I never asked."

"Of course you didn't. I'm surprised he didn't try to pin Griselda's murder on you."

"He needed me. He needed the secret ingredient for his pickled peppers. Piper, as I've told Jerry, old people quickly develop an intense craving for pickled peppers containing the secret ingredient."

"That's nauseating," Piper said.

"Not at all. In fact, some people claim that Piper's Pickled Peppers settle the stomach."

Piper made a gagging sound.

Jerry said, "So now Frank will keep feeding zombies to the giant screaming earth mother zombie so that it will keep producing the secret ingredient that makes Piper's Pickled Peppers so popular, and consumption of those pickled peppers will keep creating more zombies, and the giant screaming earth mother zombie will keep influencing Frank to keep feeding it more zombies so that it can keep growing and eventually control the world. What have I missed?"

"The nefarious activities of Senator Fred Foxtrot. But even without that, the situation seems quite gloomy."

"We're doomed."

"Where there's life, there's hope, young man."

"In the current circumstances, that's not a comforting proverb."

"What are we going to do?" Piper asked.

"We could kill ourselves now and avoid Armageddon," Jerry said, "but we'd probably come back as zombies."

"Don't do anything hasty," Zing said. "As I said, I'm pursuing some interesting lines of research in connection with this matter, and

I'm fairly hopeful that they will bear fruit and advance our agenda."

"You know, Walter," Jerry said, "sometimes you sound much more like a corporate executive than the scientist I used to watch on TV."

"That's a terrible thing to say! Well, perhaps being in upper management for all these decades has degraded both my intelligence and my humanity. That's inevitable, of course. We'd better hope that the scientific part of my mind is still working well enough that I'll be able to pull this off. In the meantime, as I said before, the two of you should look for a safe place."

"The North Pole," Jerry said.

"Mars," Piper said.

"Try to think of something more realistic," Zing said. "Hawaii would probably be a good bet, given the depth of the seafloor between here and there. I don't think the underground creature will be able to make its way to there for some time to come."

"The giant screaming earth mother zombie," Jerry said.

"The underground creature. Let's not be fanciful."

"Hawaii would be nice," Piper said. "That's assuming I still have access to my money. My father may have done something about that."

"I have savings," Jerry said.

"Enough to support two people in Hawaii for months or years to come?" Piper asked.

"Hardly," Jerry said, trying to look downcast but feeling elated because she had said the money would be supporting two people.

"Where are you going to go, Zing?" Piper said, abruptly changing the subject.

"Back to BioTyne. The guards there are loyal to me, so I'll be safe from your father's zombie armies while I continue my work."

Your father's zombie armies, Jerry repeated to himself. How the fuck did it come to this? "Will you also be safe from the insatiable giant screaming earth mother zombie?"

Zing sighed. "Really, Jerry. But, yes, I'll be safe from that creature inside BioTyne. The foundations are many layers of concrete and steel."

"Really? Why was it built that way?"

"To keep Chinese industrial spies from penetrating the facility from below, of course."

"Oh. Of course."

Jerry and Piper exchanged looks of astonishment. When they turned back to Zing, it was to see Griselda standing next to him. One of her giant, semi–skeletal hands rested on his shoulder. He was smiling happily.

Jerry and Piper stared at her in horror, unable to move even though she wasn't exercising her hypnotic powers on them.

"It's all right," the giant zombie said in that lovely voice. "I'm not going to eat anyone's brains for now. Walter has a good supply back at BioTyne. Right, beloved?"

"Oh, yes, indeed, my dearest."

"I am so confused," Jerry said.

"You killed George," Piper said. "I'll hate you forever."

The zombie rolled her eyes. A tiny part of one eyelid came free and floated down to the ground like a dried leaf. "Let bygones be bygones," the zombie said. "Men come, and men go."

"George wasn't coming and going. He was the love of my life. He was wonderful."

"All *right*!" the zombie said, her voice suddenly huge and not lovely at all. "I'm sorry. All right?"

Piper shrank back against Jerry, who put his arm around her protectively.

Griselda smiled. "See?" She looked at Jerry. "You didn't fasten the cover properly. Sunlight was shining on me. I was listening to what Walter said while I was working to release myself. I'm with him while he works to destroy that bitch. Once he succeeds, maybe then I'll eat his brains. And yours. In the meantime, I'm going to marry Walter."

Zing turned and looked up at her, his face filled with delight. "Darling!"

"But you're dead," Jerry said. "How can you...I mean, legally?"

Griselda stared at him, and he felt the familiar paralysis take hold. "I will be Zelda Zing. If you have any objections, speak now and forever hold the pieces of your head from which your brains will have been sucked out."

Zelda Zombie Zing, Jerry thought. He nodded and said, "No objections at all, ma'am."

"Death is full of compromises, young man" Griselda said. "Remember that."

"I will."

Piper put her arms around Jerry's waist and buried her face against his shoulder. She was shaking. Jerry held her, unable to speak even if he had had anything to say.

Zelda the zombie watched them thoughtfully. Then she looked down at Zing and said, "Walter, you have work to do."

"Yes, my dearest beloved darling!" Zing sang out. He floated back to his truck, his face covered with the silly smile of a teenage boy lucky in love for the first time.

Zelda tried to squeeze herself into the passenger seat. She gave up and climbed into the back of the truck. She sat there looking annoyed.

Have fun, you two crazy kids, Jerry thought. Good luck, Walter. "Good luck with your research, Walter," he called out.

Zing started the truck. He leaned out the window and said, "It's not luck, Gerald. It's the superness of science!" He put the truck in gear. He shouted to Jerry, "Don't take any wooden pickles!" Then he laughed and laughed and roared away in a shower of dust and pebbles.

When the truck was gone, Piper pulled her face away from Jerry's shoulder. "Take me home," she said.

"But your father—"

"Not the house. Your home."

"Oh. Okey dokey."

CHAPTER TWELVE

On the way back to Jerry's apartment, they drove to Marston Mall so that Piper could buy a toothbrush, underwear, a pair of jeans, and similar necessities. She had no intention of setting foot in her own house again.

"We could go by the house quickly so that you could get your car," Jerry said.

"Yes, okay," Piper said.

He could tell that even that idea frightened her. He reached over and put his hand on hers. "It'll be okay."

She smiled wanly at him. "I miss George so much."

"Me, too," he said, removing his hand.

It was now late Saturday afternoon, and the mall was packed. Fortunately, Piper proved to be an efficient shopper. Jerry was waiting for her outside a shop, holding a couple of shopping bags in each hand, staring into space and pondering his odd and unexpected future, when a familiar and hated voice spoke his name.

He closed his eyes, but when he opened them, Wendy was still there. "Golly," he said, "it's the Wicked Witch of the West."

"Still unoriginal," Wendy said. "You never were inventive. That was part of the problem, you know."

He certainly wasn't feeling inventive now. The faces of Lily and

George passed before his eyes, and his antagonistic relationship with his ex–wife seemed unimportant in comparison. He shrugged. "If you say so."

"No spirit, either. That was another part of the problem."

Jerry knew she'd list all the other parts of the problem as she saw it. He tried to tune her out.

Then Piper was next to him. She gripped his hand. "Don't speak to Jerry that way," she said, in a voice he had never heard her use before.

Wendy was nonplussed for a moment. Then she rallied and said, "I know you. Aren't you married? You seem to be pretty chummy with Jerry."

"My husband was murdered this morning," Piper said.

"Oh," Wendy said. "I'm sorry," she added insincerely.

"Jerry was my husband's best friend, and he's being a very good friend to me."

Wendy snickered. "I bet."

Piper dropped the shopping bag she had been holding. Her eyes narrowed. She stepped forward. Wendy, four inches taller than Piper, stepped back quickly. To Jerry's eyes, Piper seemed momentarily larger, as though she had absorbed something from her zombified mother. "If you ever bother Jerry again," she said, even her voice resembling her mother's, "you'll have to deal with me."

Wendy's eyes widened. Suddenly, she turned around and scuttled away.

Piper turned to Jerry. She seemed her normal size again. "Why did you ever marry that horrible woman? What were you thinking?"

Jerry remembered that, despite the screaming fights during their engagement, he had spent a lot of time thinking how unbearably hot Wendy was in her bikini panties. "I guess I wasn't thinking very clearly," he said.

"Obviously not. You need someone to keep you from making stupid mistakes like that, you know."

"I do know." He stood rooted in place, struggling with himself. How could he say what he wanted to say? It would be a terrible mistake.

"Well, come on," Piper said. "I'm done. Let's go back to your car. I'm hungry and tired. We'll go get my car tomorrow."

"Piper, wait." He took a couple of deep breaths, preparing himself. "I know this is terrible timing. I feel really bad saying this. George was a wonderful guy. He was the love of your life. I know that. It's going to take you a long time to get over his loss. I shouldn't say anything now, but I just can't help myself." He stopped.

Piper stared at him with her eyebrows slightly raised. She waited.

"I love you. I adore you. I worship you. I've felt that way since the day I met you. I want to spend the rest of my life with you. I hate myself for saying this to you now. I just can't help it."

He watched her face, trying to read something into it, but he failed. You've blown it, he told himself. Enjoy the next couple of seconds with Piper, because this is probably the last you'll ever see of her.

"Hmm," Piper said. Then she smiled. "You know what? Let's give it a try for a while and see how it works out."

He was about to hug her when she said, "Poor George. Those bastards must have eaten him by now."

Back at Jerry's apartment, they spent some time making room in the closet and dresser for Piper's new and future purchases.

Jerry looked in his refrigerator and was surprised by how little it contained. He had mostly stopped cooking after his divorce. Piper was used to having her meals prepared at home by professionals. He would have to brush up on his few rusty cooking skills and acquire a lot of new ones to keep her happy—and he was determined to keep her happy.

He looked at his watch and wondered how and when he could suggest going to bed. Or even whether. He still wasn't sure exactly what their arrangement was. Now that he thought about it, her answer in the mall had been vague, possibly deliberately so.

The telephone rang. Jerry said, "Oh, jeez, I hope it's not my idiot sister again." Then he froze, mouth open, shocked by what he had said.

Piper gave him a sympathetic look and picked up the phone. "Hello. Gerald Morgenstern residence." Her eyes widened. "Dad!"

She stared at Jerry and he stared at her.

After a while, Piper said into the phone, "I'll ask him." She put her hand over the receiver. "It's my father. He's back at the house. He wants you to come over and talk to him. He says he wants you to run the company now that..." She breathed rapidly a few times and then composed herself. "Now that George is no longer available to do it."

"Jesus! Your house?"

"His house."

"Right. His house. What do you think?"

"It could be a trap."

"Yeah, but he obviously knows where I am, so I'm no safer here than I would be there. Tell him I'll be there in an hour."

Piper nodded. She took her hand off the receiver and spoke into it. "All right, Dad. We'll be there in an hour." She hung up.

"No, you're staying here," Jerry said.

"I'm staying with you. We're together now. Get used to it."

"Whatever you say." Jerry's heart was pounding. Most of that was due to terror at the thought of going back to the Pistole house and meeting Frank, but not all of it.

Just as in the old days, they were met at the door by a butler. This was someone new, not a servant Piper knew or Jerry recognized. Nor did the butler know who they were. In addition, the butler was a zombie.

He was wearing a three–piece suit and discreet tie. He greeted them with the combination of formality, deference, and scorn that Jerry remembered hating in the Pistole butlers of long ago. But his speech was halting and slurred, his face was cracking and falling apart, and he smelled of death.

"I'm Piper Gordon," Piper said. "Mr. Pistole's daughter. This is Jerry Morgenstern. My father's expecting us."

The butler bowed slightly, said, "Please follow me," or possibly something else that sounded similar, and let the way into the house.

When Jerry and Piper entered the house, the door closed behind them. "That's very creepy," Jerry whispered to Piper.

"It's some kind of electronic door controller," Piper said. "My father was talking about having it installed before he died. It's not supernatural. Don't worry." She seemed to have regained her courage now that she was back in her own house.

"I meant the butler."

They passed other servants, all formally dressed, going about the business of a large house. Going about it slowly, for they were all zombies. Fortunately, they seemed oblivious to the two ambulatory meals walking past them.

Jerry wondered if he and Piper were the only living creatures in the house.

The butler led them up the main staircase to the room that had been Frank's office for so long, then George's for a short while, and was now apparently once again Frank's.

The butler gestured toward the office, bowed slightly, and moved away down the hallway, making not a sound. Jerry was reminded of Wodehouse's fictional butler Jeeves shimmering in and out of rooms. He was about to try to break the barrier he suddenly sensed between himself and Piper by making a joke about Jeeves and zombies when he noticed that Fred Foxtrot was in the office talking to Frank, who stood behind his desk.

"Federal funds, of course," Foxtrot was saying. "I'll handle that part if I can muster the political support. That's where you come in."

"Very important mission," Frank said hollowly. "Must have space. New worlds to conquer." He noticed Jerry and Piper standing in the doorway. "For my pickles," he said to them.

Foxtrot turned and saw them. He smiled professionally at Jerry and pruriently at Piper and then left.

"Creep," Jerry muttered.

"Hush," Piper said. She smiled at her father, her smile about as genuine as Foxtrot's professional one. "Hi, Dad. Here we are."

Frank stared at them uncomprehendingly. This was not the scary monster of earlier days, both pre and post death. This was a weak and pitiful zombie.

Awareness of who they were filtered into his expression. "Oh, yes," he said. "Thank you so much for coming. Won't you please have a seat?"

Jerry looked around. There were no chairs in the room. There wasn't even one behind the desk.

"That's okay," Jerry said. "We'll stand."

"Okay..." Frank's voice trailed away. He stared at Jerry but didn't seem to see him.

"Dad?" Piper said. "You wanted to see us."

Frank started. "Oh, yes. Oh, yes. Oh, yes. Oh, yes." He started again. "Sorry. Trouble thinking since...big hole in mountains."

"Since the giant screaming earth mother zombie in the big hole you dug in that mountain valley ate your zombie army along with my sister, you mean?" Jerry asked. "Right. Well, we'll be going, now."

"Wait!" Frank looked alert again. "Please, help me! Don't leave me alone!"

"Frank, how can we trust you? You sent your zombie army after us. They were trying to kill us."

Frank looked down. "Sorry. Bad zombie. Please help me."

"He *is* my father," Piper said. "I owe him something."

"Oh, God," Jerry said. "All right, Frank. You want me to take George's place?" Piper stifled a sob, and Jerry cursed his choice of words. "You want me to run the company for you? All right, I'll do that. Get all the zombies out of that place, though. No more zombies."

"No more zombies," Frank said, nodding.

The motion made Jerry nervous. "Don't nod so hard."

"Don't nod so hard," Frank repeated, still nodding.

"Also, no more secret ingredient."

Frank paused. A crafty–zombie look flitted across his ruined face and disappeared. Then he nodded again. "No more Zelda juice."

"Jerry, let's think about that," Piper said. "The secret ingredient is what took our brand to the top. We don't want to deleverage our unique expertise. We'd risk losing our hold on our target demographic."

Jerry stared at her. "Also," he said, "no more bullshit corporate bizspeak."

"Okay," Frank said, still nodding. "No more...that."

"We'll have to manage without the secret ingredient," Jerry said. "Besides, we no longer have a source for it."

"Do," Frank said. "Giant screaming earth mother zombie."

"Yeah, Zing told us. But what makes you think she'll give you the stuff? Expel it, or whatever."

"She said so. She told me."

"You *talked* to her? It?"

Frank nodded more vigorously. Big flakes of skin drifted down to the floor. “She talks to me. Tells me things.”

“Uh, sure.” Jerry whispered to Piper, “That thing ate his brain.”

“Uh uh, brain’s fine,” Frank said, demonstrating that death had not diminished the remarkable hearing that had struck fear into so many employees for so long.

“Dad,” Piper said, “how did you get away from that thing? We saw it eat the other zombies.”

Frank looked blank. “Don’t know. Fell asleep behind rock. Woke up here.” He shivered. “Could think again down here. Never going back there.” He brightened. “Not all my zombies eaten. Some okay. Servants in house now.”

“Oh, great,” Jerry said.

“One is cook. Good cook. Real good. Want food?”

“I’m not really hungry,” Jerry said.

“I am,” Piper said. “I wouldn’t mind a little something.”

“Great!” Frank said. “Come kitchen.”

He led the way down the stairs and to the big kitchen. That was good, Jerry thought. He suspected that the mess in the small kitchen had not yet been cleaned up. Even from this far away, he thought he could still smell it.

A zombie in a white chef’s outfit, complete with tall, white hat, stood in the center of the kitchen, his face bathed in sunlight shining through the big window over the sink, his eyes closed. When they entered, he turned toward them, opened his dead eyes, and whispered, “Catching some rays.”

“Food,” Frank said.

The chef zombie stared with interest at Piper and Jerry for a moment. Then he turned, walked over to the refrigerator, and pulled the door open. A stomach-churning odor filled the room. The light inside the refrigerator was not on.

“Yum!” Frank said.

Piper ran from the kitchen, pulling Jerry behind her. The smell pursued them across the house and out the front door. They stood outside, both fighting against the urge to vomit.

“Jesus,” Piper said, “everything’s rotting. The fridge is turned off. Is he eating that stuff?”

Frank ambled out of the house and joined them. “Leaving?” he asked. He looked disappointed. He turned his face to the sun and closed his eyes. “Mmm,” he said. “Rays. Soak it up.” He opened his eyes again. “You stay here? Nice house.”

“No!” Piper said. “I just came to get my car.”

“I’ll see you at the office tomorrow, Frank,” Jerry said.

“Uh uh,” Frank said. “I stay here. Catch rays. You work. You got good brain.” Inevitably, his gaze drifted to Jerry’s forehead.

“George’s body,” Piper said. “We’ve got to get it out of there—what’s left of it.”

“George safe,” Frank said. “Funeral home. Just industrial accident. Paid a fine. Forms all filled in.” A crafty zombie look crossed his face. “I greased palms. I ate someone.”

Jerry and Piper backed away from him.

“Find out where George is,” Piper said to Jerry. “I want him cremated. I can’t stand the thought of him coming back as a zombie.”

“Yeah, good idea,” Jerry said. He thought, our conversations keep getting weirder.

CHAPTER THIRTEEN

The odd thing, Jerry often thought as the months drifted by, was how normal everything seemed, at least while he was away from home.

He was back at work at Piper's Pickled Peppers, although now he occupied the big presidential office and spent his days feeling overwhelmed and inadequate. He got there early and stayed late and fretted about stagnant sales numbers. They weren't falling, but the company was no longer thriving as it had during George's tenure.

George.

George was dead, and all that was left of him physically resided in an urn in a niche in a wall at Heavenly Memories Garden of Rest. And yet in a way, George was as undead as any zombie. His spirit had moved with Piper from the Pistole mansion to Jerry's apartment, and now he was living there with them. For a spirit, his presence was remarkably tangible and took up a lot of room. The place was crowded.

In the evening, once Jerry got back from work and wolfed down some cold food from the fridge, he and Piper would often sit silently, side by side in matching leather armchairs, and watch the news on a huge television set—much too big for Jerry's living room—that Piper had insisted on buying.

The TV set and the armchairs took up a big part of the room. The awareness of George filled the rest of it.

She had also insisted on buying the armchairs and throwing out Jerry's comfortable, battered old couch—the couch on which he had so often masturbated while thinking about Piper, imagining that she was lying on the couch with him, although sometimes, despite himself, he had jacked off to the image of Wendy in her bikini underpants.

He told himself that Piper would surely look even hotter than Wendy in bikini underpants. He wondered morosely if he would ever find out.

At least Wendy had had sex with him—in the early days, at any rate.

After the news, Jerry and Piper usually washed up and went to bed. They lay side by side in Jerry's double bed, both dressed in nightclothes, quite chastely, until the alarm sounded in the morning. Sometimes he woke in the middle of the night to the sound of Piper crying softly. He wanted to take her in his arms and comfort her, but he never dared to. She always seemed normal again in the morning.

They never made love—never had and, Jerry feared, never would.

If he hadn't been so immensely physically frustrated, he would have been quite happy. Or so he told himself.

Outside his apartment, though, the world moved on as though nothing untoward had happened.

Frank never showed up at the office. Jerry had no idea what was happening at the Pistole mansion, and he had no wish to find out. There were no zombies at the office or—he had managed to make himself go there and check—at the factory. When Jerry went out to lunch, he rarely saw any of the creatures shambling along. Those he did see acted weak and confused and seemed non-threatening, much like the new Frank Pistole. Even the memories of the terrible events of the recent past were losing their intensity—for Jerry, at least, if not for Piper.

Perhaps, he told himself, the world really is returning to normal. A new normal. Better than the old normal! My paycheck is a lot bigger, and I'm living with Piper. Well, sharing an apartment with her.

But that's still better than in the past, he told himself as he unlocked the door to his apartment. Poor George, though, he added mechanically in his standard attempt to diminish his feelings of guilt.

When Jerry entered, Piper was standing near the front window, her eyes closed, her face bathed in sunlight. Jerry froze. He stared at her, his heart pounding with fear.

Then she opened her eyes and smiled at him. "Hi. You're early."

He breathed deeply in relief. "I guess I am, a bit. Everything okay?"

"Why wouldn't it be?"

"Why do you Christians always answer a question with a question?" She didn't laugh. No one ever laughed at his jokes. He wondered why he kept making them. "So what did you do today?"

"Went to the gym, as usual."

"Great." In his eyes, she inched ever closer to physical perfection, and he was happy that she seemed to want to keep inching.

"You should go, too," she said.

"Work. Too much of it."

"I could teach you a few basic exercises. You'd feel a lot better. Work would be easier."

"Work would be easier if I had George's brains," Jerry said. Oh, shit, he thought. Why did I say that?

Piper sighed heavily. "I used to try to get George to come to the gym, and he always refused, too. It would have made him even more wonderful. Thank God we got his body out of there before any of those bastards could eat him."

"Um, right. I'm hungry. I wonder what's in the fridge."

"You shouldn't eat cold food every evening," Piper said. "You should have a good, hot meal straight from the oven."

"Great idea!"

"There's a pizza in the freezer. I'll heat it up. Pizza was the last food I had with George. It will make me feel closer to him."

"Yeah. It will be like he's here with us. Sometimes, it feels like he is."

"What a sweet thing to say! We can pretend he's eating the pizza with us." Cheered up, she went off to the kitchen.

Jerry sighed and turned on the TV. He had no idea what was on. He just hoped that the electronic voices and images would push George aside for a while.

The screen came to life and a commercial appeared.

Perfect timing, Jerry thought grouchily.

The commercial opened with a husband and wife staring at a hole in a wall of their house from which electric wires protruded. The wife, a slender, attractive woman, was patiently explaining to her rumpled, overweight, slack-jawed husband how electricity and electrical wiring work. He stared at her with as little comprehension as though zombies had sucked out his brains. The commercial ended with the wife buying and installing the advertised product, which solved the couple's nagging electrical problems, while her husband watched helplessly.

That was followed immediately by another commercial. In this one, a slender, attractive woman patiently explained to her rumpled, overweight, slack-jawed husband how car engines work, what car brand (the advertised one, of course) is the best, and the best way to finance a car purchase. Her husband stared at her uncomprehendingly and drooled.

Just as that faded away with a final view of the wife's smug, arch, condescending smile, and Jerry breathed a sigh of relief, another commercial began. A slender, attractive woman wearing an indulgent smile used the advertised product to clean up the mess made in the kitchen by her doltish, thoughtless husband and children who had made a rare attempt to cook something. She held a can of the cleaning product the commercial was selling up to the camera and said, "You're a woman, so it's all up to you and on your shoulders all the time, but Soopershine is here to help!"

Piper came back into the living room carrying two plates, each holding three thick slices of steaming pizza. It smelled wonderful.

"That was quick," Jerry said.

"Oh, I meant to tell you. I threw out your old microwave. I bought a new one. It works super fast."

His microwave oven, his couch, his television set. Jerry wondered if he'd be the next tired old thing to be thrown out.

They sat in the adjoining armchairs and ate their pizza and watched television without exchanging a word.

Just a couple of children of zombies eating pizza, he thought. Not a very good pizza, either. Thank God there are no pickled peppers on it.

He wondered if Piper was thinking about George.

Of course she is, he told himself.

Another commercial began. Jerry groaned. "All commercials, all the time! Let's turn it off."

"Wait," Piper said. "This one is funny. I've watched it at the gym."

A slender, attractive wife was in the kitchen, efficiently making a gourmet meal. Through the window behind her, the viewers could see her incompetent husband blowing up the barbecue grill. The wife glanced through the window as pieces of her husband rained down. She shook her head and smiled indulgently.

Piper laughed.

Jerry said, "That's not—"

Suddenly, the screen filled with Fred Foxtrot's unctuous face. Very obvious masking tape and plumber's putty covered his face. A bloody gash bisected his left cheek at a 45-degree angle. Jerry was sure the gash had been applied by a makeup man and that the blood came from a red felt–tip marker.

"Fucking fake zombie," Jerry muttered.

"Good old Fred," Piper said. "You have to admire his...What's the Yiddish word? Hahtspah?"

"Chutzpah," Jerry said, pronouncing it with the proper guttural sound. "I don't admire it. I've never admired chutzpah. Anyway, I don't trust him."

"Oh, don't be silly. He's just playing the Washington game. Sshh. I want to hear what he's saying."

Blah, blah, blah, blah, blah, Jerry thought. That's what he's saying. That's all he ever says.

"I want to congratulate my fellow senators," Foxtrot was saying, "and my friends and colleagues in the House for passing, and the president for signing into law, the Restoration of Voting Rights to Interrupted Existence Compatriots Act. This is a wonderful day for America and in particular for those fellow citizens of ours who were so unfairly deprived of their sacred, God–given right to vote. I dare to hope—" he chuckled "—that most of those newly restored votes will go to Republican candidates."

His colleagues laughed loudly. It struck Jerry that, unlike the few previous times when he had seen television coverage of Foxtrot addressing the Senate, the chamber was full and the senators were leaning forward, their attention focused on Foxtrot, their manner one of deference.

Foxtrot beamed at them paternally for a moment. Then his expression switched to serious mode. "And now, if you will indulge me—" his tone said clearly that he knew that they would "—I'd like to say just a few words about the bill I introduced this morning, the Spreading the Seeds of Earth Initiative.

"The race to colonize the many livable worlds that surround us is now underway." Foxtrot's tone was somber, portentous. He might have been narrating a documentary. He paused for effect.

"Many?" Jerry said. "Like which ones?"

"Sshh," Piper said.

Foxtrot resumed. "Of course, I hope that every settlement on another world will be American, proudly flying the grand old flag and speaking American. However, due to the incompetence, misdeeds, and traitorous instincts of every Democratic president of this and the last century, there's a fairly good chance that other nationalities will land on those bountiful worlds before we do."

Groans and headshaking from his colleagues in the world's greatest deliberative body.

"Blather, blather," Jerry said. "Can we turn this off?"

"Sshh," Piper said.

"What we must ensure," Foxtrot said, "is that no matter who lands on those other worlds first, the fundamental essence of our planet, our mother Earth, will be propagated throughout space."

"What is he talking about?" Jerry asked.

Piper shrugged.

"My bill," Foxtrot said, "will establish an initiative to plant the seeds of our mother planet on the other worlds of our solar system. It will also include funds for the accelerated development of a manned mission to Mars, in hopes that we will plant our flag there first."

His colleagues frowned and shook their heads and muttered.

"Needless to say," Foxtrot said, "we will avoid that bottomless pit of inefficient and incompetent government known as NASA. My bill specifies that all of this work must be performed entirely by free enterprise."

More muttering.

"Moreover, the work will be spread across the country, with major facilities and therefore lots of jobs located in each of the states represented by the members of this chamber."

Cheers and foot stamping.

Foxtrot nodded and smiled until the noise had died down. Then he said, "Thank you, thank you. Now, good night, God bless you, and may God bless the United States of America."

"Money for his pals," Jerry said. "So that's what this is about. As usual with that guy."

"I thought you liked the space program," Piper said. "As long as we get people on the planets, what difference does it make what motive was behind it? Or who?"

"This is the most serious and sustained conversation we've had since you moved in."

"Really? God, you're right. Are you done with your pizza?"

"Yeah."

"Are you done watching TV?"

"I am if you are."

"Yes, I am. Let's go to bed."

He almost said, "It's too early for me." He almost said, "I'm going to stay up and read for a few hours." He almost said, "You go ahead." Fortunately, he said none of those things. Instead, he said, "Oh, okay. Sure."

And so at last they made love.

It was nowhere near as wonderful as Jerry had always fantasized that sex with Piper would be, but it was quite good—better than average, Jerry assured himself. He also assured himself that he was a very happy and a very lucky man. At the very least, and to his relief, the sight of Piper naked had finally deprived of their lingering power the remembered images of Wendy Kline in bikini underpants.

He couldn't forget, though, that he and Wendy had engaged in some marathon lovemaking sessions that had lasted—or had seemed to last—for hours and had left both of them happily exhausted and sleeping deeply. With Piper, sex was short, pleasant, friendly, and nice, and after both had achieved orgasm, she was the one to go to sleep while Jerry lay on his back, wide awake.

The ceiling was faintly illuminated by the light coming through the window from a far-off streetlight. He stared at the ceiling for a long time, hoping that its featurelessness would quiet his brain and send him off to sleep. Instead, he started to make out details—cracks, and patches where the paint was a different shade.

He closed his eyes and listened to Piper's soft, regular breathing for a while. There was no hint of quiet sobbing, this time. He thought he deserved congratulations for that, but her breathing didn't lull him to sleep, either.

When he accepted the fact that he wasn't going to fall asleep, he decided to go into the living room and read for a while.

He slid out of bed carefully so as not to disturb Piper. The glow from the ceiling lit the room gently to his dark-adjusted eyes. For the first time, he wondered how zombies saw the world. Did dying and coming back to life and drawing energy from the sun make their eyes work differently?

Stop thinking about zombies, he told himself. Think about Piper instead. You love her. You adore her. You just made love to her, the woman of your dreams. She looks and feels even better nude than you ever imagined any woman could.

A zombie would look at her and see only a source of brains, he thought.

Oh, fuck you, he told himself.

Moving carefully and quietly, he got his bathrobe from the closet and left the bedroom, closing the door silently.

He hadn't checked the bedroom clock. When he got to the living room, he was surprised to see that it was already 10:00 o'clock. He had been lying awake in bed for longer than he had realized. Instead of reading, he decided to watch the news.

He got a chair from the kitchen and put it close to the television set. Then he turned on the set, turned the sound down almost to the limits of audibility, and clicked to Channel Five.

He sat impatiently through the opening sequence in which the stylized *5* logo moved around the screen and bombastic music played. A deep male voice said, "Five's Alive! From our newsroom in downtown Piketon, it's the Five Action Events News! Breaking now exclusively on Five's Alive!"

The computerized effects disappeared and the newsroom appeared. It was a bizarrely high-tech studio containing a semicircular glass desk on a podium, behind which several television monitors of different sizes hung in mid-air. Images moved busily on all of them. Behind the desk sat one of Piketon's many interchangeable attractive, but not too attractive, anchorwomen.

The previous year, all of the local newscasts had used similarly moderately attractive anchormen. The year before that, the standard had been teams—one anchorman and one anchorwoman. Jerry wondered what they would all switch to next year. Barking seals, maybe. That would be okay. Or anchorzombies. That would not be okay.

"Good evening," the anchorwoman said. "We're following this breaking news that Five's Alive Action Events News broke for you exclusively on our earlier breaking news. There have been numerous reports of large numbers of mobile homes and RVs traveling in caravans entering the state from the south along Interstate 25 and exiting the Interstate near the town of Bartle's Drop, about 30 miles north of Piketon. Five's Alive viewers who were on the Interstate have called us to say that the mobile homes and RVs seem to be driven by IECs, although we have not been able to confirm that. The State Patrol confirms the existence of these caravans, but they say that there is no evidence of unusual numbers of mobile homes or RVs in the mountains in that area, so they assume that all the vehicles were passing through our region. They are monitoring the situation."

Well, that wasn't very breaking, Jerry thought.

Then it occurred to him that the caravans of zombies might be headed to the valley where the giant screaming earth mother zombie lived. He had a sudden vision of the mobile homes and RVs driving over the edge of the huge pit and being absorbed along with their passengers by the creature inside the hole. That would explain why there was no evidence of the vehicles up there.

It wouldn't explain why the zombies were heading up there in the first place, though.

"We'll have more on this breaking news after this commercial break," the anchorwoman said.

She was replaced by a commercial in which a slender, attractive young woman wearing a hard hat was building a jet engine from scratch by herself while a bunch of sloppy, dull–eyed men stood by watching helplessly and hopelessly.

The bedroom door opened and Piper came out, naked, squinting against the living–room light. "Couldn't sleep?" she asked. "What're you watching?"

"The news." Jerry aimed the remote control at the television set and turned it off. He feared the effect on Piper's mood if she saw any part of the report about zombies and the mountain area that the two of them had escaped from not very long before. "But it's over now. You know how it is on the local stations: five minutes of news and 25 minutes of sports."

"Yeah." She walked over to him, pulled his bathrobe apart, and sat down sideways on his lap. She put her head on his chest. "I'm cold."

He pulled his bathrobe as far out as he could wrapped it and his arms around her. "How's that?"

"Better." She sighed. "You're wonderful."

The telephone rang.

"Of course," Jerry said.

"I'll get it." Piper pushed herself off his lap, walked over to the telephone, and picked up the receiver. "Hello. Gerald Morgenstern residence."

Jerry loved hearing her say that. At that moment, he couldn't think of anything about her that he didn't love.

Piper said, "This is Piper. Who is this?" She paused. "Piper Pistole. Who is this?" Another pause. She frowned. "No, I'm not Jewish. Who *is* this?"

"Oh, God," Jerry said.

Piper covered the receiver. "She says she's your mother. She sounds really weird."

"That's because she's a zombie."

Piper held the receiver out to him. Jerry sighed, got up, and took it from her. "Hi, Mom."

"Jerry, Jerry, Jerry, Jerry, Jerry." Dry, whispery, cracked, conveying no real human emotion, it was a creepy parody of the disapproval he had heard regularly from his mother while she was still alive. "Why don't you try to make it up with Wendy. She was such a nice Jewish girl."

"She was a monster."

"Don't be silly. I remember when you brought her to visit us. We got along with her so well. She was so respectful and appreciative of everything."

You should have heard what she said about you after we left, he thought. "Mom, Piper is the most wonderful woman in the history of the world. I'm sure you'd love her if you met her."

"Is she smart? You're so smart, you should have a girl who's also very smart, just like you."

"Very smart. Very, very smart."

"So she's brainy, then. She has lots of brains. You should bring her down here to meet us."

Oh, shit, he thought. "Oh. Well, you know, we're so busy. I don't see how we can."

"You're ashamed of your parents? You want to hide us from your wonderful, brainy *shiksa*?"

"No, Mom, it's not that. It's just..."

Piper whispered, "What's the problem?"

Jerry covered the receiver. "She wants to meet you. She wants us to go down there and visit them."

"That's reasonable. Of course they want to meet the woman you're involved with. We should go. That's the proper thing to do."

"They're the living dead! My parents are fucking brain–eating zombies!"

Piper shrugged. "So are mine."

He had no answer to that. He took his hand off the receiver. "Mom? Okay. We'll fly down there. I'll let you know the date after I've booked the flight." He listened for a moment, then forced himself to say, "Love you, too." He hung up. He felt ill.

Piper said shyly, "Do you really think I'm the most wonderful woman in the history of the world?"

"God, yes. I've always thought that."

"Cool!"

But my mother, he thought, would prefer that I meet a nice Jewish zombie.

CHAPTER FOURTEEN

As they went through the security line at the airport a week later, Jerry was startled to see that most of the uniformed TSA personnel were zombies. Then he was startled to see that they were staring dully into space as though they were as stupid and unthinking as Frank Pistole had become. Then he was startled to realize how little difference it made compared to his previous passages through these security lines, before the zombie invasion.

Once they were through the security checkpoint and out of zombie earshot, Jerry said, "I'm beginning to think that the zombie problem is over. Maybe sunlight or whatever it is stops animating them after a while. They're dying all over again. It was scary for a while, but now we're getting back to normal."

Piper squeezed his arm. "You're such an optimist. That's one of the many, many things I love so much about you."

"Um, okay. Or, say, maybe it's Walter Zing. Remember how he said he was working on something? Maybe it's a virus, or something like that. Maybe that's what's doing this to the zombies."

"Ugh." Piper let go of his arm. "Dr. Creepazoid."

"You seemed to be changing your mind about him."

"I was mistaken. I thought he wasn't Dr. Creepazoid, but he is."

"You won't call him that if he saves the world."

"Yes, I will. I'll call him Dr. Creepazoid Who Saved the World."

"George really admired him. George would be offended by you

saying that."

"So what? George is gone. But I can see that it offends you, so I won't say it anymore."

What strange world am I living in? Jerry asked himself.

They flew first class—old hat for Piper, but to Jerry a novel experience. He loved the early boarding, the wide seats, the free champagne, and the extra attention from the flight attendants, each of whom knew his name and addressed him as Mr. Morgenstern.

He loved the way Piper held onto his arm even after they were seated, how she talked happily and excitedly about their trip, how she told the flight attendant more than once that Jerry was wonderful, how she occasionally leaned her head on his shoulder.

At least, he loved it for about the first hour of the flight. After that, Piper's behavior started getting on his nerves.

Why did she talk so much? She never had before. Why didn't she let go of him? It made it hard for him to move or relax properly in the wide, comfortable seat. Why did she keep saying he was wonderful? She used to say that about George, whereas she had had only nasty words for Jerry.

Not that he preferred the nasty words to the nice ones, but the change, which had delighted him at first, was starting to seem stranger and stranger to him.

And what about George? Jerry had resented his massive spiritual presence in the apartment until the presence suddenly disappeared. Now he felt guilty for that resentment. He also felt that the cessation of Piper's mourning was improperly sudden. Shouldn't she still be feeling some sadness? George really had been a great guy—not wonderful, maybe, but very good. How could Piper, who had seemed to love George so intensely, put him out of her mind so completely?

Zombies were scary enough. Ordinary human nature was even worse.

At Tampa, they had to go outside the main airport terminal to wait for the limousine that would take them to the rental car lot. They stepped into hot, liquid air.

Jerry groaned. "The butt crack of hell. My clothes are melting. My brain is melting. I can't breathe. Can we turn around and go back home now?"

"It'll be fun. I bet your parents know some great seafood restaurants here."

"Oh, boy," Jerry said. "There are a few things I should explain to you while we drive down there."

For the first time, he wondered if very observant Jews came back as very observant Jewish zombies, and if so, were brains kosher, and if not, what did such zombies do about eating? It was a strangely disturbing train of thought.

The rental car had been arranged by Piper. It turned out to be a very large luxury model, the purchase price of which was probably not much less than Jerry's big, new annual salary. He looked at it without enthusiasm. "I usually drive down here in my own car."

Piper shuddered. "Sounds awful. You won't be doing that anymore. That reminds me: I want you to get rid of that old junker. You need to be driving something classier now. Maybe something like this."

"I love that car!"

"You love me more."

He couldn't argue with that.

He wondered if you could store the old car in a rented garage somewhere and tell Piper that he had sold it. Then he could still drive it from time to time.

I could have the best of both worlds, he thought. In a manner of speaking.

Feeling awkward behind the wheel of the expensive monster,

Jerry found the airport exit and took the highway south toward Interstate 275. Once he was on the causeway across Tampa Bay, with water on both sides and the admittedly efficient air conditioner filling the car with cold air, he began to relax.

"Now it looks familiar," he said.

"See? You'll get used to your new life. You'll be fine." She squeezed his arm. "You're wonderful."

"Okay."

"I love how green it is on the coasts," Piper said. "I love Arapahoe, but I miss the greenery and how densely it grows and all the great seafood."

"We have seafood in Piketon."

"Pretty inferior stuff."

"You're beginning to sound like my sister."

"All right. I won't say anything more." After a very short silence, she stretched and writhed alluringly. "I feel so happy! It's because of you."

"Oh," Jerry said. God, he thought. He could never have imagined that he would start to feel just the slightest bit tired of hearing Piper say such things, but he was.

"You're wonderful," she added.

Jerry concentrated on driving.

After a while, he said, "Speaking of seafood, before we get to my parents' place, I need to tell you about the dietary laws."

"They're on a diet? I thought they ate brains."

"So, here's the thing. You know how I make a point of eating pork whenever I get the chance?"

Much later, Piper said. "And you have to have to completely separate sets of knives and forks and plates and glasses, and you mustn't ever mix them up? That's weirder than zombies."

"I haven't even told you about Passover yet. Oops. Here we are."

He pulled into the parking lot of his parents' condominium complex and parked in one of the visitor spaces.

Piper said, "We're here? Great! Let's go meet your parents."

"Wait. I want to remind you that there are zombies all over the place here, and my parents are the worst of them. Brain–eating zombies."

"Oh, pooh. I told you: so are my parents."

"Mine are worse. They suck out your soul along with your brain."

Piper laughed. "Oh, you're being silly. Who's that?"

She was pointing at one of the balconies in the wall across the parking lot. Jerry's mother stood there, waving at them slowly.

"It's my mother. Stay next to me so that I can protect you from her."

"What a sweet–looking old lady! I know we'll be great friends."

She pushed her door open, jumped out of the car, and began to trot across the parking lot, waving to Jerry's mother and calling out, "Hi! I'm Piper!"

Jerry cursed, pushed himself out of the car, and ran after her. He caught up with her in the middle of the lot. "Piper, please! We have to stay together."

"Oh, all right." She was annoyed, but on the bright side, she didn't tell him he was wonderful.

"Please wait right here while I lock the car."

He locked the car, and then they trudged across the parking lot. Both of them were feeling the heat now. Piper's semi–euphoria seemed to have evaporated, and she drooped. Jerry felt guilty for that, but at least it made her stay next to him.

The elevator was hot. The hallway was hot. When Jerry's mother opened the door at his knock, even hotter air came out from it. The stink made Jerry stomach lurch. It was the stink of decaying food and two decaying bodies.

Not that the two older and Morgensterns looked any more decayed than the last time Jerry had seen them. The opposite seemed to be the case. When Jerry hugged his mother—cautiously, holding his breath, wary of her grasp—she felt more substantial than before. This time, he couldn't feel her naked ribs. Even up close, her skin looked like actual skin, not plumber's putty or masking tape, and with only a few places where the bone showed through.

She squeezed him with frightening strength, then pushed him away and looked at him. "You haven't been eating. I have lots of food ready for you."

"Oh!" Piper said brightly. "That would be—"

"Unnecessary," Jerry said. "They stuffed us on the plane."

"Hmph," his mother said. "I can imagine what garbage they gave you. You need some good, Jewish food." She stared coldly at Piper. "It wouldn't hurt you, either."

Piper said, "Actually, Jerry, you know—"

"Yes, you're right. We have to check in. Mom, we made a reservation at a motel near here. We have to get over there. We'll be back in the morning."

"What? You're not staying here?"

"I thought it would be less awkward, considering that I'm going to be having lots of loud sex with a *shiksa*."

His mother stared at him with her mouth open. So did Piper.

Jerry had always wanted to say that to his mother, but now he realized that this might not have been the best circumstances in which to do it.

"Aren't you even going to say hello to your father?" his mother said.

"Sure. Where is he?"

"I'm Piper," Piper said. "I'm so happy to meet you."

"He's in the living room, watching television." Jerry's mother turned away and walked into the kitchen.

Piper's face fell. "Is she prejudiced against living people?"

"Um," Jerry said. "You know what, let's go into the living room. Maybe the stink is a little less horrible there."

It was, very slightly. His father was sitting in his old, soft armchair, sinking into it in a stupor while he stared at the blaring television set.

When Jerry and Piper entered the room, a commercial was playing. A slender, attractive woman was singlehandedly building a skyscraper at extremely high speed while a collection of mindless men watched her with slack jaws and vacant eyes. After she finished, she inspected the new building from the adjacent sidewalk, brushed an invisible speck of dust from its shiny wall, nodded in approval, and then quickly prepared a nutritious, hot dinner for the male onlookers, smiling smugly all the while.

Jerry's father glanced at Jerry and Piper and said, "Those guys need a good meal of brains. So, this is your *shiksa*? She's a looker. Looks brainy."

The commercial ended. The regular program, a baseball game, Jerry's father's favorite television viewing, resumed.

The camera zoomed in on the pitcher as he wound up. Jerry squinted at the screen. "Is that Finnegan? Didn't he die in a car crash last year?"

"Nu? He came back. He's an IEC. He's still the best pitcher in the league."

"But he's...What happens if he gets hit by a line drive?"

"Now you're prejudiced? IECs aren't as good as you, just because you're so smart? How are your brains doing?"

"They're fine. We're leaving now."

"You can't even stay? Your sister called. She'll be here tomorrow morning. We can have a nice family meal."

"What? My sister? You mean Lily?"

"Who else? Do you have another sister? You get involved with a *shiksa*, and now you forget all about your family?"

"But Lily's..." Dead. Gone. Eaten by the giant screaming earth mother zombie who lives in a big hole in the mountains north of Piketon. His father was imagining things. Who knew how a zombie brain worked? "We'll be back in the morning."

"You're not staying here?" His father shrugged. "All right. On your way here tomorrow, pick up some Piper's Pickled Peppers. We ran out of them."

They got out safely and headed back to the car.

"Why didn't you want to stay there?" Piper asked. "We don't have a motel reservation. You lied about that."

"It stinks in there. It turns my stomach. Didn't it do that you?"

"Only at first. I was getting used to it."

"I bet the refrigerator isn't even turned on, just like in your father's place. That's probably what caused most of the horrible smell. The food's all rotten. We couldn't eat anything there. Even apart from that, it's not safe. They'd eat our brains while we were asleep."

"That's silly. So our parents are zombies. That's just the way the world is now. We have to adjust. They wouldn't eat their own son's brains."

"They ate my sister's brains, and she's their own daughter."

"But we saw your sister! Up in the mountains."

"Yeah. She never used her brains even when she had them, so I guess she was able to function without them."

"You must be mistaken. I bet they didn't eat her brains at all. Anyway, at least you can talk to your parents. They're not all stupid, the way my father is now."

"That's true. I wonder why that is." He shrugged. "They always were different from everyone else's parents."

"Every kid thinks that about his parents."

"In my case, it was true. I've been thinking that the zombies are wearing out. They're all acting stupid all of a sudden. Maybe it's just taking longer to happen with my parents. Would you like to walk over to the beach before we look for a motel room? There's a nice pier there. We could walk out over the water."

"I guess. If you really want to."

He didn't, but he wanted to walk past the old folks' rec center again to see how the antique zombies there were behaving. He wanted to test his theory that the zombie eruption was running out of steam.

They walked across the parking lot and onto the sidewalk that led to the strip of beach that fronted the bay.

"This is nice," Piper said.

"If your definition of *nice* includes murderous heat and humidity and insects."

"You're the one who wanted to walk to the beach."

"That's true."

"That's okay. I'm happy to walk to the beach with you." She took his arm. "You're wonderful."

They didn't get to the beach.

As they were approaching the old folks' rec center, zombies began to emerge from it. They filled the sidewalk and spilled over onto the grass, forming a barrier two or three zombies deep and extending from the rec center building into the street.

"Oh, shit," Jerry said.

"Maybe they're slow and stupid and dull, like my father," Piper said. "Let's find out." Pulling Jerry along, she walked determinedly toward the line of formerly dead Floridians.

"Some day," Jerry said, "I must tell you how deeply I loathe Florida."

"Not now," Piper said.

As they got closer to the wall of zombies, Jerry and Piper slowed to a stop. They were about five feet away from the zombie barricade. They looked at the zombies, and the zombies looked at them.

Then one of the zombies began to walk toward them. It opened its mouth wide as it came. Jerry could see daylight through the a hole at the back of the creature's head. Others began to move. Soon the whole line was advancing on Jerry and Piper, mouths open, hands reaching for them.

"Oh, shit," Jerry said. "Come on!" He grabbed Piper's hand and turned and ran, dragging her with him.

His panic infected her, and she started running. Given her far higher level of fitness, that meant that she was dragging him while he gasped desperately for air.

Eventually, Piper stopped and looked back. "I think we're okay now," she said, breathing quite normally. "They're far behind, and they've stopped moving." She shaded her eyes and stared. "I think they're looking at the sun."

Jerry stood bent over, his hands on his knees, trying to breathe.

"Is that what it looks like to you?" Piper asked.

Jerry waved his hand and said nothing because he couldn't speak yet. When he was finally able to talk, he said, "Still think we should spend the night in this part of town?"

"No. You're right. Let's go find a motel."

"I know one where we'll be safe."

They went back to the car, and Jerry drove to the motel he had stayed in during his previous visit.

As they parked in front of the office, Piper grimaced and said, "This is very...downscale."

"It has lots of bright lights, and the doors are very solid."

When they had registered and were in their room with the door locked, Piper looked at the bed with distaste. "I wonder if there's such a thing as zombie bedbugs," she said.

"I wish you hadn't said that."

"The regular ones are bad enough. I bet that mattress is crawling with zombie ones."

"I stayed here before and I didn't catch anything."

"Well...All right, then. You can afford much better. If not, give yourself a raise."

"I'm trying to be a sober, responsible, prudent CEO."

"Oh, boy," Piper said. "That's a serious flaw. I'll have to cure you of that."

"I thought I was wonderful."

"But not perfect. I'm hungry. We could try to find a seafood restaurant, unless you know of one nearby."

He thought regretfully of The Gourmet Pirate. "My favorite one is deep in the heart of zombie territory. It's not very far from my parents' condo."

Piper sighed. "I was looking forward to seafood, but maybe we should try vegetarian. Zombies would avoid vegetarian restaurants, wouldn't they?"

"I've really never considered that question before, but it does make sense."

Piper turned on her laptop, connected to the Internet through the motel's wireless setup, and found a place in Tampa that looked suitable. They drove back to Tampa across the causeway and found the restaurant. They sat by a window looking out over the waters of the bay, talking desultorily, and eating overpriced and tasteless meat substitutes, while Jerry tried not to think about Studley's productions.

Afterwards, they drove around for a long time, looking at the scenery but not really taking it in.

Then they went back to the motel and went to bed early. Both of them fell asleep instantly.

CHAPTER FIFTEEN

In the morning, they drove back again to the condo complex where Jerry's parents...*lived* wasn't the word. Jerry couldn't decide what word to use. Existed? Loomed? Lurked?

He parked in a visitor's slot with the car facing toward his parents' building. "Behold," he said, gesturing toward the sun-blasted, humidity-drenched parking lot glaring white beyond the windshield. "The hellish pathway of despair. The walkway to perdition."

"Aren't you overdoing it?"

"My parents are terrifying, brain-eating zombies. No, I'm not overdoing it. I don't even know why I'm here."

"You have to learn to be more tolerant of other people's faults, Jerry. No one's perfect."

"You are."

She grinned "Really?"

"Well, really close."

"Thank you, Mr. Romantic." She kissed his cheek. "That's okay. I still think you're wonderful. Come on." She opened her door. "I'm going to make friends with your mother today. Really. That's my goal for my first visit here."

"First? Oh, God."

But she had left the car and closed her door, so she didn't hear him.

His mother answered the door, as usual. She hugged Jerry and said, "Hello, dear." She seemed even more substantial than the day before, but Jerry thought he must be imagining that.

Piper said, "Hi! I'm so glad to see you again."

Jerry's mother turned and walked toward the kitchen.

"I'm not going to give up," Piper said to Jerry. "Her reaction to me is strange because she's an IEC."

"Zombie!"

"Zombie."

"And that's not why—Never mind. Let's get this visit over with." He put his arm over Piper's shoulders protectively, and they went to the kitchen.

The stench inside the condo seemed a bit weaker. Jerry wondered if he was getting used to it, as Piper had said she was.

When they got to the kitchen, both of his parents were seated at the kitchen table. Jerry's father was reading the newspaper and Jerry's mother was watching the small kitchen television set that she had always preferred.

A commercial was playing. In the commercial, a slender, attractive woman, a scientist of some sort—you could tell because she was wearing glasses and a crisp, white lab coat—was describing her latest important discovery to a lecture hall filled with other attractive, slender women wearing glasses and crisp, white lab coats and slack-jawed, bewildered men wearing rumpled, off-white lab coats.

"Did you bring the pickles?" his father asked.

"Sorry. I forgot."

His father grunted. "Of course you did. You always forget everything. I don't know what good those big brains of yours are." He stared at Jerry's head for a while and then became aware of Piper, who was clutching Jerry's arm and smiling nervously. He stared at her head for a while, then grunted and turned back to his newspaper.

"How long does it take to drive from here to Piketon?" his mother asked.

"About three days. But I flew this time."

"We're not talking about you," his father said. "We're thinking of renting an RV and driving up there ourselves."

"It's a long drive for someone like you," Jerry said. "Someone who's not young, I mean." Someone who's dead, he thought. What if your hands fall off while you're driving?

"There's something up there we want to see."

"I'll send you pictures. Just tell me what it is."

"No, dear," his mother said. "It's calling to us. We have to see it for ourselves."

"It's...a long drive," Jerry repeated lamely. He was sure that they meant to drive up to the big hole outside Bartle's Drop and jump into it, feeding themselves to the giant screaming earth mother zombie. He didn't know how he knew it, but he was convinced of it. Even though they were brain–eating zombies and they terrified him more now than they had when they were still alive, he didn't want them to do it. He also didn't see how he could stop them.

There was a loud knocking at the front door.

Jerry's father said, "If it's those kids again, tell them we're not giving to any charities. Tell them not to come back." As his wife turned to go, he said, "Wait a minute. I changed my mind. Tell them to come in. I'd like to talk to them." He licked his lips.

Jerry and Piper exchanged looks of alarm.

Jerry's mother left the kitchen. They heard her open the front door and say, "Oh, hello." Then they heard her walking slowly back toward the kitchen. She entered the room, and right behind her came Lily.

"Hi!" Lily said. "We're all together! Isn't this nice? Hi, Piper!"

"Uh, hi," Piper said. "I'm really confused."

"By what?"

"By why you're still alive," Jerry said. "We saw you jump into that hole and get eaten by the giant screaming earth mother zombie." The weirdness of what he had just said echoed in his own ears, and he looked at his parents to see how they were reacting to it. They were both staring at him dully, apparently without any reaction at all.

"Oh, don't be silly," Lily said. "Mother didn't eat me. I was just visiting with her for a while. Also, the great thing is, Mother's no long screaming."

"Huh?" her mother said.

"Not you, Mom," Lily said.

"Well, yeah," Jerry said. "She's well fed now. We saw that."

Lily stared him with narrowed eyes. "You saw things up there in the hills that you shouldn't have. You should stop thinking about them. Wipe them from your mind. From your brain." Her gaze shifted to his forehead.

"Please don't do that," Jerry said.

She smiled and kept staring. Jerry felt more and more nervous. "Mom," he said, "make her stop."

"Huh?" his mother said.

Suddenly, Lily started sniffing the air. She frowned. "They're everywhere, Jerry. You can never rest. Bathroom." She left the kitchen.

Jerry's mother sat back down at the kitchen table. The television set was still on, but it was background noise being ignored by everyone. Both older Morgensterns sat at the table and stared into space.

Jerry caught the word *Arapahoe* and paid attention to the TV. A brief news item was on. It had something to do with Fred Foxtrot and accusations that he was profiting illegally from a giant corporation that had been set up with government funds because of his Spreading the Seeds of Earth Initiative, which had recently been signed into law.

Big surprise, Jerry thought.

Yet another commercial began to play depicting a slender, attractive woman demonstrating vast intelligence and knowledge in contrast with a stupid and sloppy man.

"Mom," Jerry said, "do you mind if I turn that off?"

"Huh?" his mother said.

Jerry clicked the power button on the front of the set. The screen went dark. "That's better," he said.

His father said, "Huh?"

There was a yell from the bathroom. Jerry's parents didn't move. Jerry and Piper ran from the kitchen and down the hall.

Jerry turned the handle of the bathroom door, but it was locked. He knocked on the door. "Lily! Are you okay?"

"She was eaten," Piper whispered. "How can she be okay?"

On the other side of the door, Lily yelled, "Back! Ah hah! Gotcha, you little devils!" Then there was silence.

Jerry knocked again, more tentatively this time.

The lock clicked and the door opened. Lily stood in the opening, smiling. "Don't fuck with Mother," she said.

"Never," Jerry said. "Are you okay?"

"Yep. I'm going to watch television now. Are you two staying here?"

"Elsewhere."

"Hmm. All right." She walked off in the direction of the living room.

"What is going on?" Piper asked.

"Weird stuff. As usual in my family. No, this is weirder than usual. I wish we hadn't come. Let's try to talk to my parents for a while, and then eventually we'll be able to leave. Let's see if we can change our flight to an earlier one—maybe one that leaves this afternoon."

"Their feelings will be hurt. You talk to them. I'll try to talk to Lily. At least she acknowledged my existence."

Jerry grabbed her upper arms. "Be careful!"

Piper smiled. She freed her arms from his grip and put them around his neck. She kissed him and then hugged him quickly. "You're so wonderful." She let go of him and followed Lily.

He didn't feel wonderful at all. He felt utterly bewildered. He couldn't understand what was going on, he had no idea why Lily was still alive, and he didn't know what to do next.

He wondered into the kitchen. His parents were sitting exactly as he had left them, both of them still starting into space.

"Mom, Dad," Jerry said, "I really think we need to talk about this plan of yours to drive up to Arapahoe."

His father turned toward him. For a long while, the old zombie said nothing. Then he said, "Not going Ara–...Ara–...Stay here."

"Well, that's a relief. Are you having some kind of problem talking?"

His mother said, "Huh?"

His father said, "Brains."

A hand grabbed Jerry's arm painfully. He screamed. Then he saw that it was Piper. He pretended that he had been coughing.

"We're leaving. Now," she said. "Come on." She began pulling him from the room.

"Mom, Dad, 'bye," Jerry said. "We're going now."

His father stared at him uncomprehendingly. His mother raised her right hand with apparent difficulty and moved it back and forth slowly in what seemed to be meant as a goodbye gesture. Her little finger fell off.

"Oh, God," Jerry said.

Piper pulled him from the kitchen and down the hallway to the front door. Outside, she kept pulling. They took the elevator down and then walked even faster across the suffocating parking lot.

She didn't stop pulling until they reached the car. Once they were inside with the doors locked, the engine started, and slowly cooling air blowing on their faces, she finally relaxed a bit. "We're going back to the motel to get our luggage and check out," she said. "Then we're going straight to the airport. We'll get the first available flight home. I'll even fly economy class."

"What happened? Did Lily attack you, or something?"

"You won't believe what happened."

"My parents are brain–eating zombies. My sister was eaten by a giant screaming earth mother zombie, and now she's walking around and talking as if nothing happened. I'll believe just about anything."

"Okay. So. I followed her when she said she was going to go into the living room and watch TV. Remember?"

"I remember."

"When I got there, she was sitting in that armchair your father uses. The TV was turned off. She was just sitting there facing toward it. She wasn't moving."

"She was watching the blank screen? Weird."

Piper shook her head. "It was worse than that. Her face was blank. Completely blank."

"Well, that's not surprising. I told you: my parents ate her brains. No wonder her face was blank."

"I don't mean blank as in empty of feeling. I mean blank as in no features. In fact, she didn't even look like a human being. More like a flesh–colored...thing with Lily's clothes sort of draped on it."

"What kind of thing?" This visit had affected Piper more badly than he had realized, Jerry thought.

She waved her arms in frustration as she tried to find the right words. "I mean...I mean...Like a cylinder with a pointy–roundy end where her head should have been."

"Pointy–roundy?"

"Yes! Pointy–roundy! Like the end of an octopus's tentacle."

"Hmm. Well, that's certainly strange."

"You don't believe me."

"It *is* a lot to absorb."

"You promised you'd believe me, and then you didn't." She started crying.

He tried to put his arms around her, but she pushed him away. "Don't do that. Don't touch me. Fuck you." She cried harder. Then she turned to him and flung her arms around his neck. "I'm sorry. I shouldn't have said that. You're wonderful."

"Pseudopod."

"What?"

"Pseudopod. I was trying to think of the word. What you described, it sounds like a pseudopod—a pseudopod of that monster in the hole in the ground in the foothills back home."

"The giant screaming earth mother zombie?"

"Yeah. Unless you know of another monster in a hole in the ground in the foothills. Maybe that's all she is. Maybe that's how she showed up again after being eaten. She's just part of that creature. God, this just keeps getting worse! Is that why you came into the kitchen all panicked like that? Because you saw that pseudopod thing?"

"No. When I saw that, I couldn't move. Not because of fear. It was amazement. I was just frozen in place. I must have gasped or made some other kind of sound. Suddenly the thing changed back into Lily. It just sort of...flowed back into her shape. It was shaped like her, with her proper face, and her arms and legs, and with her hair on top. It looked at me and said, 'Oh, hi, I didn't see you standing there.' Then it stood up and it started walking toward me. It said, 'I didn't give you a hug yet. Let me give you a hug.' *That's* when I came into the kitchen all panicked like that."

Jerry put the car in gear. "This really is the butt crack of Hell. The seafood doesn't make up for it."

"I want to go home."

He backed out of the parking space. "Absolutely. We'll be safe there."

No, we won't, he told himself. We'll be even closer to the giant screaming earth mother zombie. This must be the end of the world.

CHAPTER SIXTEEN

Despite himself, and to his own surprise, after they got back to Piketon, Jerry found himself so immersed in trying to increase sales for Piper's Pickled Peppers that he didn't worry about the end of the world.

Things had changed in his hometown during the few days of his absence. Now, when he left the office and went for a walk in downtown Piketon, he saw more zombies again. Fortunately, they were dull and stupid, and so they longer frightened him. But now and then he would pass someone on the street, a stranger, someone he had never seen before, who would give him a knowing look and a conspiratorial smile, someone who looked like a perfectly normal, living human being, and he would know that it was a zombie. No, he suddenly realized one day, not a zombie: an extension, a pseudopod of the giant screaming earth mother zombie. The thing in Florida that looked like Lily was not unique.

Worst of all was when one of those creatures, those pseudopodia, while passing him, would say softly, "Hello, Jerry."

What were they up to? How did they know his name? Why didn't they attack him?

Maybe, he thought, the giant screaming earth mother zombie has developed intelligence and these pseudopodia are extensions of its brain as well as its body. Maybe some part of Lily's brain survived in the giant creature. That must be the case, considering that the pseudopod that had looked like her in his parents' condo had seemed to know everything the real Lily had known. So maybe the underground monster had family feelings toward him. Which, he thought, would actually make it morally superior to the late real Lily. He felt immediately guilty for thinking that.

Maybe the creature was just toying with him, amusing itself. Maybe it was trying to drive him crazy, either for pleasure or in order to learn more about human nature. If so, it was succeeding. Every day, he felt closer to the edge of insanity.

The creepiness factor of the pseudopodia smiling knowingly at him and saying his name in their soft voices increased every day. He realized that during his walk through downtown between the office and the bus stop, he welcomed the sight of actual zombies. He felt safe around them. He liked seeing them standing stupidly on the sidewalk, staring up at the sun. He experienced increasingly warm feelings toward them. When he saw someone he thought was a pseudopod of the giant screaming earth mother zombie, he tried to adjust his path so as to keep a brainless zombie between him and it. When he did that, he wanted to say thank you to the zombie. He never did so because that would have been just too creepy.

He wondered where Walter Zing was and if the scientist was really doing anything to save mankind. He also wondered how he could possibly be thinking of Walter Zing as a savior. He could see no evidence of salvation from that quarter.

One morning, as Jerry walked toward the office, a pseudopod stepped in his way.

It looked like a middle-aged man, slightly overweight, balding. It smiled at him.

Jerry stopped walking and stood tensely. This was it! The giant screaming earth mother zombie had lost interest in whatever game it had been playing with him, and now it—or one of its pseudopodia, anyway—was going to eat him.

Jerry looked around quickly. There didn't seem to be any other pseudopodia nearby. Maybe he could make a run for it.

"Hey, Jerry," the pseudopod said. "Watch this."

Astonished, Jerry forgot about running and watched.

The pseudopod turned away and pointed toward one of the dry, cracking, flaking zombies standing silently nearby, face upturned to the sun, eyes closed, a happy smile on its face. At least, the creature wore what Jerry thought was a smile. It was hard to tell since it had so little face. An almost naked skull gleamed in the bright sunlight it seemed to be enjoying.

"Come to Mama," the pseudopod said.

The zombie lowered its gaze and bent its empty eye sockets at the pseudopod. "Oookaaay," it said slowly in a muffled, cracked voice. It was like the sound of pieces of dry leather being rubbed together.

The pseudopod pointed toward the curb. The zombie shuffled creakily across the sidewalk and stopped when it reached the edge.

"Step down into the gutter," the pseudopod said.

The zombie stepped carefully off the curb into the gutter. To Jerry, its movements looked painful. He wondered if its joints were breaking down despite the sunshine.

"Bend down and look into the storm drain," the pseudopod said.

The zombie didn't move.

"Bend down!" the pseudopod said sharply.

The zombie turned its fleshless face toward Jerry. Jerry thought he read fear and an appeal in the empty eye sockets. He told himself he must be imagining it.

The pseudopod spoke again, in a still louder and more commanding tone. "Bend down! Look into the storm drain!"

The zombie moaned. Slowly, awkwardly, its knees and hips bent until it was sitting on its haunches. Tiny particles of skin and flesh floated down from it like gray snow. It put its hands on the concrete of the gutter and lowered itself until its face was level with the opening of the storm drain. It uttered a sigh, or possibly a sob.

A half-dozen thin, white strings began extending from the storm drain. They waved slowly in the air. Jerry had the impression that they were looking around, or perhaps sniffing the air, searching for something. He thought that there was something leisurely about their movements, as though they knew there was no need to hurry.

These was the same things he had seen in the foothills, waving in the air above the giant hole Frank Pistole's zombie army had dug. How could the giant screaming earth mother zombie have extended its tentacles this far? Or had it extended itself? Had it managed to grow through the earth, through the underground watercourses, through the sewers? How big was it?

Slowly, gently, irresistibly, the tentacles slid around the shivering zombie—shivering, but apparently unable to break the spell and get out of the way. They wrapped around and around him, and then it was too late for him, even if he had been able to move.

They flipped him onto his side and began dragged him toward the drain.

He was too big to fit through the drain opening.

Jerry turned away from the scene. The other zombies on the sidewalk were watching the action. They seemed unable to tear their dull gazes away from what was happening. Jerry thought he saw horror and fear in their faces, but he didn't see how that could be the case with such horrible, fearful creatures.

Jerry couldn't see any other human beings. He seemed to be alone with the zombies and the pseudopod and the tentacles.

"I'm going to work now," he announced.

"Not yet," the pseudopod said. "Keep watching."

It was a command Jerry was unable to resist. The pseudopod's voice controlled him even more completely than the voice of Piper's dead mother had been able to. He turned back and watched.

Nothing had changed during the few seconds when Jerry hadn't been watching. The zombie lay motionless on his side up against the storm drain opening with white tentacles wrapped around him, just as before. Now that Jerry was looking again, movement began.

More tentacles emerged from the drain and wrapped themselves around the zombie. The zombie, freed from the spell that had controlled him, began to squirm weakly. It did no good.

The tentacles tightened. Jerry heard cracking sounds. The zombie made a strange whining sound and then stopped struggling. The powerful tentacles squeezed and pulled, and the zombie elongated and became thinner.

Jerry observed it all with detachment. He felt like a dull zombie himself. He thought that if the zombie had been a living human, there would have been a lot of blood. He was glad that there wasn't.

Eventually, the zombie was slender enough to fit through the drain. The tentacles pulled him through the opening, and he disappeared.

"Show's over," the pseudopod said. He grinned at Jerry. "Cool, huh? You should go to work, now."

"Yes," Jerry said mechanically. "You're right. Thank you for the show."

He walked away at his normal walking pace—neither hurrying in panic or shuffling along the way the zombies did. His mind was blank.

After a couple of blocks, the pseudopod's mental control over him faded away. Or perhaps the pseudopod released him from its hold at that point. Full awareness suddenly returned, along with panic.

Jerry spun around. No one was following him. He could still see the crowd of zombies two blocks away, but the sidewalk around him was empty. He shivered in horror and resumed walking toward his office, rapidly now.

The pseudopodia were toying with him. That one could have made him feed himself to the tentacles in the storm drain. They're toying with me, he thought, or they have some reason for not killing me. This isn't the end of the world. It's more like the day after the end of the world.

It could have been even worse, Jerry told himself. The giant screaming earth mother zombie was stealing the identities of the dead. He wondered how he'd feel if he encountered a smirking pseudopod that looked and sounded and acted like George. He wondered how Piper would feel. Thank God she had the poor guy cremated, he thought. And also that the ashes aren't in the ground, where the giant screaming earth mother zombie might find them.

Although, he thought, now that the creature is sending out these extensions of itself that are the size of human beings, what's to stop it from grabbing the urn containing George's ashes from the Heavenly Memories Garden of Rest?

Oh, crap, he said to himself. Why did you have to think of that?

By the time Jerry reached the office, he was yearning for mindless, excessive work to drive what he had seen from his mind.

His wish was granted. As he was crossing the open space between the elevator and the door of his office—a light, open, inviting space, now that Frank was no longer there—a figure sprang up from the one of the couches and said, "Boss! I've been waiting for you!" It was Myron Henderson.

Myron had started out as the replacement for the stupid kid from the mailroom whom George had sent into Frank's office with a pickle. He had ascended from the mailroom almost immediately and had continued to rise in the company.

"Don't call me boss," Jerry said mechanically.

"Sir!"

Jerry sighed. "What's up, Myron?"

"Orders are up, sir!"

Jerry stopped walking. "Really? That's good news. I wonder what happened."

"Well, I mean one order, sir. One big order. Look at this. It was just faxed in."

Jerry took the sheet from his hand. It was a huge order for pickled peppers—about half as many jars of pickled peppers as the company currently produced in a year.

Must be some kind of weird hoax, Jerry thought. Maybe it's a trick by a competitor.

He looked at the company name at the top of the sheet. "The Spreader Corporation," he muttered. The logo was a capital S inside an oval, all done in shades of green. "I've never heard of them," he said. "What do they do? Make those gadgets that spread grass seeds? And why would they want so many pickled peppers? Check them out. See if they're legit."

"I already did, sir. They're legit. Mysterious, but legit. The company's only a month old. They've been ordering lots of different things from a number of companies lately. They pay up front, and their checks don't bounce."

"Up front?"

"Look there." Myron pointed at the bottom of the sheet where it said in bold, capital letters PAYMENT UPON ACCEPTANCE OF ORDER.

"Damn," Jerry said. "Hell, we'll need that money to expand our facilities and start another shift. Myron, this is just the shot in the arm we needed."

"I know it is, sir!"

"Tell them the money is non–refundable."

"You bet. Say, Boss, would you like me to handle all of this for you? I'd be happy to work with Facilities and HR on starting up another shift. I'll also talk to the Spreader people about the time we'll need to marinate all those pickles. Oh, and I'll see about getting the new supplies ordered."

Jerry laughed. "You're really ambitious, aren't you, Myron?"

"I sure am, Boss!"

"All right. You're in charge of this account. I dub thee Sir Myron of Spreader. Go forth and spread. I'll figure out some kind of raise."

"Cool! Thank you, Boss!" Myron rushed away to the staircase that led down to the peon levels. He disappeared as the stairway door closed behind him. He always took the staircase. The elevator was too slow for him.

What a putz, Jerry thought. I shouldn't complain. Corporations are built on putzes like him. And he is taking on a bunch of work that I'd rather not do myself.

Buoyed up, Jerry went into his office, where he spent some time browsing the Web and playing solitaire just because he could and no one dared say anything to him about it. Except Piper, of course, but she wasn't there.

A couple of relaxing hours later, he realized that no one had disturbed him, he felt much better than before, and he hadn't thought of pseudopodia, tentacles, or storm drains in all that time.

As the days and then weeks passed, Jerry thought about the pseudopodia, the tentacles, and the storm drain less and less often until he never thought about them at all. Not during the day, at least. All three showed up in terrible dreams that he was fortunate enough not to remember after he woke up.

Piper's Pickled Peppers, Inc. was buzzing with activity these days. The company was now renting office space on some of the lower floors of the building and negotiating for even more space. The order from The Spreader Corporation seemed to have had a magical influence on the rest of the world. Orders were coming in from everywhere. Jerry could imagine himself presiding over a company that occupied all fifteen floors of the current building.

Maybe I should think about buying the whole building, he thought. We could rename it. Piper Tower. Piper Spire.

Maybe I should be worrying about what happens when we finally run out of the secret ingredient, he thought.

Maybe you should try to enjoy life for a change and stop fretting, he told himself.

Myron Henderson had to visit the fifteenth floor so often to report to Jerry or to confer with him that Jerry moved him into a big office of his own on the top floor. Myron had become indispensable. He had also started to look around Jerry's office with a proprietary air whenever he was in there.

Some day, Jerry thought, I'm going to have to feed that kid to a zombie.

Some day in the future. For now, Myron was working hyperkinetically, Jerry was working less, and the company was booming. Jerry was able to spend more time away from the office, more time at home, in the big, new house in Redland Heights that Piper had insisted they buy so that they could leave "your ratty little apartment."

That would have meant more time with Piper if Piper hadn't continued to spend her days at the gym. Ah, but the results of those hours at the gym! Jerry assured himself that he should have no complaints.

He had never discussed Myron with Piper, but she seemed to

have picked up on his distrust of his indispensable subordinate. She visited the office rarely, and on some of those occasions, she encountered Myron. She never passed up an opportunity to insult him, sneering at his enthusiasm, his mannerism of speaking with exclamation marks, and his youth. Once she asked him if he needed a towel so that he could wipe away the wetness behind his ears.

Jerry was touched by her loyalty, although he worried that one day Myron would tire of her insults and quit the company. Fortunately, Myron's response was always to smile politely and rush back to work.

It was the middle of the week, and Jerry was at home in the middle of the day.

He had told his staff that he would be working at home. In fact, he was surfing the Web, playing Solitaire, staring out the window, wishing Piper were there, and forcing himself to sip from a large glass of expensive single-malt scotch. He hated the stuff, but he felt he ought to learn to like it. It seemed appropriate to his position. The giant television set was showing a documentary about World War One. It was depressing and awful, and it suited Jerry's mood perfectly.

The front doorbell rang.

Jerry set the glass down with a feeling of relief and went downstairs to answer the door. Piper had wanted a butler, but Jerry had put his foot down at that. He had put it down a bit hesitantly, a bit timidly, but he had put it down. When the bell rang, they answered the door themselves. Actually, Jerry was always the one who answered it. Piper was willing to allow that, but she refused to answer the door herself.

Jerry opened the door. Walter Zing stood on the front porch.

"Let me in!" Zing hissed. He looked around nervously.

Jerry stood aside, and Zing scurried into the house.

Jerry stepped outside and looked around. He saw nothing suspicious. He shrugged and went back in, closing the door behind him.

"Can you trust your servants?"

"We don't have any."

"Really? In a place this size? I'm surprised Piper agreed to that."

"She agreed because I promised I'd do everything myself."

"My goodness. Including the dusting and vacuuming?"

"Of course."

Zing looked at the floor. "Hmm. Perhaps you should consider hiring someone for that job."

"You came here to criticize my housekeeping?"

"Oh, no. Of course not. I came here to show you something."

"Okay. Go ahead."

"I can't show you here. We have to go downtown."

"Why didn't you call me and have me meet you downtown?"

Zing frowned. "That's very clever of you, Jerry. It hadn't occurred to me. In any case, I have to be careful. We'll take your car."

Jerry had no wish to go downtown. He had every wish to stay where he was. "Are you in danger?"

"Oh, yes, indeed. The humanoid extensions are looking for me constantly. They want to kill me. They seem to be able to find me no matter where I go."

"Humanoid extensions," Jerry muttered. "Oh, you mean the pseudopodia."

"Pseudopodia!" Zing said delightedly. "That's excellent. I'll call them that from now on. Very good, Jerry. And let me congratulate you on the site of your house, as well."

"Well, yeah, the view's pretty good." It's much better when Piper's part of the view, he thought.

"Oh, I'm not talking about the view. I meant the underground watercourses. Or rather, the lack of them. The creature in the foothills has no natural pathway to reach you here. You must have investigated carefully before moving in here."

Jerry's knees felt weak. "I didn't even think of that! Piper chose this place. I think it was because of the number of bedrooms and bathrooms and closets and stuff like that." He thought of the tentacles that had emerged from the storm drain and captured the zombie. "I should have thought of that. But it wouldn't matter anyway, though, would it? The giant screaming earth mother zombie can travel through the sewers, so it could come right up through the toilet. Oh, God. I'll never be able to use the toilet again."

"That hardly seems practical. You do raise an interesting point, though. So you still call the creature the giant screaming..."

"The giant screaming earth mother zombie. You know, because it's giant, and Lily said it was screaming, and—"

"Yes, yes." Zing waved his hand. "I get it. That's a rather cumbersome name, though, don't you think?"

I think this is another one of those very strange conversations, Jerry thought. "Yeah, I guess it is," he said.

"But you're on the right track," Zing said. "Don't give up. Let me see...We could use the initials. SEMZ. Semz. You know, I like that!"

"What about the G? The 'giant' part?"

"Gsemz?" Zing shook his head. "No, I'm sorry. That just doesn't work. Semz it is. As you know, proper nomenclature is very important in science. I haven't decided on the proper scientific name for the creature yet."

It occurred to Jerry that if he could lead Zing sufficiently off track and deeper into his world of science, he might forget all about going downtown. "It has a scientific name?"

"It will, once all this is over and I have time to work on a paper about it. But that's in the future. Right now, we have to go downtown."

Jerry sighed. "My car's in the back."

"Does the driveway go all the way around the house? It looks like it does."

"Yes."

"What a nice design. I'd better park my car behind your house to keep it out of the sight of the pseudopodia."

"How would they recognize your car?" Jerry asked.

Zing was already on the way out and hadn't heard him. "I'll meet you behind the house," he called out.

Grumbling to himself because he had no one else to grumble to, Jerry locked the front door behind Zing and then crossed the house and went out through the back door. One of the few things he liked about the house Piper had chosen was that, despite its size, it had only one door in the front and one in the back. Having only two ways for zombies to get in made him feel safer.

Zing was pulling around the house as Jerry was locking the rear door behind himself. The car was unfamiliar to Jerry, but not so the license plate. It read BT STUD.

Zing got out of his car. "Is that your car over there, Jerry? Let's go. Why are you smiling?"

"Nervousness. I smile when I'm nervous. I was thinking about the mysterious ability of the pseudopodia to find you."

"They're fiendishly intelligent, positively fiendish. I suppose I should say that Semz is fiendishly intelligent, since the pseudopodia are merely its extensions."

Jerry thought about white tentacles slithering through sewers and up through toilets and stopped smiling. "Yeah, let's go."

They went.

CHAPTER SEVENTEEN

Jerry exited the freeway at Kennedy Drive and then turned east onto River Drive. "We're getting close," he said. "Where exactly did you want to go."

"Oh, anywhere," Zing said. "Just downtown. That's where the pseudopodia seem to cluster."

"Wait a minute. They're chasing you. They want to kill you. You're running from them. And now you want to find them deliberately."

"Yes. Exactly. Isn't science super?"

"What does this have to do with science?"

"You'll see."

"I don't want to see," Jerry muttered.

He pulled into a parking lot and was lucky enough to find an open space despite it being the middle of the working day. They got out and Jerry put enough money into the appropriate slot in the big, yellow box to let his car stay where it was until midnight.

That's weird, he thought. I'm worried about the car getting towed away when I'm heading into the heart of downtown to get myself killed and I won't be back to get my car. I hope Piper will mourn for me longer than she did for poor George.

"Okay," he said to Zing. "Let's step boldly forth."

"I think a cautious approach would be better," Zing said.

It was around noon. People were walking by, jostling each other on the sidewalk, and the street to their right was full of traffic. Jerry couldn't see much point in caution. He wasn't even sure how to be cautious. He tried nonetheless. He kept looking from side to side, and occasionally he would turn around and look behind him. Everyone he saw looked perfectly normal, and no one seemed to be paying any attention to them.

"I don't see any sign of pseudopodia," he said.

Zing held a finger to his lips. "You will," he whispered. "They're everywhere."

"I think you mean 'almost everywhere,'" Jerry said. "They're obviously not really everywhere because, you know." He sliced his hand through the air in front of him, demonstrating that there were no pseudopodia occupying that space.

Zing frowned. "Hmm. You're right, of course. That's an excellent observation. I can see why you were addicted to my television show."

"Uh, huh," Jerry said.

The pedestrian traffic was becoming heavier and the storefronts were becoming more crowded together.

"Well, this is pretty much downtown," Jerry said. "We can keep going, but it won't get any downtowner."

Zing grabbed Jerry's arm. "I think we're downtown enough," Zing said. His voice trembled.

Suddenly, almost magically, the human pedestrians had disappeared. Jerry and Zing were surrounded by a circle of pseudopodia. The one who had forced Jerry to watch the zombie being destroyed by the tentacles had worn a bland expression. It hadn't looked friendly, but neither had it looked menacing. These pseudopodia all looked terrifying.

Jerry and Zing stood uncertainly, wanting to run but not seeing any chance of breaking through the encircling creatures.

"Zing!" the pseudopodia all said in one low, hoarse voice. The name seemed to run around the circle like a long echo. “Zzzziiiinnnngggg!”

Then there was silence. Even the traffic had vanished from the street.

Ahead of them, a manhole cover in the sidewalk rose up and slid sideways with a heavy, grating sound. Thin white tentacles arose from the dark opening and rose high into the air above them.

Jerry knew what came next. He hoped it wouldn’t be too horribly painful and that it wouldn’t last long. He closed his eyes.

One of the pseudopodia said, “Bring me Zing!” The rest of them laughed simultaneously and maniacally.

Jerry decided he had to see that. He opened his eyes, but by now they were all silent. “Did you guys have to practice that for a long time?” he asked.

The pseudopodia ignored him. They were focused on Zing.

“Watch this, Jerry,” Zing said.

He put his hand in his trousers pocket and pulled out a test tube with a rubber stopper in its opening. He raised his arm and threw the test tube down onto the sidewalk. The glass shattered.

The tentacles whipped down toward Zing.

Just before they touched him, their ends shriveled and dropped off. The tentacles retreated. They waved wildly in the air. Jerry could see them shriveling from their tips back along their bodies. In a few seconds, the tentacles had vanished entirely.

The pseudopodia made a loud, incoherent noise and rushed forward. Then they stopped. In one voice, they howled. Starting with the ones closest to Jerry and Zing, and progressing back through the crowd, they shivered, wavered, lost their human shape, and collapsed, melting down into piles of multicolored glop. The glop began to evaporate in the strong sunlight.

Zing nodded. “Excellent.”

Jerry waited for his heart rate to slow back to normal. Then he said, "Did you do that to them?"

Zing smiled happily. "Indeed I did. Rather, I should say that Studley did it to them. A very special Studley. That's what was in that test tube. It's a version I perfected only this morning. So I rushed over to get you so that we could test it."

"That was the test? *You hadn't tested it before?* Are you crazy?"

"I knew it would work. Studley does what I ask of him."

"Great. Give him a medal."

"I can't," Zing said sadly, looking down at the sidewalk. "They're all dead now. All those Studleys."

"You made a weapon that works against the pseudopodia and those tentacles, and then you destroyed it? Wonderful."

"Not at all. I tested the weapon, and now I must mass produce it. I could only make a small quantity at the facilities I have where I've been hiding. Now I need much bigger facilities."

"I'm all for that. Turn those Studleys out by the millions."

"I already did." Zing pointed at the sidewalk. "Now we'll need billions. Trillions. More than that."

"So how're you going to produce them in those numbers?"

"That's why I wanted you along for the test. It was really a demonstration. You're the only person I trust, Jerry. Well, you and my hardy band of followers and Grizzy, of course. You're going to convert part of the Piper's Pickled Peppers factory into a production facility for me."

There's a bizarre kind of balance and symmetry to that idea, Jerry thought. "We're getting very low on the secret ingredient," he said.

"You're bargaining about saving the world?" Zing said. "I'm very disappointed in you."

"I have become a soulless CEO."

Zing stared at him for a moment. "You do remind me a bit of Frank in his younger days. All right, then. You let me use your factory to produce the new Studleys, and I'll also tackle the problem of the secret ingredient supply."

"Does Griselda support you in this fight against the giant screaming earth mother zombie? I thought she was going away with you in wedded bliss."

"Grizzy sees Semz as her rival. In their own way, each of them wants me." Zing smiled. "It's rather sweet, don't you think?"

"I think that either way, the ending doesn't look promising for you."

"Pessimists don't save the world, Jerry. When can we get started? I have a lot of work ahead of me."

"Right away, I guess. We're downtown anyway. We might as well go over to the office and I can start setting things up for you."

"Which way? Let's go!" Zing was bouncing up and down with eagerness.

"Back to the car, of course."

"Can't we walk? How far is it?"

"Not far, but I'm not willing to encounter any more of the pseudopodia or those tentacles while I'm with you. We'll drive. I have my own reserved space in the underground parking garage nowadays. It's good to be the king."

Zing puffed out his chest. "Did you hear their howl of despair when they realized that they had met their match? They'll keep their distance now!"

"Walter, they're not afraid of you. They might be afraid of your Studleys. Do you have any more test tubes full of them in your pockets?"

Zing's chest collapsed again. "Well, no. That was the only one in existence so far. Perhaps we should return to your car and drive."

"Yeah."

"It's a nice car, by the way. Quite expensive and luxurious. And quite a step up from the old rattletrap you were driving before."

"Uh huh." It's good to be the king, Jerry thought, but it's even better to be the queen.

Ever since he had started using the space reserved in the underground parking garage for the president of Piper's Pickled Peppers—what he thought of as the Big Cheese Space—Jerry had felt more than ever like a poseur. He always half expected uniformed guards to spring out of hiding and arrest him for illegally parking in the space reserved for the actual PPP big cheese. This time, and for the first time, as he pulled in and turned off the smoothly purring engine of his absurdly overpriced new car, he wasn't thinking about that at all. He wasn't even thinking about Piper's horrified reaction a month earlier when he had suggested that he buy a used version of the car instead of a new one. Instead, he was thinking that the underground parking garage must be close to the water table and natural underground water courses and unnatural ones such as sewer lines.

He hurried Zing away from the car and to the elevator, looking around nervously all the while. Once the elevator door closed behind them and he felt the car rising, Jerry relaxed. He was safe at last.

"Have you ever watched construction workers putting up a building like this?" Zing asked.

"Sure."

"It's fascinating, isn't it? I admire the way they put up the central core first. That would be the elevator shaft, like the one we're in. It also contains the stairwells. I've always wondered if all the electrical lines and water and sewage lines are in that core, too. Do you suppose they are? They'd be right out there"—he knocked on the wall of the elevator car—"next to us. Intriguing thought."

Jerry saw tentacles writhing up the pipes right beyond the wall, and he moaned. "We're not going to be safe from that monster anywhere."

"Which monster?"

"The giant screaming earth mother zombie."

"Ah. Semz. Possibly not. That's why we have to get my production line up and running right away."

The elevator door opened, revealing the pleasant waiting area of the fifteenth floor. It looked peaceful and safe. Jerry knew that was an illusion. No place was safe.

He led the way to Myron Henderson's office. "Boss!" Myron said in surprise. He sprang to his feet and came around his desk. "I thought you were taking the day off. I mean working at home."

"Don't call me boss. Myron, this is, um, Ferdinand Archduke. He's going to be working on a special project for me. It's a new way to, um, make our pickled peppers even more irresistible."

"Cool, Boss! Sir!" He stuck his hand out. "It's great to meet you, Mr. Archduke."

They shook hands.

Myron said, "You look kind of familiar. Have we met before?"

Zing brightened. "You're young, but did you ever see the old television show—"

Jerry grabbed Zing's upper arm and squeezed so hard that the scientist yelped. "You have never met him before, Myron."

"His name sounds familiar."

"No, it doesn't. You've never heard it before."

"Okay, Boss."

"Good. So. We're running two shifts now, right?"

"Right, boss. Even with that, we're at capacity. If we could snag another customer like Spreader Corporation, we'd need a third shift.

Twenty–four seven! Wouldn't that be great?"

Jerry shook his head. "Third shift will be Dr.—I mean Mr. Archduke and his staff. They'll be using our facilities then."

"What's third shift?" Zing asked.

"Graveyard," Jerry said.

"Night shift," Myron said. "Midnight to eight a.m."

Zing looked shocked. "That's inhuman!"

Jerry stared at him, willing him to stop talking. "Well, that's what all of this is really about, isn't it, Ferd?"

"Ferd," Zing repeated with a look of distaste.

Myron said, "Mr. Archduke, can you let me know how many workers you'll need? And their qualifications? Also, I'll need a list of equipment you want installed. And of course Mr. Morgenstern will have to approve all the expenses."

"Approved," Jerry said.

"I'll be using my own staff," Zing said. "You've already met them, Jerry."

Jerry thought about the group of Zing's supporters he had encountered in the mountains after escaping from the giant screaming earth mother zombie, and he quailed at the thought of them being humanity's last, best hope. "Right. What about equipment?"

"We'll take care of that," Zing said. "I would like to look the place over first."

"Myron's your man for that," Jerry said. He preferred to avoid the factory. "Myron, why don't you take him over there now?"

"Sure thing, Boss. Let me take care of a few things first. I'll meet you down in the parking garage in about fifteen minutes, Mr. Archduke."

"No need to be formal," Zing said. "Please call me W—"

"Call him Mr. Archduke," Jerry interrupted. "Let's keep it formal. Ferd, let's go to my office and chat for a few minutes."

When they were in Jerry's office and he had closed the door, he said to Zing, "For God's sake, remember your fake name."

"Hmph. Why do I have to have a fake name?"

"We can't trust anyone. Even if we can trust Myron, what happens if he gets his brain eaten by a zombie and then the zombie gets absorbed into the giant screaming earth mother zombie?"

"Semz," Zing said. "Well, so what?"

"Then the pseudopodia would know everything he knows. That seems to be how it works. That's what happened when the giant screaming earth mother zombie ate my sister."

"Semz. So?"

"So they'd know where you are. The pseudopodia. The tentacles."

"Oh. Ah. All right. But why didn't you let me choose my own pseudonym?"

"It was a spur of the moment thing. We didn't discuss it ahead of time."

"When I was a boy, I wanted to be Roy Rogers. You could tell Myron that you made a mistake and my name is actually, um, Rogers Roy."

"Oh, yeah, that wouldn't make him suspicious at all. No. You're stuck with Ferdinand Archduke. Ferd to your friends."

"It sounds so silly."

"You're right. Let's go down to the parking garage."

Downstairs in the parking garage, when Myron emerged from the elevator, Jerry said to him, "It occurs to me that we're going to need guards at the factory during the third shift. Actually, for all three shifts. A lot of guards."

"But we don't have any guards there now, Boss. I mean, except for the ones in charge of that special inner room."

"The inner room contains a trade secret. That's why we have those guards there. What Mr. Archduke and his people will be working on is an even greater and more valuable secret. There are people who will want to get inside and steal it if they find out it's there. Dangerous people. Very dangerous people."

"Our competitors are a pretty mild-mannered bunch, Boss."

"These are a different bunch. They're not mild-mannered at all. They're...Middle Eastern, Moslem, terrorist, start-up pickle makers who are experts at disguise."

Myron's eyes grew wide. "Wow! We'd better hire some really tough guys, then!"

"With no scruples."

"And really big guns!" Myron licked his lips. "Cool!"

"See to it. We're all depending on you."

Myron almost saluted. "Yes, sir! Mr. Archduke, my car's this way. Don't worry about a thing, Mr. Archduke. I'm on the job. I'm *always* on the job."

Zing gave Jerry an annoyed glance and then followed Myron away across the parking garage.

Jerry sighed in relief. Suddenly, he had no confidence in Zing. He didn't believe that the scientist could manufacture his new Studleys in sufficient quantity or in time. Even if he could, Jerry didn't see how he could broadcast the little devils widely enough to kill off all the pseudopodia. And even if he could do that, there was still the matter of the giant screaming earth mother zombie itself.

The world is doomed, Jerry thought. We're all going to be eaten by that thing eventually. Might as well just accept it. I'll try to enjoy the time that's left. Maybe Piper's home early from the gym.

Whistling, feeling strangely light and free because of his acceptance of the inevitability of doom, he went to his car and drove home.

Unfortunately, Piper wasn't there. Fortunately, cold beer was.

CHAPTER EIGHTEEN

Walter Zing e-mailed regular progress reports to Jerry at the end of each week. They were usually one sentence long and said things like "This week, successfully synthesized REDACTED" or "Produced REDACTED grams of REDACTED." Jerry deleted the e-mails.

After a few weeks of this and growing frustration, Jerry summoned Myron Henderson to his office to see if he knew anything.

"One time, I tried to get in there during third shift to inspect things, Boss," he said, "and they wouldn't let me in. The same guards I hired! They stopped me! With guns and passwords and electronic communications and everything. It was cool."

"So you didn't find anything out?"

"Not about what was happening inside the plant during third shift, but the commander of the guards told me they've stopped a few attempts at infiltration."

"Really?" Jerry felt alarmed, nervous, and sick to his stomach at this news.

"He said they looked just like real Americans. Man, those Moslem, terrorist, start-up pickle makers really are masters of disguise. Just like you said!"

"So what happened? No one told me about this. Did they turn them over to the police?"

"Negatory, boss. They shot 'em."

"Shot them!"

"They didn't want to bother you about it. I told them how busy you are. Yep," he nodded, "shot 'em. He said they disappeared right away. He said it was almost like they dissolved or something."

Jerry shivered in fear. Those damned pseudopodia! The guards had only been a precaution. Jerry hadn't really expected the pseudopodia to find Zing. How had they tracked him down? At Jerry's orders, Zing had obtained new license plates. That should have helped keep him hidden. Belatedly, Jerry realized that the pseudopodia had probably infiltrated the Department of Motor Vehicles. They've probably infiltrated all government agencies, he thought, from Federal all the way down to local. That would have made it easy for them to find out what Zing's new license plate was, and then they could easily have followed his car to the pickle factory.

They haven't done anything yet, though, he thought. They could probably get inside easily enough. They could kill someone like Myron and replace him with a pseudopod.

He stared hard at Myron, who looked back at him expectantly while bouncing from one foot to the other.

If Myron has been replaced, Jerry thought, how would I be able to tell?

"Well, tell them to stay on the lookout," Jerry said. "These guys are really dangerous. The guards did the right thing. Shoot to kill."

When will the tentacles appear in the men's room? he asked himself. Sprouting right out of the urinal! Jerry squeezed his thighs together protectively.

What are they waiting for? he wondered.

They *are* waiting, he realized. They didn't kill me downtown when they had the chance, and they're not doing anything now. They need me for something. Or they need the factory. Maybe they don't know what Zing is working on. If they ever find out, they'll probably just kill all of us, no matter what they want this place for.

I think I need to find out just what kind of progress Zing has made, he thought.

"Myron, would you please go over to the factory and tell Mr. Archduke to come to my house this evening to give me a progress report?"

Myron looked puzzled. "Why don't I just call him and tell him to e–mail it to you, boss?"

"Good God, man! Have you no idea how fiendishly ingenious these Moslem terrorist pickle makers are? They've probably hacked into our phones and e–mails accounts."

Myron's eyes widened. "Wow! Okay, Boss. I'll go over there right away."

"Thanks." He's not a pseudopod, Jerry thought. They couldn't duplicate that.

Three hours later, Walter Zing showed up in Jerry's office.

"What are you doing here?" Jerry asked him. "You're all exposed. Where are your guards?"

"Calm yourself, Jerry. Our troubles are over. I brought this." He held up a gallon plastic bottle labeled Distilled Water.

"I assume that's not distilled water."

"It's Studleys. New and improved Studleys. These are even better than the ones I used before. And there are many, many more of them back in the factory. I believe we have enough of them now to—" he coughed modestly "—save the world."

"We go outside and sprinkle them on the pseudopodia? Like what the hero in a vampire movie does with holy water?"

"I have no idea. I've never seen a movie about vampires. But, no. This is much better and more powerful. You see, I hypothesize that Semz controls the pseudopodia by means of telepathic control via its tentacles. So rather than bothering to attack the pseudopodia, I intend to pour this jar full of Studleys into the water supply. That will destroy the tentacles that must have infiltrated the plumbing and sewer systems of the city. That in turn will destroy the pseudopodia."

"You hypothesize?"

"We don't have time for the kind of careful, thorough, rigorous testing I would prefer. Sometimes, science involves taking risks."

"And if it doesn't work?"

"Back to the drawing board," Zing said cheerfully.

"How do we start? Do we have to go to wherever the main water treatment plant is for Piketon and dump the Studleys in there?"

"Eventually, yes. For the first test, however, I'm going to dump my Studleys into the toilet in the men's room on this floor."

"That won't do any good. The Studleys will just get flushed away to...wherever it is that sewage goes away to."

"The sewers, obviously. That's where most of the tentacles are. I'm convinced of it. That's the best avenue by which Semz would invade the city."

"How will we know if you're right?"

"We'll take a walk through the city and see what happens."

"Are you crazy?"

"No, but I do have a sense of adventure. Science requires it. You'll come with me, of course. You can't be a coward all your life, Jerry."

"That was my plan."

"What would Piper say if someone told her that you'd chickened out?"

"Apparently, in addition to a sense of adventure, science requires extortion."

"Occasionally. Oh, come on, Jerry. This is why you pay yourself the big bucks. It'll be fun."

"No, this is not why I pay myself the big bucks. Oh, all right. Lead the way, Archduke."

Zing muttered something. It sounded like "Roy Rogers," but Jerry couldn't be sure.

They went to the men's room, poured the contents of Zing's plastic bottle into one of the toilets, and flushed it. Jerry wondered if there would be some effect—the screams of dying tentacles, perhaps—but there was nothing.

"Well, that was anticlimactic," he said. "So now the world is safe?"

"Far from it," Zing said. "At most, this part of the city is safe. This was just the first step, after all. Come. Let's go downstairs and go for a walk."

Despite his bravado, when they reached the glass doors on the ground floor that led out onto the sidewalk, Zing hesitated.

"Ah," Jerry said. "Now it's real. Do you want to go back up to my office?"

"Of course not." Zing pushed the doors open and stepped out onto the sidewalk.

At first, the only figures they could see were normal human beings. There were no zombies in the area and no one that looked like a pseudopod.

They walked down the sidewalk, first slowly and cautiously and then faster. Jerry began to relax. "Looks like it worked, Walter. They're all gone."

"Yes, indeed. I have to admit, I'm relieved. Let's go this way."

Ahead of them was an intersection. A zombie leaned back against the wall at the corner, his face turned up to the sun, his eyes closed. Zing and Jerry walked around him cautiously, but the zombie was as unaware of their presence, as all the zombies were now.

Zing turned the corner. Jerry was close behind him.

They found themselves face to face with a wall of pseudopodia three deep. Their usual bland, smiling, amiable expressions were gone, replaced by snarling fury.

Zing and Jerry turned around immediately.

Another wall of pseudopodia had formed behind them.

"Oh, dear," Zing said.

Jerry said, "Oh, shit."

Tentacles writhed out of somewhere and waved threateningly above them.

"Oh, great," Jerry said. "The missing ingredient."

The tentacles faltered, slowed, stopped moving. Then they shriveled up and broke into small fragments that blew away in the light breeze. The pseudopodia collapsed into piles of colorful goo.

"Success," Zing said. His voice shook.

"That was actually a bit close," Jerry said.

"True. Fortunately, the Studleys are still at work, down there in the sewers. These Studleys are a tougher bunch than the first version, the ones I had in the test tube. This version will survive for much longer, and it will continue to track down the Semz extensions and counteract them."

"I hope that means kill them."

"I've never liked the word *kill*."

"Use whatever word you like." They turned back toward the office. "What matters is that your little Studleys seem to be doing the job. I think you just saved the human race, Walter."

"It does look that way, doesn't it?"

They passed the zombie at the corner. It opened its eyes and looked at them speculatively. "Catching some rays," it whispered.

They walked faster and left it behind.

"Great," Jerry said. "The pseudopodia are under control, but now the zombies are waking up again."

"We can deal with them later," Zing said. After a long pause, he added, "I think."

Once they were back in Jerry's office, Zing's bravado returned. He stood straighter, took up more space, and spoke with big arm gestures. He was again the heroic scientific crusader that Jerry had seen once before. "Oh, by the way," he said, "I've solved the problem of the secret ingredient."

"That's wonderful!"

"Oh, it was nothing. Once I turned my attention to the problem, it solved itself."

"How?"

"Studleys."

"They seem to be the answer to everything."

"Not quite everything," Zing said. "They haven't brought about world peace. Ha, ha. Well, not yet, anyway."

"Let me guess. You modified some Studleys so that they produce the secret ingredient."

"Excellent, Jerry! Well done. Yes, and I installed a container of them inside that special, secret room you have inside the plant so that—"

"How did you get inside that?"

"It was never locked after George was killed."

"Damn. I'll have to put Myron on that."

"As I was saying, I installed a container of Studleys and hooked it up so that there is now an endless supply of the secret ingredient."

"Endless until those Studleys wear out and die. What do I do then?"

"Oh, they'll never wear out. These are much improved Studleys. All you have to do is keep feeding them."

"Feeding them what? Sugar water? Expensive beer?"

"Cockroaches. Those turned out to contain the perfect

combination of ingredients for the Studleys' work."

"Ugh. There are probably a lot of those in the factory."

"Dead cockroaches. Live ones won't work."

"Why not?"

"I haven't figured that out yet. Anyway, one or two dead cockroaches a day will do the trick."

"I'll put Myron on it," Jerry said.

"And I must return to work," Zing said.

Myron Henderson knocked on the door of Jerry's office as Zing was preparing to leave. Myron never quite went away, Jerry realized. It's a good thing for him that I need him, Jerry thought, or I'd be tempted to feed him to the zombies.

"Hi, Mr. Archduke!" Myron said. "Do you need anything from me?"

"Not at all. I've delivered my progress report to Jerry, and now I'm off to save the world." Zing walked away rapidly toward the elevator, his head high and his chest thrust out.

"Wow!" Myron said. "Mr. Archduke really takes pickle research seriously, doesn't he?"

"It's life and death to him. Did you want to tell me something?" Or are you just making sure that I remember your existence in case a promotion opens up.

"It's The Spreader Corporation, Boss. They want to know if we'd be willing to sell them one of our production lines."

"What the hell? Why do they want that?"

"I asked, but they were kind of vague. They said that they need to ensure a pickled pepper supply for some personnel who'll be setting up a new regional headquarters in a very remote location where delivery of supplies is rare and unreliable. They'll be sending their people out there with lots of our pickled peppers, but they're afraid that the supply will run out, so they want to be able to produce new pickles on site."

"Their people must really love pickled peppers. Our pickled peppers. You said they have lots of money, didn't you?"

"Lots and lots."

"Well, okay, then. We'll charge them an arm and a leg for our beat–up old equipment, and we'll use their money to replace it with shiny new stuff. They could just buy the new stuff themselves, but we won't point that out to them."

"They also want a five–year supply of our secret ingredient."

"Hell, no! Not on your life!"

"I told them you'd probably react that way, Boss."

"Five–year supply! Where are they going? Antarctica?"

"It does seem kinda weird. Okay, Boss. I'll try to make a deal just for the production line."

Jerry nodded. "Good."

Myron left, and Jerry was forced to admit to himself that the company would be in trouble if he fed Myron to the zombies.

Maybe just an arm or a leg, Jerry thought. He'd still be able to function.

The day was far from over, but Jerry felt exhausted and ready to go home already. That was hardly surprising, he thought, considering what he had been through on the street below, and considering too that he was no longer used to working more than a couple of hours a day. Thanks to Myron, he reminded himself.

It is good to be the king, he reminded himself as he got up to leave.

As he drove his overpriced car up the exit ramp from the parking garage toward the street, Jerry could see, silhouetted against the bright sunlight, pedestrians crossing in front of him on the sidewalk. He blew his horn impatiently. "Peasants," he said. "Get out of my way."

Holy cow, he said to himself, you really are a CEO, aren't you?

Jerry went back to being that most rare of CEOs: one who shows up for work every day. He was less lonely and unhappy in his big office on the fifteenth floor than he was in his big, empty house. The nights at home were good because Piper was there. The days, when she was away at the gym, or shopping, or having long lunches with her friends, were empty and pointless and made him feel empty and pointless himself.

It struck him as odd, when he thought about it, that he had lived alone fairly happily for years, except for the brief period when he had lived with Wendy Kline—and after the thrilling beginning, that had been much worse than living alone. Now, after having lived with Piper for only a few months, he couldn't stand being alone in the house.

He wondered if it would have been better if they had stayed in what Piper had dismissed as his crappy little apartment. Perhaps it would have been better for him, anyway.

Zing, according to the regular progress reports he was now e-mailing to Jerry, was producing vast quantities of Studleys and improving them with each new batch. He was dumping his little darlings in the sewers, in the rivers, and once in the city's main water treatment plant.

The attempts at infiltration had fallen almost to zero, Zing reported. He believed that this was due to the ongoing destruction of the pseudopodia by the Studleys.

Jerry's cautious observations seemed to bear this out. Only twice did he encounter what he thought were pseudopodia during his walks through downtown Piketon. He couldn't be sure that they really were pseudopodia because they both scuttled away from him in fear. He enjoyed that.

The zombies were acting more like their old selves. That was worrisome at first. Later it became frightening. Jerry wasn't sure that the end of the world had been averted, after all.

Piper began to spend more time at home and less at the gym or out with friends. The reduced gym time hadn't made her any less physically wonderful as far as Jerry could see, and he was delighted with the change in her habits. Still, he was surprised. When he asked her why she had changed, she said, "Partly, I was beginning to feel like some kind of gym zombie, mindlessly spending my days there lifting weights and swimming and running and lifting weights and...Mostly, I just think I ought to be spending more time with you."

"Great!"

"You're so wonderful, you know."

"Oh. Okay." The feeling of strangeness that had overcome him before when she had said that returned abruptly. She had told him so often in years past that George was wonderful and that he, Jerry, was worthless. The sudden change in his status and the apparent disappearance of all memory of George never ceased to unnerve him. Human zombies and giant screaming earth mother zombies were bizarre enough, but he sometimes felt that they weren't the strangest things to have come into the world.

There were moments when he caught himself wondering if this was really Piper. Was it possible that the Piper he had adored for so long had been replaced by a pseudopod so cunning in its imitation of Piper that he couldn't tell the difference even when they were making love? Or could Piper have had some of her brains sucked out by a zombie—perhaps her father? How else explain her frequent assertion that he was wonderful, or the fact that she never, ever mentioned George?

There were other things she didn't mention. In spite of saying that she wanted to spend more time with Jerry, she didn't seem to have much to say to him when they were at home together. Much as they had in the early days at his apartment, they spent their evenings silently watching television. Fortunately, they didn't sit in adjoining armchairs. Instead, they shared a love seat Piper had bought. They sat pressed against each other, holding hands, silent, while they watched one shallow, boring show after the other on the giant screen attached to the wall on the other side of the room.

They even watched commercials as uncritically and unresponsively as they did everything else.

They were watching one that was a fine example of compact storytelling. In the first few seconds of the commercial, a slender, attractive female astronomer discovered that a giant asteroid was rushing toward the earth and would destroy it within days. Ignoring the rumpled, overweight male astronomers in their shabby white lab coats—Jerry awoke from his stupor for long enough to wonder why astronomers would wear lab coats—she contacted the White House. The next few seconds showed the president, a slender, attractive woman, conferring earnestly with the Cabinet, composed mostly of slender, attractive, alert women but with a few dull-eyed, slack-jawed, overweight men thrown in. Then, stopping only to put on lots of She!—the advertised makeup product—the astronomer and her crew of slender, attractive women took off atop a rocket to destroy the asteroid. Jerry wanted to point out that an astronomer would be very unlikely to be qualified to lead such a mission, no matter how slender, attractive, and well made up she was, but Piper's silence unmanned him. By the time the commercial's sixty seconds were up, the all-woman crew had destroyed the asteroid and returned to earth to accept the thanks of a grateful world and the puzzled stares of rumpled, overweight men who didn't understand what had just happened. All of the women were still perfectly made up, thanks to She! Shouldn't you be using She! too?

At that point, the front doorbell rang.

Jerry sprang to his feet. "I'll get it!" he felt relieved at the chance to escape and upset that he wanted to escape from Piper.

When he opened the door, he was surprised that it was dark outside. His evenings were slipping away with disturbing speed.

A dark figure stood on the front porch, a man silhouetted against the glow of a distant streetlight. Suddenly terrified, Jerry flipped the switch for the porch light.

Walter Zing stood there, smiling happily, bouncing up and down as though he had been infected by Myron Henderson. "Jerry! May I come in? I have something very exciting to tell you."

Jerry stood aside and gestured at Zing to come in. He looked outside quickly and then locked the door. The fear of zombies, pseudopodia, and murderous tentacles would never leave him, he suspected.

Jerry led the way to the kitchen. Unlike the Pistole house, this house had only one kitchen, but it was almost as large as Jerry's old apartment, and it was filled with shiny, new appliances and equipment that cost more than all of the contents of Jerry's old apartment. He never felt quite comfortable in this kitchen, but still it felt like a more natural place for a conversation than anywhere else in the house, especially when he was talking to someone Piper disliked. He could hear the television, so he assumed that she was still in the room they had set aside for the giant screen. That was just as well. She seemed unable to keep from voicing her dislike when she was around Zing.

"Is Piper here?" Zing asked. "I think she should hear about this, too."

"Is that really necessary?"

"Yes, I think so."

"She's watching television. This way." Jerry heard the sounds coming from the television suddenly change, as though Piper had switched channels. When they entered the television room, the screen was filled with the odious face of Brother Steve. The preacher's face was covered with sweat, and he was loudly denouncing something or other.

Jerry knew that Piper detested Steven Flexman and all other television preachers just as much as he did. He divined immediately that she had switched channels when she realized that Zing was in the house in the hope that playing Flexman at high volume would drive the scientist away.

"Ah!" Zing said as they entered the television room. "Brother Steve Flexman! I see that you like to watch him, too, Piper."

Piper grumbled.

"Yes, indeed. He's fascinating to watch. Of course, everything he says is pure twaddle, but clearly he knows that. What's so interesting is how carefully he phrases his twaddle. He knows just what buttons to push and how to push them."

"How interesting," Jerry lied.

Piper made a face and reached for the television remote control.

Jerry assumed that she intended to search for something that would drive Zing away since Flexman had failed her. "Perhaps we should just turn the TV off, darling," he said. "Dr. Walter says he has something to tell both of us."

"Not just yet, please," Zing said. "Brother Steve is working up to his climax."

Piper made a sound of disgust.

"The word 'twaddle' reminds me of Big Jim Tweddle," Zing said. "I like to listen to him for the same reason I like to watch Brother Steve. Tweddle's a master of manipulation. He's been off the air for the last couple of weeks, though. I wonder why."

Jerry didn't bother trying to come up with a reply to that. The three of them watched Brother Steve in silence.

"The godless, the atheists, the unsaved," Brother Steve was saying, "will tell you that there is nothing beyond this world. But I'm here to tell you, my friends, that there is indeed something more, something out there, something that we must all aspire to. There is another world, my friends, a cleaner, fresher, purer place than this. That other world is Mars."

"Wow!" Piper said. "I didn't expect him to say that."

Perhaps Brother Steve's immense live audience didn't expect him to say that, either, but it didn't seem to matter to them. They applauded and shouted "Amen" enthusiastically.

After the applause and shouting had died down, Brother Steve continued. "Next month, a patriotic, God-centered, private company—not the government, not NASA, not those demon-supporting, Jesus-denying socialists in Washington—in obedience to the command God gave us in the Book of Genesis to go forth and multiply, will launch a special rocket with a special crew to spread the seed of Earth to another world, to the planet Mars!"

Shouts of "Praise Jesus!" and "Amen!"

"This congregation," Brother Steve said loudly, "will be sending along a special shipment of Bibles for that wonderful crew to read during their voyage."

"Hallelujah!" "Amen!"

Brother Steve smiled down at his sheep paternally. When the bleating continued without signs of dying away, a look of annoyance crossed his face. He held up his meaty hands. The noise subsided.

Brother Steve resumed. "And now—"

He stopped. A look of surprise appeared on his broad, sweaty face.

"What the—" he said.

Then he shouted in an immense voice, "Jesus fucking Christ!

Glop!"

His features disappeared. The fat man standing on the pulpit changed into a fat, smooth-surfaced white thing. The white thing collapsed into a big puddle of disgusting colored things.

The camera remained focused on the pile of goo while the congregation fled screaming, fighting each other viciously to get to the exits.

"How interesting," Zing said. "That glopping sound is the very same noise I heard at the end of Jim Tweddle's very last broadcast. It does make you wonder just who else in the public eye is in reality a Semz pseudopod."

"Semz?" Piper asked.

"That's Walter's name for the giant screaming earth mother zombie," Jerry explained.

"Weird," Piper said. "Also creepy."

"It also makes you wonder exactly when Brother Steve was replaced," Jerry said. "Wouldn't his congregation have noticed?"

Zing thought about that. "I can't remember any point at which his message or speaking style changed. The transition was undetectable."

"This has been a memorable evening," Piper said. "Thank you for coming over, Dr. Zing."

"Oh, but I haven't told you what I came here to talk about."

"Perhaps some other time. I'm exhausted from all this excitement."

"I'm afraid it can't wait," Zing said.

Piper sighed in resignation. She turned off the TV, which was still showing the slowly evaporating pile of glop that had been the imitation Reverend Steven "Brother Steve" Flexman.

"The Studleys have been doing their work gallantly and with great courage," Zing began.

Jerry held up his hand.

"Yes, Jerry?"

"They're bacteria. They don't have feelings or thoughts, right? So you can't really say that they're being gallant and courageous, can you?"

"Jerry, if you keep interrupting me with silly questions, I'll never get through with what I came here to tell you. I could be here all night."

"Stop asking silly questions," Piper told Jerry. "Darling," she added.

"Thank you, Piper," Zing said. "Now, then. The Studleys have been working away, as I said. My staff is producing them in large numbers and dumping them into all sorts of appropriate places, including the water company's reservoirs."

Piper looked bewildered. Jerry said, "I'll give you the background later. Darling."

"And as we've all seen, out on the streets and just now on television, the Studleys are doing their work magnificently."

"Courageously, even," Jerry said. "I would go so far as to say gallantly."

Zing beamed at him. "Yes! Indeed." His smile disappeared. "However, I have been able to determine that some pseudopodia have survived and seem to be protected from attack by the Studleys. Semz is protecting her children. She's walling them off somehow. I don't know how she's doing it, but she certainly is a formidable opponent."

"She?"

"It. Don't call it 'she.' It's dangerous to anthropomorphize in the sciences."

"I'll try to remember that."

"This means that our current method of distributing the

Studleys—"

"Those gallant, courageous little guys," Jerry said.

"Yes, yes, they certainly are. As I was saying, our current method of distributing them still leaves Semz and her core cadre of pseudopodia unharmed. Oh, and presumably her tentacles, as well."

Jerry shivered. This really was no joking matter, he realized. "Maybe if we ignore her, she'll go away. She's isolated up there in the mountains. She can't spread any more because of the Studleys."

"She's far too clever and determined for that," Zing said. "Left alone, she'll find some way to spread and threaten the world again. We have to destroy her. The only way I can think of is for us to deliver gallons of Studleys directly into that hole she lives in. To the extent that Semz has a brain, that's where it is."

"By 'us' you of course mean your little band of daring scientists."

"No. By 'us' I mean you and me."

"Why—" Jerry was about to whine, "Why me?" But then he noticed Piper watching him, so instead he said, "Why, that sounds very exciting, Walter. Will it be a problem that I don't know anything about bacteria? Anything at all?"

"Of course I'd prefer it if poor George were still alive," Zing said.

Jerry sensed Piper stiffening.

Zing went on obliviously. "That boy had an almost intuitive understanding of bacteria. He would have been perfect for this mission. Well, well." He sighed and shook his head. "We can't change the past, can we?"

"No, we can't," Jerry said. "I assume your gallant and courageous band of scientists will be accompanying us?"

Zing shook his head. "Oh, no. They're much too valuable to risk. Perhaps you haven't realized it, but this is going to be a very dangerous mission."

"Now that you mention it, I can see that it would be."

"Yes. I have to be there myself. After all, I'm responsible for the very existence of Semz. My Studleys brought her into being. And I need someone with me to complete the mission in case the tentacles catch me and wrap around me and crush me into a gooey mess similar to what we just saw on television."

"That's a very graphic image," Jerry said, thinking of the very high chance that the tentacles would catch *him* and wrap around him and crush him into a gooey mess. He tried to think of some way of getting out of this mission of Zing's but again he became aware of Piper's gaze. It was full of admiration.

He said to Zing, "I assume that you're thinking of a helicopter or a small airplane, so that we can drop the Studleys directly into the hole?"

"Oh, no. That would be too risky. We'd be too good a target for the tentacles, and I don't think we'd be accurate enough, anyway. We'll only have one chance to save the world, so we can't afford to miss. Also, I don't know how to fly a helicopter or airplane. Do you?"

Jerry shook his head.

"So you see, if we used such a vehicle, we'd be risking a pilot's life in addition to our own. I can't accept that responsibility. No, we'll take my truck. I'll have the Studleys in a big tank in the back of it. All we have to do is back right up to the hole. Then we'll get out of the truck, lower the tailgate, open the tank, and let the Studleys pour out into the hole and do their job."

"It sounds...so simple."

"The best battle plans always are. More complexity means more chances for something to go wrong. I read that long ago in a boys' history of the Civil War. When I was a boy."

While Jerry was trying to think of an objection that would make sense and wouldn't extinguish the admiration in Piper's glance, Zing said, "I believe we're all set. I'll need a few days to get everything ready. I'll be here to pick you up early Friday morning. All right?"

Unable to speak, Jerry nodded.

"Excellent! Piper, you have a very brave and good man here. Goodnight, everyone!" Whistling, he left the room.

When they heard him let himself out and close the door behind him, Piper flung her arms around Jerry's neck and her legs around his torso, and she kissed him madly and repeatedly, saying, "You're wonderful! You're so brave! You're so wonderful!" between kisses.

Then she released him and said, "Bed!" She grabbed his hand and pulled him toward the bedroom. Jerry went willingly enough, trying not to think that this might be one of the last nights he would spend with Piper.

CHAPTER NINETEEN

Jerry went in late to work the next morning. He was tempted to not go in at all. Piper wanted him to stay in bed with her, and the temptation to do so was immense. But so was the call of duty. He might have only two more days to spend with her, but he also wanted to make sure that the company was doing well before Friday arrived, because Piper would be dependent on income from the company for the rest of her life.

So he tore himself from Piper's arms, showered, dressed, nibbled a little something in the way of breakfast, got into the expensive car he disliked, and drove downtown.

He parked in his reserved space in the underground garage, jumped out, locked the door quickly, and hurried to the elevator doors, looking nervously over his shoulder all the while. He didn't know if he was more frightened of lurking zombies who had regained their intelligence or of giant screaming earth mother zombie tentacles coming up from the floor drains. Both terrified him as much as anything possibly could. Telling himself that the tentacles no longer existed because of the gallant, courageous Studleys didn't help.

Jerry took the elevator up to the fifteenth floor. He got out and started across the reception area toward his office.

Myron Henderson popped out of nowhere. Not for the first time, Jerry wondered how Myron managed to appear suddenly and disappear just as suddenly. It was an enviable ability.

Myron was jumpier than normal. He was sweating and looked afraid. "Don't go in there, Boss!"

"Why not?"

"There's someone in there! Some scary, creepy old guy. He says it's his office."

"Call Security. Have them escort him out of the building. Don't call me boss."

"But, Boss, sir, he says his name is Frank Pistole."

"Oh, God."

"He wants pickles."

"No pickles!"

"He says he really needs a pickle. He kinda whined. It made him a bit less scary. I mean, it would have if his voice wasn't coming out through a hole in his cheek."

Jerry was tempted to send Myron in there with a pickle, but he reminded himself that the company needed Myron and Piper needed the company. "No pickles," Jerry repeated. "Go back to work, Myron. I'll take care of this."

Myron was clearly relieved. "Are you sure, Boss?" he asked, saying what he assumed his boss wanted to hear.

"I'm sure." Jerry waited while Myron scuttled away, exuding gratitude, and then he headed for the office he had come to think of as his.

But what about after Friday? he asked himself. If you don't come back from Zing's mission, someone will have to run this company, and Myron isn't ready for that job. Frank may be the best choice.

Jerry walked into the presidential office as casually as if he had seen Frank there only yesterday. "Hi, Frank. How are you on this wonderful morning?"

Frank Pistole raised his eyes from the sheet of paper he had been reading. "Hmph. It's sunny. That's the only thing that's wonderful about it. Who is that annoying young man who was just in here?"

"Myron Henderson."

"Get rid of him."

"Frank, he's in charge of our biggest account. He saved the company."

"Really? Well...Competent, is he? Smart?"

"Oh, yes. Very brainy kid." Instantly, Jerry regretted his choice of words.

Frank licked his lips. "In that case, we'll keep him. So the company's doing well?"

"Very. Extremely. It's just sailing along. You don't need to think about it all. You can just go back home and...sunbathe."

Frank stared at him dully. "Catch some rays," he said slowly.

Jerry shivered. Myron was right. Frank's voice was coming out of his mouth and through a slit in his cheek. It was only apparent when he spoke and the moving air made the slit widen.

Frank blinked a few times and looked more alert again. "I've been looking at the numbers. You're right. The company's doing well. Where's George?"

"Uh, George is dead, Frank. Don't you remember?"

"He is? What happened?"

"Your late wife killed him."

Frank looked bewildered. Jerry considered reminding him of the events in the factory, but then he decided it would be better not to. Clearly, Frank was still not his old undead self, and that was a good thing, since that old self was an evil zombie mastermind with a fearsome zombie army. Jerry also thought it would be best not to mention that George had died by having his brains sucked out.

"Who?" Frank asked.

"Zelda. Griselda Pistole."

"Oh. Why did she do that?"

"She didn't tell me."

"So who's running the company?"

"I am."

"You! But you're just..." Frank's voice trailed away. Then he said, "Okay."

"Everything's under control, Frank. You should go back home. Lie on the back lawn. Work on your tan. Catch some rays. Soak it up."

Frank stared at him for a long time. Finally he said, "Gotta write a check."

Jerry sighed. The old battles refused to end. "Brother Steve is no longer with us, Frank." When Frank didn't respond, Jerry said, "And Fred Foxtrot is so far behind in the polls that any money you give him would just be wasted." That was pure invention. Jerry hadn't seen any polls for the upcoming Senate race. However, he doubted that Frank watched the news nowadays.

Frank grunted. "Don't care about them. Coupla bozos. Mother spoke to me."

"What? Who?"

"Mother. Our mother. In the hole in the mountains."

Jerry took a step backward. "How do you mean, Frank?"

"In my mind. She spoke to me in my mind. It was strange."

"What did she say?"

Frank frowned, trying to remember. "Something about killing."

Jerry took another step back. "Maybe you just dreamed it."

Frank shook his head violently. His left ear fell off. "Don't dream. Dreams stopped when I..." He frowned more deeply. His forehead made a popping sound. "Was I in a coffin? I remember that." His voice rose. "Why did you put me in a coffin?" He began to stand up.

"That was just a dream," Jerry said quickly. "Sometimes when you lie in the sun, you fall asleep. You probably dream then."

Frank stared at him suspiciously, but he sat down again. "I like catching rays."

"Of course you do. You should go home right now, while it's still sunny out, and—"

"Mother told me to write a check. Company checkbook. Gimme. Gotta write a check."

"To whom, Frank?"

Frank looked crafty. "Secret."

Jerry couldn't imagine what strange idea was running through the remnants of Frank's brain, but he did know that he couldn't let the old zombie go back to writing company checks to his personal pet causes, as he had done before dying. It had damaged the company then and it would do so now. That meant it would injure Piper.

"It takes a while to get the company checkbook. We keep it locked away for security reasons. Why don't you tell me who you want to write the check to, and for how much, and then you can go home and catch some rays, and I'll take care of the check."

Frank looked at him through slitted eyes. At least he tried to. One of his eyelids was mostly missing, so the effect wasn't what he was trying for. "Dunno if I can trust you."

"Of course you can. Look what a good job I've been doing running your company."

"Yeah. You're a smart kid. Brainy."

"So who's the check to? And for how much."

"Spreader Corporation. A million billion zillion dollars."

"Oh. Okay. They're our biggest customer."

"Yeah? They buy lots of pickles from us?"

"Lots."

A crafty look spread across Frank's face. He giggled. "Play a trick on Mother," he whispered loudly. "No check. Send them extra pickles.

A million billion zillion extra pickles. That's less than a million billion zillion dollars, right?"

"Much less."

"Okay." Frank stood up.

Jerry backed up quickly.

Frank said, "Going home. Catch some rays." He stood there blinking and frowning as though he were trying to recapture his lost mind. After a while, he gave up and walked out of the office in a wavering line and to the elevator.

When the elevator door closed behind Frank, Jerry collapsed into the desk chair. His heart was hammering. He realized that he was sweating heavily.

If you can't even deal with a normal-size zombie with half a mind, he asked himself, how are you going to be able to attack the giant screaming earth mother zombie?

It will only be an issue for a second or two, he replied. And then I'll be dead.

CHAPTER TWENTY

On Friday morning, Jerry awoke to the insistent chiming of the front doorbell.

For a few seconds, he fought to shut the sound out and hold onto the fading remnants of a dream. He felt Piper leap out of bed and gave up the fight.

"Wake up!" she said. "It's the big day. I thought you wanted to get up early. Why didn't you set the alarm?"

Jerry groaned and pushed himself to a sitting position on the edge of the bed. "I thought I had." The doorbell was still chiming. "That must be Zing. Can you let him in while I shower and get dressed?"

"Ugh. The creepazoid. All right." She put on her robe and left the room.

Gotta be clean and properly dressed for the big day on which I'm going to get killed, Jerry thought as he stumbled into the bathroom.

He shaved and showered quickly. That woke him up. He brushed his teeth. Breakfast was out of the question. His stomach was tied in knots. What was the point, anyway? Was breakfast the most important meal of the day on which he was going to be killed?

He hoped Piper hadn't prepared any food for him. Probably not. He hoped she was being polite to Walter Zing. Probably not.

By the time he was descending the stairs, 10 minutes had passed since he had forced himself out of bed. Not bad, he thought.

He could hear voices from below—Piper's voice, then Zing's, and then a third voice, an unforgettable one, the lovely zombie voice that hypnotized.

Jerry froze on the staircase. The sounds from below ceased. He forced himself to begin moving again.

The three figures were motionless when he entered the big front parlor. They were staring at each other like awkward strangers at a party wondering what to say next. They all turned to look at him.

Piper looked relieved by his presence. Zing looked at Jerry and then at his watch in silent reprimand. Griselda the zombie giantess smiled at him and said, her astonishing voice surrounding and caressing him, "The young hero arrives."

Piper snarled at her.

Griselda stared at Piper for a moment and then said, "Sometimes you remind me of your father. That's not meant as a compliment."

Jerry said, "Mrs. Zing. How nice to see you again."

"I'm sure it is," Griselda said, looking at him intently.

Jerry looked away to avoid Griselda's hypnotic stare. He felt pleased with himself. "I'm surprised to see you here."

"I'm going to be joining you in your assault."

Startled, Jerry looked at her. "You are? Why?"

Griselda looked angry, which made her look even larger and more terrifying. "That bitch," she growled.

"Er," Jerry said, "which one? Be more specific."

Griselda smiled again. "You have a spine. I like that. I wonder how it tastes."

Piper moved to Jerry's side and grabbed his arm.

Griselda laughed. Then she looked angry again. "That monster in the mountains. That thing."

"Semz," Zing explained.

"Ah," Jerry said, "the giant screaming earth mother zombie."

Piper shivered.

"Yes," Griselda said. "Her. She tried to murder my stud." She put her huge arm around Zing and hugged him. He winced in pain. "No one murders my stud but me." She bent down and kissed the top of Zing's head. Jerry tensed in horror. He expected her to bite into Zing's skull and suck out his brains, as she had George's. But she raised her head again and released Zing, who stepped away from her with a look of relief. "I've told you, Stud," Griselda said, "That if anyone is going to kill and eat you, it will be me."

"Yes, beloved," Zing said.

"I intend to do exactly that after we kill off this Semz bitch."

"I believe you, my darling."

"Good." Her gaze drifted back to Jerry, or more precisely to his head.

Jerry could almost feel fingers sliding over his scalp, examining the size and shape of his skull, sizing up his brain. "I think we should get going," he said.

"We should have been on the way by now," Zing said. "Why weren't you ready and waiting for us?"

"Because I forgot to set the alarm."

"A Freudian slip," Zing said. "An expression of your fear. Quite understandable."

Griselda snickered. Even her snicker was beautiful and seductive.

"Hey!" Piper said. "Don't you talk about my man that way!" She gripped Jerry's arm fiercely. "He's brave and fearless, he's my knight, and I know that he is eager to go gloriously into battle."

Jerry realized that he had never asked Piper what kind of fiction she read. He suspected that their tastes were very different.

"That's the spirit!" Zing said. "Let's go!"

"I'm coming too," Piper said. "Jerry and I will go into battle side by side."

"Oh, I don't think so," Zing said.

"I also don't think so," Jerry said.

"Well, I do think so," Piper said.

"Now you remind me more of me," Griselda said.

Zing shifted away from his zombie love. "You need to stay behind so that you can run the company and save the world," he said to Piper. "Just in case we fail."

"You're not going to fail," Piper said.

"Well, it is possible. And in this case, failure would almost certainly mean…that Jerry would no longer be available to run the company."

Piper stared at him with a puzzled look. Then understanding dawned. "You mean there's real danger? Actual physical danger?"

Griselda said, "No you remind me of yourself when you were a not very bright child."

"Very extreme danger," Zing said. "Semz is a terrible and deadly adversary."

Piper flung her arms around Jerry, buried her face in his chest, and burst into tears. "I don't want you to go! Jerry, stay here! Let them get killed. They don't matter."

"That's a fine way to talk about your mother," Griselda said.

"Fuck you," Piper said, her voice muffled against Jerry's chest. "Jerry, you don't have to go."

Jerry stroked her hair until he felt her sobbing fade away and stop. "The thing is," he said, surprising himself, "if Walter says he needs me, then I really do have to go."

She raised her tear-stained face and looked at him. "You really are a wonderful knight in shining armor. Come back to me in one piece. I'll have a really hot reward for you."

Griselda made a noise of disgust. "Not in front of your mother!"

she said.

"Also," Piper said, "bring me the dragon's head. We'll have it mounted and hang it on the wall over there." She indicated which wall with her head.

"It doesn't have a head," Jerry said.

"Well, a piece of a tentacle, then."

"We'll mount a tentacle and hang it on the wall?"

"I'll be the only gal at the gym who has one of those."

"I'll do my best."

"Can we please leave now?" Zing said plaintively.

They went outside. Piper hung onto Jerry. She kept pulling his head down and kissing him. Jerry wondered why he wasn't enjoying that more. He decided that it must be because he was about to go up into the mountains to be crushed and eaten by the giant screaming earth mother zombie.

Zing's huge pickup truck was parked in front of the house. The back of the truck held an enormous, white, translucent tank much like the tanks filled with green gunk that the landscape service sprayed on Jerry's lawn a few times a month. This tank appeared to be filled with a colorless liquid. The tank was held in place by thick straps that passed over its top and were anchored in the holes spaced along the sides of the truck.

"What's that?" Jerry asked, pointing at the tank.

"Studleys," Zing said proudly. "In fact, super Studleys."

"What makes them super?"

"Can't tell you. It's super secret. But I can tell you that they're far, far more powerful and durable than the Studleys I had in that test tube I used in the city a while ago. And obviously there are far more of them in that tank than there were in the test tube." Looking at the tank, Zing smiled happily. "There are enough of them in there, and they're powerful enough, to wipe out Semz and to follow her extensions underground wherever they go and wipe them out, too."

"Great! Where do you plan to dump all of them?"

"Oh, in the hole in the mountains, of course."

Jerry had known that would be the answer, but he had hoped to be pleasantly surprised. "That...won't be easy."

"Nothing worth doing in life is easy, Jerry."

"Please don't speak in clichés, Walter."

Zing looked momentarily annoyed. "I thought I had made that up. Well. All we have to do is back the truck up to the edge of the hole, drop the tail gate, and open the outlet valve in the tank."

"Meanwhile avoiding the murderous tentacles and the protective army of angry zombies."

"Well, yes. It won't be a trivial matter, of course. As I said, nothing worth—"

"Right."

Piper pressed Jerry's arm against her side. "Mother," she said, "you will protect him. I'm ordering you to."

Zing gasped. He looked frightened.

"Ordering me?" the zombie said loudly. Her voice was less beautiful and seductive than normal. She frowned angrily. "*Ordering me?*" Her expression softened. She chuckled. "Now you remind me of my mother. She was an insignificant little squirt, too. All right, daughter. If it's convenient, I'll protect your man for you."

Zing let out his breath.

"She frightens you more than the creature in the mountains?" Jerry muttered to Zing. Maybe that's because he's living with Griselda, he thought. Sleeping with her, if he's doing that. Jerry found that image simultaneously terrifying and disturbingly exciting.

"Thank you, Mother," Piper said. "I will continue to call you 'Mother.'"

Her mother scowled at her.

"So everything's settled," Zing said with forced heartiness. He pulled a key ring from his pocket and jingled the keys together. "Let's get going. I'm driving. Jerry, you're in the passenger seat. Grizzy…"

She glared at him. "I know." She went to the truck and climbed easily into the back, where she sat down, squeezed between the tank and the side of the bed, her back against the back of the cab.

Zing walked around the truck and climbed into the driver's seat. He started the engine and leaned over and looked impatiently at Jerry through the passenger window.

"I'd better go," Jerry said to Piper.

They hugged. Then Piper pushed away. "Go," she said. "Slay the dragon."

Jerry turned and walked toward the truck, trying to look manly and strong. He climbed in, closed the door, and looked out the window, expecting to see Piper waving forlornly at him. But she had gone back inside the house.

He turned the other way and looked through the small window in the back of the cab. He could see the tank and Griselda's right shoulder. "Why is she coming with us?"

"She insisted," Zing said. He started the truck and headed down the driveway. "She said I'd need her to protect me from Semz and the zombie army."

"So why do you need me?"

"You're here in case Grizzy isn't able to protect me. She can't fit inside here, so if they get me, you'll have to back the truck up to the edge of the pit and dump the Studleys in."

"You seem remarkably cheerful."

"Yes! This is so exciting!"

"Why didn't you bring one of your doughty scientific crew along, instead of me?"

"Oh." Zing waved his hand dismissively. "They've been a

disappointment to me, I'm afraid. Perfectly good researchers," he added hastily. "Quite good at the necessary R&D for the super-Studley project. But not one of them is a man of action. None of them wanted to participate in this mission. Can you imagine that?"

Jerry shook his head. In his mind's eye, he was nodding emphatically.

Zing laughed. "I can't imagine one of them being called a knight in shining armor by his lady fair. Ha, ha!"

"Ha, ha," Jerry said.

The traffic on both sides of Interstate 25 seemed normal to Jerry. He didn't know what he was expecting. Crowds standing beside the highway to salute him and cheer him on, maybe, or signs praising him. Instead, as on every day, the world was filled with people going about their business and not thinking about zombies or the end of the world or Jerry Morgenstern.

"It's not fair," he said.

"What isn't?" Zing asked.

"Life."

"Ah." Zing glanced over his shoulder, looking through the small window at Griselda. "Well, sometimes it works out all right. Have courage."

I could use a lot of that, Jerry thought.

Zing turned off at the Bartle's Drop exit and headed west and up into the foothills. He took a dirt road and then another and then another. It was a route Jerry was unfamiliar with.

"You've spent a lot of time up here, haven't you, Walter?" Jerry said.

"Recon," Zing said in a strong and manly voice. "Learning the territory. I know every rock up here."

"Impressive," Jerry said. The rocks all look the same to me, he thought.

They went up a hillside. The road diminished to a narrow trail. Then even that faded away into the rocks and sketchy wild grass of the mountains. Zing continued more slowly, the truck jouncing up and down and from side to side.

Griselda yelled angrily. Jerry turned to look at her. She was bracing herself against the side of the truck with one hand and holding the big tank in place with the other. "You really did need her along," he said to Zing.

Zing smiled. "I will always need her along."

Until she kills you and eats you, Jerry thought.

They reached the top of the hill. Zing slowed the truck to a stop and put it in Park. He pointed through the windshield. Below them lay the familiar valley with the huge hole in the center.

"Well," Jerry said. "Here we are. I thought it would take longer to get here." He had hoped it would take longer.

The zombie army waited for them, standing silently in a circle around the hole. It was a smaller army than the one the creature had eaten the last time Jerry was here. Or maybe those were pseudopodia, not zombies. From this distance, Jerry couldn't tell. He didn't think it made much difference. Slender, white tentacles waved high in the air above the hole and the waiting army.

"If they can see us," Zing said, "then they apparently don't realize that we're a threat. Semz must think we're just hunters, or something of that sort. Let's not give them a chance to organize." He turned and spoke over his shoulder. "Hold on, my darling. You, too, Jerry," he added.

He slipped the gearshift into Drive and stepped on the accelerator.

They roared down the hillside, bouncing wildly. Griselda yelled angrily. Jerry shrieked. Zing laughed wildly. "Isn't this exciting?" he shouted.

"If you get killed," Jerry shouted back, "it will be a great loss to science!"

"True. But we need momentum."

The army was rushing together into a clump to block them. The tendrils had ceased their random movements and were all aimed in the direction of the onrushing truck.

"Watch this!" Zing shouted.

He spun the wheel. The rear end of the truck skidded sideways in a long curve on the dirt and grass. Zing straightened the wheel and pushed the gearshift into Reverse. They had completed a one-eighty turn and were now rushing backwards toward the densely packed bodies.

They smashed into the waiting zombies. Jerry felt the truck bouncing over their bodies. He glimpsed surprised faces and detached limbs flying past the side window.

The truck ground to a halt.

Zing put the truck in Park and turned the ignition off. "Oh, dear," he said. "This is unfortunate. They're piled up around the wheels, and we're not quite to the edge of the hole yet. I'll have to get out and work with Grizzy to clear them away. You stay here."

"Okay!"

"Slide behind the wheel. Once we've cleared a path, you'll back the truck up the rest of the way. Keep the doors and windows locked."

"Okay!"

Zing gripped Jerry's left shoulder in a manly and painful manner. He grinned. "If they get me, it will all be up to you."

Oh, they'll get you, Jerry thought.

"Here I go!" Zing shouted. He was still grinning. He opened the door, jumped out, and slammed the door shut behind him.

Jerry slid into the driver's seat and focused on making sure the windows and doors were locked. When he looked out, he saw Zing fighting off zombies and pseudopodia. Or trying to fight them off. He was no match for them. They were pulling him down.

Next, they'll smash their way in here and get me, Jerry thought. I'm going to die the way people always die in zombie movies. Then I'll come back as a zombie myself, and I'll go home and try to eat Piper. I hate this.

He heard a roar. The truck shook as Griselda leaped off the back and into the fray.

Jerry pressed his face against the window, trying to see what was happening. He could see zombie body parts flying up into the air. Then what appeared to be a pseudopod, smiling blandly, shot up a few feet and changed into multi–colored glop in mid–air. Griselda stood tall in the middle of the melee. Jerry heard pseudopodia yelling and Griselda roaring. The truck rocked. Things banged against it. He considered starting the engine and driving forward and far, far away. He fought down the temptation.

After a few minutes, the sounds and banging stopped. Everything was still. Griselda leaned down and then straightened, pulling Zing to his feet. The scientist was bedraggled, his face puffing up from where he'd been punched and his clothes covered with pseudopodia glop, but he was grinning widely. His mouth formed the word "Wow!" but Jerry couldn't hear him through the closed windows.

He could hear Griselda, though. In an enormous voice, she shouted at Zing, "Your stupid plan sucks!"

Jerry agreed completely.

A tentacle whipped down and wrapped around Zing. It began to squeeze even as it lifted him from the ground. Zing's face turned purple. His eyes bugged out. His mouth opened and his tongue protruded.

Griselda shouted, "Bitch!" She grabbed the tentacle next to Zing's body and tore it easily in two. Then she tore the rest of it off him just as easily.

Zing fell against her, gasping.

Griselda pushed him away. She turned toward the hole and waved her fist in the air. She shouted again. "Bitch!"

Between them and the pit, a forest of tentacles waved. But they waved uncertainly, as though the giant screaming earth mother zombie wasn't quite sure if she should attack Griselda.

The tentacles would be enough to stop the truck, though. Even without the zombie and pseudopodia army, the mangled remnants of which lay scattered about them, there was still no way to back the truck up to the hole and pour the Studleys in.

Feeling guilty about not being part of the action, but also feeling safe for the moment, Jerry opened the door and got out. "What do we do now?" he asked. He pointed at the tentacles. "We can't drive through those."

Griselda laughed. All the beauty had disappeared from her voice some time ago. Now it was harsh, loud, ugly, and frightening. "That bitch tried to hurt my Walter," she said. "I'm going to take care of her."

She yanked at the straps holding the tank in place. They snapped as though they were strings. She undid the tailgate and dropped it. Then she slid the tank halfway out, bent down, put her right shoulder under it, and stood up holding it on her shoulder, her right hand keeping it in position. The tank sagged a bit in the middle but didn't break.

"Uh, how much does that thing weigh?" Jerry asked Zing.

"What? Oh. Well, it's a cylinder. About 200 centimeters long and 150 centimeters in diameter, almost filled with a liquid that's roughly the same density as water. You figure it out."

"Oh. Okay." It doesn't really matter, Jerry thought. I bet it's really heavy.

"Roughly 3,500 kilograms," Zing said absentmindedly.

"So, in pounds, that would be..."

"7,700. Grizzy, what are you—"

"I'm doing what has to be done, my super science stud. Looks like I won't be eating you, after all. Sorry." She set off at a trot toward the hole.

The tentacles whipped toward her and then whipped away. It was as though they—or the giant screaming earth mother zombie of which they were a part—were frightened of Griselda. One tentacle touched her, and she tore the end off it with easy contempt. The rest kept their distance after that.

At the edge of the hole, Griselda paused. She reached over her head with her left hand and tore a long rip in the tank. The colorless liquid gushed out over her and into the hole. Still holding the tank, she leaped in.

"Grizzy!" Zing yelled.

Roars came from the hole. Grizzy's roars, Jerry assumed, but he couldn't be sure. Perhaps the giant screaming earth mother zombie was actually screaming. Above the hole, the tentacles whipped around furiously. Pieces of something flew up into the air and fell back into the hole. The ground trembled. Jerry and Zing staggered and grabbed the truck to keep from falling.

Then it all subsided. The sounds died away. The ground movements stopped. The waving tentacles collapsed into the hole and disappeared from sight.

The two men walked forward cautiously. They reached the edge of the hole and looked over.

There was nothing in front of them. The hole went down into

darkness. There was no sign of a bottom, no sign of the monstrous creature that had inhabited the hole, no sign of its tentacles or its pseudopodia or its captive zombies, and no sign of Griselda.

Jerry looked at Zing. The scientist was ashen faced. He trembled. His knees gave way and he began to pitch forward into the hole.

Jerry grabbed his arm and pulled him backward to safety.

Zing stood staring into space. He seemed unaware of his near escape from death or of Jerry's actions. "Oh, Grizzy," Zing whispered.

"I'm so sorry, Walter," Jerry said insincerely.

"She was the love of my life," Zing said. "And now she's gone. Forever."

Thank God, Jerry thought. "I'm so sorry," he repeated.

Suddenly Zing straightened. He grew thoughtful. He looked down at the ground. "Although, it occurs to me that perhaps..." He smiled. "Hmm."

Oh, God, Jerry thought. This will never end.

CHAPTER TWENTY-ONE

Zombie numbers began to increase again after the battle in the mountains. Jerry encountered them everywhere. They seemed energized again. They stared at his head and the heads of other living humans in a possessive way, as if to say, "Enjoy those brains for now, but remember that they're on loan. They belong to us."

This should have terrified Jerry. At one time, it would have. But by contrast with the pseudopodia, zombies no longer seemed so terrifying, and the pseudopodia had all disappeared completely.

Still, he felt much more relaxed when he was at home with all the doors and windows locked than he did when he was walking through downtown, edging past zombies standing with their faces turned to the sun, or when he was dealing with the ever more assertive Frank Pistole.

Piper didn't like having all the doors and windows locked. When the weather was mild, she liked having all the windows open and a breeze flowing through the house. She also liked to sit on the patio behind the house so that she could enjoy the fresh air and their expensively landscaped garden. She laughed at Jerry's fears and assured him that he was so wonderful and so very much her knight in shining armor that no zombies would dare come near their house.

Jerry didn't find this reassuring. He wanted to tell her that he was far from being a valiant knight. He felt more like a terrified peasant.

It didn't help that Walter Zing had also disappeared since that day in the mountains. Jerry hoped that the scientist and his gang of brilliant but cowardly followers were working diligently on a way to eliminate zombies. Possibly Zing was generating yet another variety of Studleys, one with a taste for zombie flesh. However, it also struck Jerry as possible that Zing was spending his days searching for Griselda, hoping that she had somehow survived underground and that he could resurrect her.

About three months after Griselda's leap into the hole housing the giant screaming earth mother zombie, Jerry said to Piper, "We could move. Both ourselves and the company headquarters. Or at least my office. Somewhere way north in Alaska, up where it's dark for months on end, and even in the summer the sun doesn't get very high. Zombies would avoid that place like the plague."

"What would I do up there?"

"We could build a gym onto our new house."

"Don't be silly. You're talking nonsense."

Sometimes Piper reminded Jerry of his mother.

He didn't want to be reminded of either of his parents. They kept calling him and plaintively asking when he was coming down to see them again.

"Why don't you?" Piper asked.

"They're not my parents. They're zombies."

"Of course they're your parents."

"You told your mother she wasn't your mother after she murdered George."

"Poor George. If she hadn't murdered him, we wouldn't be together. She was actually looking out for my best interests. That's what mothers do."

Poor George, Jerry thought.

"I never realized you were so antisocial," Piper said. "You're still wonderful, but you are antisocial."

"Am not."

"Are too. You don't want to see your parents, you never want to go out with other couples, and you don't invite any of your subordinates over to dinner."

"My subordinates? Your father never invited me over to dinner."

"No, but we did. George and I."

"Well, George did. You always spent the time insulting me and acting like you wanted me to leave."

She laughed and shoved him playfully. "I'm surprised you ever took any of that seriously. I always enjoyed seeing you, even before I started falling in love with you."

"So you were just kidding when you told me that I was stupid and worthless and that George should fire me?"

"Of course!"

"Oh. Okay. But why should I invite my subordinates? George was my friend. I'm not friends with any of them."

"It's good business practice. It keeps them tied to you."

"Where did you hear that?"

"Fred told me."

"Oh. Him."

"We should have him over, too. He might be president someday. It would be really useful to the company to have a friend in the White House."

"Man, if Fred Foxtrot became president, that really would be the end of the world. We'd be looking back at the zombie apocalypse with nostalgia."

"Don't talk about Fred that way. What do you have against him?"

"He's a crook. He's a slime ball. He turns my stomach. Worst of all, he's a Republican."

"You're a rich, powerful CEO now, darling. You need to become a

Republican, too."

"I'd sooner have a zombie eat my brains."

Piper laughed gaily and hugged him. "Oh, you're wonderful!"

"You were horrified when your father said he'd promised you to Foxtrot. That day in the factory."

Piper shrugged. "Life is change. Besides, that wasn't Fred's doing. That was my father's idea. Some sort of deal he had in mind, I guess. He was probably thinking that having his daughter be First Lady would be very good for Piper's Pickled Peppers. You know how he is."

"Yeah, I do know." Life is change, Jerry repeated to himself.

Piper said, "Invite that Myron Henderson guy over for dinner next Saturday night. 6:00 p.m. We'll start with him."

"That awful kid! Why him?"

"Because you need him. Also, he's interested in space stuff, so we can watch the launch together."

"What launch? And how do you know he's interested in space stuff?" But Piper had left the room, and Jerry was left grumbling and feeling sorry for himself. Myron Henderson! Here, in Jerry's own house! His refuge from the world and from zombies! He'd rather have a zombie in the house than Myron. No, he realized, that wasn't true at all, but it did feel good to say that to himself.

At work the next day, Jerry forced himself to ask Myron to dinner. The kid accepted with glee.

"By the way, Myron," Jerry said, "I hear you're interested in space stuff."

"Gosh, Boss." Myron looked shyly at the floor. "Thanks for being so interested in what I do outside the office. I'm really flattered!"

"Right. Okay. So you are interested in it, then?"

"Oh, yeah! All my life!"

"There's some kind of big launch coming up on Saturday, right? That's when you'll be over at the house."

"You didn't know about that? Wow! I'm really surprised, Boss."

Jerry suppressed the urge to choke the kid with a pickle. "What is this big launch, Myron?"

"Golly!" Myron took a deep breath.

Jerry sensed a lecture coming on. "Give me the executive summary."

"Wow! You bet! You know that there's a planet called Mars, right, Boss?"

"Yes, Myron. Assume I'm a little bit smarter than the average CEO."

"Oh, okay. You know about the Spreading the Seeds of Earth Initiative, right? That bill that Senator Foxtrot pushed through?"

"Yeah, I remember that one." Jerry remembered it only vaguely. When he saw Foxtrot blathering away on the television screen, he tuned it out. He was surprised to learn that one of Foxtrot's many bills had actually become law and moreover had had any kind of effect on the world. "That was pushing private exploration and settlement of Mars, wasn't it?"

"That's right, Boss!"

Jerry felt as though he were being patted on the head.

Myron continued. "The first crew and ship are ready to go. They'll be blasting off on Saturday night at about 10:00 o'clock our time."

"Good. We can all watch it on the enormous television screen we have in our special television room."

"Wooow!" Myron said. "Thanks, Boss!"

"It's the very least I can do for such a valuable employee, Myron."

"Oh, gee, Boss. I'll be there, Boss! Six o'clock, right?"

"Right. I'll e–mail you the directions."

"That's okay, Boss. I know where your house is."

Jerry left the office early. It was about 2:00 o'clock when he got home. Piper was there, as was usually the case now. As it always did, her presence in the house filled him with happiness.

He heard her voice when he opened the front door. He wondered whom she was talking to. Maybe Zing was back! No, Piper's tone sounded much too friendly for that. That also ruled out her father. She was probably on the phone with one of her gym buddies, he decided.

He yanked off his hated tie as he passed through the living room and threw it on the couch. His sport coat followed.

All the windows were open, and a breeze was stirring the air. He had to admit that it was pleasant. Piper's voice was coming from the back patio, as far as he could judge. She must think that the protective aurora of my knightly valor extends all the way out here from downtown, he thought.

He pushed the screen door open, stepped out onto the patio, and stopped.

Piper was sitting at one of the small tables on the patio, holding a cup of coffee, and laughing merrily. Sitting across from her, smiling in the unctuous way that was the only way he knew how to smile, was Senator Fred Foxtrot.

Jerry groaned.

Piper turned at the sound. "Darling!" She put her cup down, pushed her chair back, sprang to her feet, and threw herself at Jerry. She flung her arms around his neck and kissed him madly. "I'm so glad you're home! Fred stopped by. Isn't that great?"

Foxtrot rose to his feet and stepped around the table with his hand outstretched and his unctuous smile, looking a bit forced, still in place.

Jerry couldn't avoid touching the man's flesh, but he tried to make the handshake short. Foxtrot seemed to feel the same way.

"Senator," Jerry said, nodding and radiating hostility.

"Morgenstern," Foxtrot said, nodding and radiating it back.

"Fred has some really exciting news," Piper said. "He's leaving us."

"That *is* exciting news," Jerry said. "Thanks for dropping by."

Piper laughed as though Jerry had made a wonderful joke. "No, no, that's not what I meant. He's leaving office. He won't be our senator after this weekend."

"I wanted my old family friend to be the first to know," Foxtrot said, putting his hand on Piper's shoulder. Noticing the look on Jerry's face, he removed his hand again. "I've already told Frank, and now I'm on my way to a press conference, where I'll make the official announcement about my retirement from office."

"He'll be moving on to a higher office," Piper said. "Isn't that great?"

"Yeah, congratulations," Jerry said. Jerry wondered what that office might be. It was almost two years until the next presidential election and the next gubernatorial election in Arapahoe, so Foxtrot wasn't running for either of those offices. Some appointed position, then? Jerry couldn't think of an appointive office above janitor that Foxtrot was qualified for. Maybe Ambassador to Lower Shitstain.

"It seems a shame to give up the power of a senator," Jerry said. "You've introduced a lot of bills in your career. Now you're going to be…What, an ambassador, or something? Cabinet secretary?" God forbid that he be an ambassador, he thought. We can't afford a war with Lower Shitstain.

Foxtrot smirked. "Can't tell you, I'm afraid. That's confidential information at this point. I will tell you that it's a much higher office than U. S. Senator, though. I'd better leave now. My press conference is scheduled for 4:00 p.m. Why don't you watch it? I'm sure all the local channels and all the national news channels will be carrying it."

"Oh, that's exciting!" Piper said. "Isn't it exciting, Jerry?"

"Oh, yes. Very exciting. So you'll be revealing your new office during the press conference, Senator?"

Foxtrot shook his head. "No. I'll be revealing it this weekend. I can't talk about it till then."

Foxtrot left, and Piper rushed to turn on the huge television set. "I don't want to miss any of that press conference!"

"It won't even start for almost two hours," Jerry told her.

"I want to be ready." She paged through the onscreen program schedule. Her expression turned from excited to puzzled. "It's not listed. I looked at the local TV stations and all the main cable news channels, and I don't see it."

Jerry laughed. "Darling, no one gives a shit about that asshole—except for him, of course."

Piper said, "I wish you wouldn't talk that way about—Ah hah!" The screen switched from the onscreen schedule to the local Fixed News station. Fred Foxtrot's enormous face filled the background. In front of that, a plastic anchorman and a plastic anchorwoman smiled insincerely and prattled away about Arapahoe's junior senator and speculated about his hastily arranged press conference, which they assured the viewer their station would be covering live and in full.

"See?" Piper said. "Fred is a very important man."

"They're starting early. You can turn it off for now."

"I'm gonna keep watching it in case they say something important. Do we have any pickles in the house?" She noticed Jerry's horrified expression and said, "Dill pickles."

"I'll check." He went into the kitchen, forgot all about looking for dill pickles, and poured himself a very large glass of Scotch with a small number of small ice cubes. He stared at the glass for a while in an estimating kind of way and then added more Scotch.

Carrying his glass, he wandered upstairs to his study. He felt like escaping from reality by surfing the Web for a while. He swallowed a mouthful from his glass and felt moderately escaped almost immediately. He looked at the weather forecast, deleted spam from his e–mail, and argued with online acquaintances on his favorite social network, explaining to them how mistaken they were about this and that.

Time passed. His glass had become empty. He was feeling very escaped indeed. It was almost 4:00 o'clock. I'll pour myself more Scotch before Foxtrot starts talking, he thought. That will help me get through it.

You'll be drunk, he warned himself.

Not drunk enough, he replied.

He noticed a new e–mail message that had just appeared in his account. More stupid spam, he thought. He tried to focus on the subject and whom it was from, but his eyes and mind weren't cooperating. He double–clicked on the message to open it.

It read, "Be sure to watch the launch on Saturday night."

He frowned and concentrated.

It was signed "Lily" and it had been sent from his sister's e–mail address. Suddenly, he was sober.

He stood up quickly. His chair rolled backwards, halfway across the room. He backed away from the computer as though he feared that tentacles or a pseudopod in the shape of Lily would emerge from it and grab him. In fact, that was exactly what he was afraid of.

He went downstairs to the kitchen, poured himself a fresh and even larger glass of Scotch, and went to the television room.

Piper was still glued to the giant screen. "No dill pickles?" she asked over her shoulder.

"I didn't find any."

"Damn. I'm really craving them."

"Are you pregnant?"

She spun around and stared at him, looking startled. "I never thought of that! I'd better find out. Oh, wouldn't that be wonderful? To have your wonderful little baby?"

"I was a rotten baby. My mother said so."

"Oooh. I bet you were cuuuute and sweeeet."

"Oh, God." He swallowed a lot of Scotch. "Look." He pointed at the TV screen. Foxtrot had appeared.

Foxtrot stood behind a lectern to which a few microphones were attached. He smiled his usual big smile, although it struck Jerry as hesitant and uncertain. A very small crowd of reporters stood in front of the podium—far fewer, Jerry suspected, than Foxtrot had expected. They all looked bored.

Foxtrot opened with a wordy, rambling statement that Jerry could make nothing of. It seemed to be about the wonderfulness of America and Fred Foxtrot.

"Well, this is pointless," Jerry said.

"Sshh," Piper said.

"It has been an immense honor to serve this great country and state for so many years," Foxtrot concluded. "And now, as I look back over my many years of service and my significant accomplishments—"

"Are you resigning, Senator?" a reporter called out.

Foxtrot looked annoyed. "Yes. That's what I was saying."

"When?" another reporter shouted.

"Immediately. I'll be discussing my successor with the governor—"

"What are you going to do instead?"

Foxtrot looked crafty. "I can't tell you now. You'll know before the weekend's out."

"Why are you quitting? Does it have anything to do with the Justice Department's investigation?"

Foxtrot assumed an air of outrage. "I am innocent of all charges. This is a witch hunt by Democratic appointees in the Department of Justice."

The reporters laughed. One said, "What about those anonymous deposits into your offshore accounts, Senator?"

"I have no offshore accounts. That's a malicious lie. Thank you for attending, ladies and gentlemen. Be sure to watch the launch this weekend of the first Mars settlement ship, made possible by the Spreading the Seeds of Earth Initiative that I introduced into the Senate. Thank you, good night, God bless you, and may God bless the United States of America."

Foxtrot and his press conference disappeared from the screen, replaced by the previous two news anchors. They looked at each other in puzzlement, clearly wondering how they were going to fill up the time now that Foxtrot had given them so little material to work with.

Piper switched off the television set. "You're right," she said. "That was kind of disappointing." She brightened. "Oh, well, at least the launch on Saturday will be exciting."

"I guess. It would be more exciting if Myron Henderson weren't going to be here watching it with us."

"Oh, gosh! I forgot all about that dinner! I need to start planning."

"Don't plan anything. Let's just order a pizza." He could tell she wasn't listening.

Myron began to act as though he and Jerry were not just boss and subordinate, but friends as well. He smiled and nodded at Jerry in a specially familiar way devoid of his former subservience. That subservience had annoyed Jerry, but this assumption of familiarity annoyed him even more. As the weekend approached, when others were present, for example in meetings, Myron would make what he must have thought would seem to the others to be in–jokes that only he and Jerry understood.

Jerry began to fantasize about throwing Myron into the hole in the mountains. There might still be something dangerous down there.

At around 5:30 on Saturday evening, Jerry found Piper in the dining room preparing for their guest.

"Not ready yet?" he asked her.

"Don't worry. Everything will be ready by 6:00. You'll make the right impression on…What's his name, again?"

"Myron Henderson. He'll be here early. He's that type."

"Oh, don't be silly. I don't think Myron's that type at all."

The doorbell rang.

"Yes, he is," Jerry said.

"Well, delay him. Take him into the living room and give him a drink and chat for half an hour."

"Hmph." Jerry walked toward the front door. Maybe it's not Myron, he thought. Maybe it's a brain–eating zombie. That would be better.

It was Myron. He was grinning madly. "Wow, this is beautiful, Boss. What a great neighborhood."

Myron would never have wanted to visit me in my crappy little apartment, Jerry thought. Gee, I miss that place.

"Is that a bunch of flowers, Myron?"

"Yes, Boss. I thought I should bring flowers for your lovely wife."

Jerry winced. "Come on in." He stood aside. "Why don't you take those into the kitchen. I'll show you the way." He raised his voice. "Oh, Piper," he called.

"Great, Boss." Myron headed for the kitchen without waiting for Jerry.

Excellent, Jerry thought. I can get started on the drinking by myself.

By the time he got the kitchen himself, glass in hand, weaving a bit, about 20 minutes had passed. Piper was doing a good acting job. Anyone who hadn't heard her verbal jabs at Myron during their few prior meetings would have believed that she was happy to see their guest. When Jerry came in, she said to him, "Oh, Darling, look at the flowers Myron brought." She had put them in a vase. "Aren't they beautiful?"

"Mm," Jerry said. He had no opinion about flowers.

She picked the vase up. "I'm going to put these in the center of the dining room table. Is that drink for Myron?"

"Uh uh."

"Well, get him one."

"Oh, that's all right, Jerry," Myron said. "I don't drink alcohol."

"Coke?" Jerry asked. "Pepsi? Sprite? Mountain Dew?"

"Hmm." Myron frowned in thought.

"We don't have any of those."

Myron laughed. "That was a good one, Jerry. Why don't we watch television? The launch should be coming up soon." He walked away into the television room.

You're lucky I'm halfway drunk, Jerry thought. Otherwise I'd kill you.

By the time he reached the television room, the screen was on and Piper and Myron were sitting on the love seat. Piper shoved Myron and said, "Don't be a fool, Myron."

"Sorry," he said. He got up and sat down in the armchair next to Piper's end of the couch.

Piper looked at Jerry and patted the seat next to her. Jerry sat down heavily, then shifted over so that he was touching Piper. All was not right with the world because of Myron's presence, but at least it was a bit better now. "So, what's the sit, as Walter would say?"

"Please don't remind me of Dr. Creepazoid," Piper said.

"There've been delays, and they're still loading supplies," Myron said, "but the crew is ready to go aboard. They're about to give their farewell speeches."

In the center of the screen, Jerry saw what appeared to be the lowest section of a giant rocket. It was attached to a metal gantry. Looping pipes and cables led from the gantry to the rocket. Workers in hard hats swarmed around both. A ramp led from the ground up to an opening in the side of the rocket, about ten or fifteen feet above the ground.

"Now, that's the way an interplanetary spaceship should look," Jerry said. "It's just like the ones in old movies."

At the foot of the ramp was a lectern with a microphone attached to it. A few reporters stood in front of it. They chatted with each other, glanced at their watches, and looked bored.

"Must not be a big crew," Jerry said. "That's strange."

"Look at that," Piper said. "It's just like at an airport."

A train of luggage trucks, looking identical to those used to at airports, had pulled up beside the rocket. Workers in hard hats appeared from somewhere off camera and began sliding big crates from the luggage trucks into an open-sided elevator built into the gantry.

"What the hell?" Jerry said. He squinted and leaned closer to the screen. His first impression had been correct. On the sides of the crates, two logos were stamped. One was the familiar triple-P of Piper's Pickled Peppers. Next to it was a capital S inside an oval, colored in shades of green. "Look there." He pointed.

"Those are our shipments to the Spreader Corporation!" Myron said excitedly. "Wow! They're taking our pickles to Mars!"

"That's so cool," Piper said. "Thanks for getting that contract and saving the company, My."

"Oh, that's okay," Myron said with transparently false modesty. "Just doing my job, Pipes."

"Sshh," Jerry said. "This must be the crew."

A small group of human figures, dwarfed by the rocket behind them, shuffled onscreen and arranged themselves behind the lectern. In the front of the group, commandeering the microphone, was former Senator Fred Foxtrot.

"It's Fred!" Piper said in delight. "That must be the new job he was talking about at his press conference. He's the spokesman for the Mars settlement program. Cool!"

How did he manage to snag that gig? Jerry wondered. The man was just a minor ex-politician under investigation by the government.

Jerry's gaze drifted to the uniformed crew standing behind Foxtrot. Jerry wasn't surprised that they looked bland and indistinguishable from each other, but he was surprised by just *how* bland and indistinguishable they looked. A shiver ran down his spine.

Foxtrot beamed at the press and began to speak. "Blah, blah, blah," he said.

"Oh, God," Jerry said.

"Sshh," Piper said.

The reporters looked bored.

"Blah, blah, blah," Foxtrot continued. "And blah, and blah, and blah."

Jerry felt himself falling asleep.

"Blah, blah, our brave mission commander," Foxtrot said, gesturing toward the crew.

One of the uniformed figures stepped forward, nodded at the

reporters, and then stepped back into the bland group.

"Holy shit!" Jerry said. "It's Lily!"

Foxtrot introduced the rest of the crew, but Jerry paid no attention. He was focused on his sister, or on what seemed to be his sister. As he stared at her, her face smoothed out. She looked less like Lily by the moment and more like the bland figures to either side of her.

"And now, as we prepare to depart from our great mother, the Earth," Foxtrot intoned, "I'd like to thank my former colleagues in the United States Congress for passing my bill, the Spreading the Seeds of Earth Initiative, and the president for signing it into law. Thanks to my bill and the funds allocated by it, we have built and stocked this great ship—" he gestured over his shoulder "—*Seeds I*, only the first of a mighty fleet that will spread the seed of life to other worlds. Our great Mother Earth will be recreated throughout the Solar System and eventually throughout the universe."

"Oh, man," Myron said, "they're gonna be buying a lot of our pickles!"

Behind Foxtrot, the uniformed crew was filing up the ramp and into the ship.

"My friends," Foxtrot said, "God bless you, and may God bless...the planet Mars. Farewell." He turned and trudged up the ramp after the crew.

"What the hell?" Jerry said. "He's going with them? To Mars? He's going to be president after all? Of Mars?" Tens of millions of miles away, where the Department of Justice won't be able to get him, Jerry thought. Canny bastard.

Piper sobbed. "Farewell, Fred! We'll miss you."

Foxtrot stopped at the top of the ramp for one final wave. Then he stepped through the hatch, joining the uniformed crew, who were just visible beyond the opening. A metal door slid down, closing the hatch and hiding the crew and Foxtrot.

It was a proper ending to the scene, Jerry thought. Foxtrot and the last of the pseudopodia—for that was surely what they were—were now safely shut away behind thick metal and were about to be blasted off into space and be sent far, far away.

The last trace of the greatest danger was about to leave the earth, he thought. He sipped some whisky and tried to ignore the distraction of the muttered conversation and occasional laugh behind him. The zombies were still around, but he was sure that Walter Zing was working on that problem. Things were definitely looking up.

At last, he thought. The worst is behind me.

About the Author

David Dvorkin was born in 1943 in England. His family moved to South Africa after World Two and then to the United States when David was a teenager. After attending college in Indiana, he worked in Houston at NASA on the Apollo program and then in Denver as an aerospace engineer, software developer, and technical writer. He and his wife, Leonore, have lived in Denver since 1971.

In addition to non-fiction, David has published a number of science fiction, horror, mystery, and Star Trek novels. He has also coauthored two science fiction novels with his son, Daniel. For details, as well as quite a bit of non-fiction reading material, please see David's Web site, http://www.dvorkin.com.

www.ingramcontent.com/pod-product-compliance
Lightning Source LLC
Chambersburg PA
CBHW060602310726
48982CB00008B/1206/J

* 9 7 8 1 7 3 4 5 6 3 6 4 1 *